LET YOU GO

EMILY BEAN

ALLY

I was dying.

My five-year plan was going to have to be condensed significantly. I could feel my heart pounding in my chest, almost as if it was trying to make its way up and out. Perhaps it would like to find a new body.

One that had longevity.

This was all I could think about as I sat waiting for a doctor to confirm my biggest fear. I tried to focus on the random paintings that had been placed haphazardly on the walls. I had always wondered who it was they hired to decorate medical rooms; to select low-budget wall art that would be the witness to other people's sorrows.

The woman across from me reminded me of my mother. Tattered purse, worn-out boots, black pants that could pass as workout attire or dressy. Her shirt had some bedazzled trim at the top. She pulled a compact mirror out of her purse and checked her reflection. Satisfied, she snapped the mirror shut and shoved it back into her bag. The other woman sitting next to me had well-done blonde highlights. It was questionable whether she had had Botox. I watched her scroll through her phone and tap her foot impatiently. I imagined she had a beautiful white kitchen and ate only salads with grilled chicken for dinner.

"Ally?" My name cut through the silence in the room, and it took me a moment to realize I was being called back by the nurse. Standing up, I smoothed my shirt down over my stomach and smiled. Neither of the women looked up when I walked by. I wondered how they could go through their day so uninterested in their surroundings. People watching was one of my favorite pastimes. If the circumstances were different, I would have enjoyed sitting here for much longer, just to see who came and went.

"How are you today?" The nurse didn't wait for my response. "Follow me this way, we are heading to room 11, at the end of the hall."

I scrambled after her. Room 11. This must have been a sign. Eleven was my favorite number, but this didn't feel like a lucky moment.

Before I settled into the room, she took my height and weight. Why did they have to check your height every time? Did they expect adults to keep growing? She marked down my blood pressure and asked me all the regular questions. Just as quickly as she arrived, she was gone and I was left to sit alone for God knew how long while I waited or the doctor to confirm my suspicions.

Finally, there was a soft knock at the door, and I straightened up.

"Ally, hi. I'm Dr. Jacobson." He extended his hand, and I peered down at his hairy knuckles. Reluctantly, I shook it, making a mental note to properly wash my hands in the small sink before I left. "So," he continued, "the nurse tells me you are concerned that you may have cancer?"

I sensed a whisper of impatience in his body language, as if he had somewhere better to be. That I was making this all up. I frowned. He thought I was overreacting. "Yes. Based on my symptoms, I am quite certain that is the issue."

He nodded, looking bored. "Can you tell me about your symptoms?"

Fighting the urge to roll my eyes at his dismissive tone, I swallowed my agitation. "Bloating, discomfort in the pelvic area, fatigue, a frequent and urgent need to urinate, occasional nausea..." I tried to say firmly, but I heard my voice trailing off.

Dr. Jacobson's eyebrows rose ever so slightly. One would have thought his partner would alert him that he was in need of an eyebrow trimming. They were quite thick. I took a quick glance at his ring finger, which was occupied. It was helpful for me to focus on this minor detail, rather than the very large and inconvenient detail of why I was here in the first place.

"All of those symptoms do match up with ovarian cancer," he said, his voice still passive and unbothered.

I nodded, pleased with this statement. I knew I was correct in my diagnosis. Although I was devastated that my life was slipping through my fingers, I was also relieved. This way I wouldn't have to inform my husband, Cade, about the plans I had made.

"However, there are a few other symptoms we would typically see," the doctor said, clearing his throat before continuing. "Abdominal pain, constipation, a mass, bleeding, and more. Before we jump down that rabbit hole, I'd like to rule out a much stronger possibility."

I bristled. Could he have been suggesting that I did not have ovarian cancer?

"While I appreciate your opinion, Doctor, I am almost certain there is something very wrong with me." He smiled sympathetically and waited for me to quiet, but I continued, "I have never felt so out of sorts in my life."

"Ally, I'm not suggesting that what you are feeling is invalid. What I am suggesting"—he paused to put his pen in the pocket of his jacket—"is that it sounds like there is a strong possibility that you are pregnant."

My stomach dropped, and my heart seemed to skip many

beats. My brain seemed to short-circuit as I tried to come up with a response. It was suddenly too hot in this room. Beads of sweat ran down the front of my chest, which was both alarming and embarrassing. The familiar feeling of nausea prodded at me as I connected the dots. This had to be a mistake. I took extreme precautions against this sort of incident as it would interfere with my five-year plan immensely. The thought of being trapped here in this small, New England town made my whole body start to shake. It was too much for me to handle.

I could not move forward if I was pregnant.

"Ally?" The doctor was speaking to me again, and I took a moment to pull myself out of my internal spiral. I blinked slowly at him, and he continued, "I am going to send a nurse in to give you a pregnancy test, and we can go from there." He was already halfway out the door, smiling at me as if this was a good thing. As if I had been waiting my whole life to receive news like this.

When the nurse returned, she instructed me to urinate into a cup, which seemed unsanitary, but I obliged, eager to move this process along and exit the building as quickly as possible. While I waited, I scrolled through my phone, observing countless notifications from my friends and family. Today was my birthday, but I certainly didn't feel like celebrating. I felt like crawling into a hole and staying there for the rest of eternity.

Approximately forty minutes later, I was standing back at the receptionist's desk, booking my next appointment. My mind was swirling. Tears threatened to make themselves visible, but I had spent decades keeping them at bay, so I did what I did best; I held them in and straightened out my shoulders.

The receptionist had a round little chart that reminded me of one of those children's books that changed shades when you turned the dial on the side. It spun and spun until she matched today's date with the following months. As I watched, I made a mental note to switch to a different doctor. This one was clearly behind the times, using a piece of decorated cardboard to determine my due date. I shifted my weight to my other foot, and heat rose in my body. I wanted to rip my coat off and perhaps my sweater, too, but I didn't. Instead, I cursed the receptionist in my head as sweat pooled in all the wrong places.

"Alrighty then, handy little chart, isn't it? Now you can book all your appointments ahead of time, so you don't need to worry and wonder." The receptionist seemed thrilled with this announcement, and I fought the urge to reach across the desk and rip her precious chart in half. Instead, I smiled, thanked her, and headed for the door.

Once I was outside in the fresh air, my enthusiastic façade faltered as my mind raced with what to do next.

It would have been easier to accept the cancer diagnosis.

That I was prepared for. This I was not.

I could not be a mother.

I clenched my fists in frustration, which reminded me that I was clutching the ultrasound picture in my left hand. I peered down at it, releasing my grip slightly, trying my best to focus on the dark shadows of the image that seem to blend rather than the stark reminder that there was an intruder currently living inside of me.

Its grainy appearance was already crumpled, but that didn't matter.

I wouldn't be displaying it on my fridge like I had seen pregnant women do in the movies.

A trash can sat a few feet ahead, waiting. As I passed by, I casually tossed the picture in, then I began to type Cade a text. I wouldn't be telling him about this predicament.

Having a baby did not fit into my plan.

It would have completely derailed us.

There was no way we would ever come to an agreement. How would we compromise when we both wanted completely different things?

I refocused on my phone and sent the text.

Meet you at Killian's in 30?

An unnecessary annoyance stirred in my gut at his near-immediate reply.

I'll get our favorite table.

Lovely, I thought as I got into my car and backed out of the parking lot. Just dinner at our favorite table while I panicked internally about the invasive species inhabiting my insides. I shook my head and tried to focus on the positives, but I couldn't stop thinking about the baby and how I was annoyed with Cade for a reason I could not pinpoint. So, I let myself think about the reasons I should have been annoyed with him. The things I had assumed I would get over once we were married, but I was still waiting. Like the fact that he left paper towels everywhere in sad little heaps after he dried his hands with them. Or that he always whistled after he got out of the shower. Or that he sometimes napped with his eyes slightly open. The first few times I found him like that, I thought he was dead.

The blinker on my car clicked happily as I waited to turn at the light just before Killian's. It made me feel organized. Official. It was just the confidence boost I needed before I headed inside the restaurant because I was unsure of how I would keep this from Cade. He was very in touch with my emotions when he wanted to be, which I understood. I imagined it was difficult to keep up with my constant reactions to the world as a highly sensitive person.

My steering wheel was slightly sticky from the hand sanitizer I generously applied to all my frequently touched objects after I left the building. My stomach flipped and flopped at the toxic smell. The waves of nausea started to creep in. I needed to get the bottle out of my car. Immediately. Rolling down the window, I took the poisonous little bottle and tossed it out. It landed with a comforting thud on someone's front lawn. Usually, I was against littering, but this was an unfortunate circumstance.

I spotted Cade's sleek BMW already parked near the entrance as I pulled into the parking lot. I felt hot all over again. Too hot. It was as if all my nerves had turned into a thick layer of plastic wrap, suffocating my skin. I did not know how I was going to navigate this. The tears were building back up like white-hot daggers behind my eyelids. I slammed the steering wheel, forgetting about the stupid sticky residue as I peeled my hands away.

I distracted myself from the tears by thinking about a hot dinner roll slathered with chilled butter. After I consumed a few rolls, I would feel better. Maybe then I would change my mind and consider telling Cade. I just wasn't sure how he was going to react when I explained that I could not have a baby. That I had other plans. Plans that did not involve him.

When I pulled open the double doors to the restaurant, I didn't hear the typical music that usually welcomed me when I came here. Frowning, I realized it was quite dark. Where was the hostess? Did they have an incident with the electricity? I wasn't sure if I should turn around and leave, so I stopped. Perhaps I'd missed a text from Cade. The feeling of heat was back, climbing up my body like an imposter.

Just as my hand located the cool covering of my phone case in my tote, the lights switched on, and suddenly, there were people everywhere.

Screaming, "Surprise!!"

All the people I knew. I wanted to hide. I wanted to put my hands over my ears and yell. I wanted to be anywhere but here. Secretly pregnant and forced to socialize.

In the center of the crowd was Cade, sharply dressed in a navy suit. I could tell by the way he was standing there, relaxed and confident, that he knew he looks good. A sharp pang hit me as I thought about how thrilled he would be to have a baby. I pushed the thought away and focused on the crowd. Next to Cade was my mother, Lorrie, and Julie, my best friend.

How had I not seen this coming? I should have known. It was the looming diagnosis that distracted me, of course. I had been so focused on the possibility of the inconvenient little life inside me that I let my guard slip. Under normal circumstances, it would be very hard to surprise me, but Cade and Julie had gotten lucky. I made a mental note to scold Julie later.

Julie. Oh dear. Seeing her now was almost more than I could handle. My stomach swam with guilt. It crept up into my chest and settled there, as if to remind me it wouldn't be leaving anytime soon. Knowing how badly she wanted what I now had, how would I tell her I am pregnant? The idea of not telling her flickered through my brain, and I tried to let it settle there.

Slowly, the reality that I wouldn't be able to tell her floated down around me like a quiet snowfall. I didn't know how I was going to navigate this without Julie by my side, but what other choice did I have?

All I wanted at this moment was a few hot buttered rolls and quiet. I could feel the tears coming. Burning again like hot pricks at the back of my eyes. If only Cade had chosen this moment to pay attention to my emotions. I assumed that at this point, it was clear to someone who knew me well that I was on the verge of a meltdown.

Instead of crying, I smiled my best smile and covered my mouth with my hands, suppressing the pretend scream of excitement. Everyone squealed with delight, and Cade rushed over to me, planting a kiss on my forehead. I forced down a gag. The potent smell of alcohol seeped through his pores and directly into my nostrils. It was not often that he tucked into the bottle, but when he did, I found it absolutely revolting. I braced myself for his upcoming slurred speech. When he got drunk, he dropped his R's and suddenly he sounded like he was from South Boston. I could not pinpoint why, but it had always bothered me.

My mom was right behind him and gave me a big hug, plopping a party hat firmly on my head. I did not like the feel of the fabric one bit. She knew I didn't like hats. She knew I didn't like surprises.

They both knew I didn't like crowds.

"Mother," I said through gritted teeth. "I'm taking the hat off." She was wearing the only party dress she owned. The same one she had had since I was little. Her hair was pulled back with a scrunchie, but not one that was in style. Another pang of guilt shot through my chest. She deserved so much more in her life. A life where she didn't have to spend every waking moment working. A life where she was loved and supported by her husband. A life where things got to be easy for her. Where she could be happy and free.

"Were you surprised?" Cade asked, whisking the hat off my head. "You really had us waiting! What took you so long? I thought you might have gone and gotten lost at the shopping center," he joked, winking at my mother.

Another flash of heat pulsed through my body. I ripped my jacket off, causing Cade to frown. This must have been a common pregnancy symptom, I thought. It was very unsettling.

I needed to sit down.

I needed quiet.

I needed the nice table in the corner that we always sat at with the hot buttered rolls.

I did not need this.

Definitely not this.

NANCY

IT WASN'T HEALTHY TO BE OUT DRIVING AROUND AND stalking friends after dinner, but it was always the evenings that left her feeling lonely. If her children knew what she was doing, they would definitely have her committed to one of those old folks' homes. Nancy shuddered at the thought. She'd rather someone just put her out of her misery than desert her at one of those facilities.

Nancy lifted her foot off the gas and allowed her car to creep by Lorrie's house one more time, taking in the overgrown grass and tattered front steps. The driveway needed weeding, and the garage looked like it was one windstorm away from crumbling to the ground.

She muttered to herself and drummed her fingers on the steering wheel. Even if Lorrie had been home, Nancy wouldn't have told her, yet she couldn't keep driving in circles ruminating on the news she had just received. The phrases tumbled around in her brain, refusing to be ignored. *"There is no cure... At the rate it is progressing... Due to the nature of the disease...."* She couldn't remember the rest of what the doctor had said.

How ironic.

Nancy released a shaky breath just as her Bluetooth rang, startling her. She still wasn't used to the sound of the phone infiltrating all her speakers and rattling her bones in one swoop. She clicked through an array of buttons on the steering wheel, figuring one of them had to be the right one. Finally, the ringing stopped, and her daughter's voice replaced the fleeting moment of silence.

"Mom. Where are you? What are you doing?" The questions boomed into the car. Nancy winced. Julie was awfully pushy, and it seemed the trait was growing stronger with age.

"I'm out running errands, dear. Is everything all right?" She didn't want to tell Julie that she was bored. It would just reiterate Julie's idea that Nancy needed more companionship. Sighing, she took a left at the lights. She may as well go home and watch the new drama on Netflix everyone was up in arms about.

"Mom, did you forget about tonight? About Killian's? About Ally? It's her thirtieth birthday. *Remember*?" She said the word remember very slowly, as if she were helping a two-year-old sound it out for the first time.

Nancy slammed on the brakes in the middle of the street, pressing her forefinger and thumb against her forehead. She needed to be more careful or Julie was going to catch on.

Julie sighed on the other end. "Lorrie is looking for you. I can't believe you aren't here."

Nancy frowned. What day was it? She could have sworn it was Thursday. "Ally's party is tonight? But I thought it was on Thursday?"

Julie groaned with annoyance on the other end. "*Mom*. It *is* on Thursday. Today is Thursday. Today is the party. Right now is the party." There she went again, sounding out the words as if Nancy was inept. "Where are you?" she hissed on the other end.

Nancy drew her head back into the headrest, trying to escape her daughter's angry voice.

She didn't have a good explanation. She honestly didn't know why she was driving around in this neighborhood. Was it part of her diagnosis, or was she just becoming the annoying mother who couldn't keep everyone's schedules straight? That was one of the hardest parts about what was wrong with her—the confusion about the confusion.

"I am sorry, Julie! I got my days mixed up. I can be there in twenty minutes." She pulled a U-turn in the middle of the street and waved sheepishly at a man who was getting his mail. "Sorry," she mouthed to him.

By the time she pulled into Killian's, Nancy had gone through all the reasons she might have been late. None of them were believable. There wasn't much she could say, but she had to come up with something because this wasn't the first time that she had messed up plans with Julie, Lorrie, and Ally.

It wasn't her fault, really. She had little control over her situation. There was only so much the medicine could do to keep her on track. The doctors explained that there wasn't a cure, but she could manage most of her symptoms with a prescription and help from her family and friends. Eventually, it would consume her, this memory issue. She knew how it would end. After she had left the specialist's office, she had googled end-of-life care for this sort of thing. As her cognitive memory deteriorated, so would the rest of her body. It would be slow. Embarrassing. A burden to her children. Her life would dissolve into a mess of adult diapers and around-the-clock care. Most likely, in a place she would not recognize. Someone would have to spoon-feed her soft peas and pat her encouragingly on the knee as if she were a toddler.

"NO!" she yelled out loud. She wasn't going to let herself go there. She wasn't going to think about the fact that she might never see her daughter become a mother or enjoy her retirement years spoiling her grandchildren with loud toys and too much candy. For now, she knew the main issue was that she hadn't told her family or her friends. The doctor considered it a problem. She didn't. She hadn't told anyone, and she intended to keep it that way. She had everything she needed at home to keep herself in line. As long as she came up with a system and kept all her ducks in a row, there shouldn't be any more mishaps until much later. If only Dean were here to help her feel less like a burden. To hold her hand and reassure her that everything would be all right.

Nancy was still sitting in the car outside Killian's mulling over what to say to Julie, when suddenly there was a loud tapping on her window. "*Mom?* What in the world are you doing?" Julie was prying at the door handle of the car, trying to open it. "Unlock the door. Are you okay?"

Nancy shook her head to shift back into focus and fumbled for the lock on the side of the door. "Sorry, dear. I was just thinking about dad." Nancy winced, knowing that was somewhat of a cop-out and also that it would get Julie to back off.

Sure enough, Julie's face softened, and she put her hand out. "Come on, Mom. Everyone is missing you. I was wondering what was taking you so long, and I happened to look out the window and saw you sitting here with a blank stare. Are you hungry? There are a ton of appetizers, and the bartender makes a mean margarita." Julie was already grabbing Nancy's purse and searching around the back seat for God only knows what. "Did you bring a gift?" Shit. A gift. She had forgotten to get a gift.

"Oh, silly me," she sang. "I completely forgot to bring the gift! It's sitting right on my counter at home. I'll just head back and get it now. I won't be long." Nancy shifted back into driving position, reaching for the ignition.

Julie groaned and threw her arms in the air. "No. Absolutely not. Ally is turning thirty, not five. She won't care. You are not leaving. You are coming inside to keep Lorrie busy so she doesn't send Ally over the edge." Julie was practically pulling Nancy out of the car while she scolded her.

"Okay, Jules. Are you sure you're all right? You seem awfully on edge lately." Her daughter had always been snappy, but over the last few months it seemed to have worsened. As if everyone was out to get her.

Julie narrowed her eyes and spun on her heel, leaving Nancy with no choice but to follow her inside to the lion's den.

JULIE

Julie pushed open the double doors and allowed the moment to embrace her. She knew she looked good. Everyone's eyes settled over her like a warm blanket as they took her in.

Her beauty.

Her confidence.

Her long black hair.

Her blue eyes and warm smile.

Her ability to take charge and make things happen.

But Julie didn't care about how beautiful she was. Being beautiful, being confident, being everything she was would never get her the one thing she wanted more than anything else in the world.

A baby.

She walked briskly over to Ally and her mother, aware that her own mother was hurrying along at her heels, like a scared little bird.

Julie really needed to be gentle with her mother, but she kept doing weird shit. She was constantly pushing Julie's buttons and giving her no choice but to be brash. That was Julie's nature, anyway. It was how she moved through life, keeping everyone a clip away so they didn't see what was really going on in her smart little head. A sad story sat there, waiting to be uncovered.

Waiting for someone to reach out and pluck it from her brain.

To expose it to the world.

To uncover who she really was.

Ally was sitting at one end of the bar, twirling a cocktail stirrer around in her margarita instead of drinking it. Julie squinted and watched her best friend sit in the discomfort of the evening. Her chest tightened as she took a long sip of her own drink in an attempt to push down the feelings of guilt. Julie had known Ally would balk at all the attention initially, but she also knew that Ally would come around after everyone settled down and maybe even enjoy herself. They were similar in that way; they both liked things to be their ideas. The minute someone else told either of them to do something, they immediately resisted.

That was probably why Julie had been so put off by Greg lately.

He kept trying to tell her how things were going to go.

Julie forced him out of her mind and tried to focus on Ally.

She seemed off. Distant in a way that Julie couldn't put her finger on.

Leaving her mother to fend for herself, Julie sauntered over to Ally, placing her clutch delicately on the bar. Ally was still swirling the contents of her drink, completely ignoring her.

"Ally. Earth to Ally. What is going on with you?"

Ally let go of the stirrer and looked up at Julie, her expression pinched. "You know I hate surprises. And crowds. All of this." She sighed, making a sweeping motion. "Why didn't you tell me?" Ally mumbled, scrunching her nose. "I know, I know. Let me guess, Cade insisted."

Julie took another big sip of her drink. "I knew you were going to be awkward about it, duh. But I figured you would at least have a few drinks and lighten up."

She watched as Ally pulled the complimentary bowls of mixed nuts and tortilla chips toward herself, shoving some into her mouth and eyed her suspiciously. "You seem out of it, more than usual," she said, pointing to the chips. "I have never seen you eat bar food in my entire life. Something else is going on. What is it?"

Ally sat up straighter, furrowing her brow. "I am famished and irritated." She squared her shoulders and folded her hands in front of her, pretending to be proper. "Plus, I have turned a new leaf. I am not going to be as concerned about germs as I once was. Life is too short."

Julie laughed and grabbed a chip, sloshing into the salsa. "You never cease to amaze me, you know that? Also, I don't believe you for one second." She nudged the bowl back toward Ally. "But seriously, what is going on?"

Julie could see the impatience flashing in her eyes. She knew it well.

"It's nothing. Cade is simply annoying me, and I'm tired. I wanted a quiet dinner. Not to see everyone I have ever met in the last ten years."

Julie frowned and flagged down the bartender. "Well, I am sorry, but what did you expect with Cade? You know he loves a good party. He wasn't going to settle for anything less than all of this."

Ally rolled her eyes dramatically.

"You know," Julie continued, "that's one of the things I appreciate about you and Cade. You are both so different. He really brings out the social part of you. Helps you come out of your shell a bit."

Ally wrinkled her face in disgust and scoffed.

Julie laughed and turned back to the bar. It was true. Ever since Cade and Ally found each other, Ally had become more comfortable in social situations, even if she didn't want to admit it. Cade really was a gem in every way. Julie wished she had more of that with Greg. Someone who was really invested in every aspect of her, even the challenging parts.

As if Ally could read her mind, she leaned forward toward Julie, lowering her voice, "You better be careful, or I am going to force you to discuss why Greg isn't here right now."

At the mention of Greg's name, Julie stiffened. He wasn't here because he didn't want to be. Because he didn't seem to care about her anymore. Because, she thought to herself, our marriage might be ending.

Julie narrowed her eyes. "That, my dear, is off-limits for the foreseeable future." She looked out into the crowd of people to avoid Ally's gaze. "Uh-oh. Look who is headed our way."

Ally groaned and sank down in her chair. "My mother is relentless tonight. I wish she would leave me alone."

"Don't worry; I'll handle it." Julie hopped off the bar stool and stood to greet them. "You both look beautiful tonight," she gushed, embracing them in a hug. "Mom, I'm glad you found Lorrie. And Lorrie, you and Cade pulled off quite the party."

Lorrie smiled and leaned over to plant a kiss on Julie's cheek. "Isn't it grand? Cade really is the best. He handled everything." She clasped her hands together and beamed. "I just helped him with a few guest contacts and with the menu!"

Julie turned to look at Ally. She knew that Ally would have a snarky response. It was one reason they had become best friends. Both of them really struggled to find patience with their mothers, but for very different reasons.

"What? Finding the bar and showing up?" Ally mumbled, scowling.

"Ally, dear. What has gotten into you tonight? I thought you would be thrilled with all of this!"

Julie watched Lorrie's face fall in defeat, causing a growing pit of guilt to form within Julie's stomach. The poor woman tried so hard and had been through so much, but would never admit this to Ally.

"Mother, I like to know what to expect and to have a plan."

"Yes, well, of course, but some of the best things in life are a surprise; now, stop being ungrateful, and come say hi to all of the guests."

Ally slinked off the bar stool and followed her mother into the crowd of people, leaving Julie and Nancy alone. Her mother had a happy-go-lucky smile plastered across her face as if she hadn't just witnessed all the tension unfold in front of her.

Julie looked around and lowered her voice to whisper to her mother. "Something is up with Ally. She nearly tackled her mother just then."

Nancy moved closer to Julie and frowned. "She is fine, dear. Where is Greg? I haven't seen him yet."

Julie's chest tightened. She didn't want to get into this with her mother right now. "He had to work late. I'm not sure if he will make it."

"Oh, what a shame. He works too hard. Tell him he needs to speak to his boss. It's not healthy to be at the office so late on a Saturday night."

"Mom. It's Thursday, remember?"

"Right, yes." Her mother laughed, reaching into her purse and pulling out a lipstick.

Julie sighed, trying hard to find compassion for her mother, but it was as if her body fought her every single step of the way. What someone would normally find endearing about her mother, Julie found annoying. What another daughter may cherish, Julie wished away.

She hated that she was like this.

She knew later she would lie in bed staring at the ceiling trying to justify why she had been so short with her mother.

Then she would spiral out, text Ally, admit to all the mean things she had said, and vow to start over the next day.

Every time she was around her mother, she told herself that it would be different. That she would be patient. That she would be kind. That she would be understanding. That she would be grateful.

And every time she failed miserably.

Being around her mother catapulted Julie back into that dark spot right between rage and resentment where she was held against her will, unable to fight the words that flew out of her mouth like tiny bullets, hitting her mother over and over again until Julie was left to pick up the fragments of the conversation, promising, once again, to be better the next time.

ALLY

I was in my bed, listening to the sounds of Cade getting ready to go on a run. The clink of his toothbrush on the bathroom vanity. His fast footsteps trailing down the stairs. The jingle of our dog Archimede's collar as he followed Cade around the kitchen, beside himself with excitement. The opening and closing of the fridge. Cade filling his mason jar. The sound of it landing back down on the countertop.

What an idyllic world he was living in, oblivious to my predicament. To *our* pregnancy predicament, I reminded myself. Yet, would it be ours if I didn't tell him? It would be much easier, I decided. To keep it quiet. To keep it to myself. Just like I had with my five-year plan to break out of Eastwood and see the world. The more that you involved others, the more opinions you had to juggle. The more bodies you had to dodge and manage.

"Ally! Are you sure you don't want to come with me?" Cade's voice cut through my brain, and I winced, rolling over to face the window. "I'm asleep," I whispered into the pillow. Waiting, I held my breath.

Just go already.

"She must be snoozing, bud," he said to the dog. I stayed frozen until finally he sighed in disappointment, his footsteps fading away from the stairwell, replaced with the effervescent jingle of Archimede's collar. A part of me felt relieved he had left, while the other part filled up with guilt that he was oblivious to what was happening. This was the first big secret I had kept from Cade, and it seemed to follow me around like a pesky fly that got stuck indoors in the summer.

I needed nourishment. Something with carbs. A bagel. An onion bagel with veggie cream cheese. Even though that concoction was out of my realm of ordinary, I couldn't prevent my mouth from salivating at the thought of the first bite.

Before surrendering to the strange craving, I needed to wait until Cade was out the door. I turned and looked out the window, waiting for them to depart. My journal was sticking out from underneath the pillow, calling to me. I grabbed it and flipped hastily to the first page where my plan was written.

I stared at the words I'd written six months ago.

Quit my soul-sucking job as an accountant within the next two years.

Continue exposure therapy (get used to loud noises, uncomfortable fabrics, and dirty venues).

Break Cade's heart by telling him I do not want to start a family. I stopped at this one. Should I cross it out? Alter it? What happened now that I was actually carrying a baby? I fidgeted \with the cover of the journal, adding a temporary question mark as a placeholder.

Start resistance training, and hike my first 4,000-footer. This would help get me into shape for my travels. I planned to hike the Inca Trail to Machu Picchu.

Sell my car and our home, so I have the appropriate funds for travel. This would require me explaining to Cade that we would need to split the equity from our home. I did not think he would take this well, and my heart clenched at the thought.

Sign up for WWOOF in New Zealand. I would have to make sure I was able to interview several host families before I committed to this one. What a disaster it would be to travel for over twenty-four hours only to end up with a family I could not contend with.

I lifted my head and peered out the window once more. Cade and the dog were traveling happily down the road away from the house. Off into what should have been a wonderful Saturday morning. This was becoming more complicated by the minute. Pulling out my phone, my fingers swiped to the App Store. It was almost as if they were moving against my will. I wasn't fit to be a mother. It wasn't something I had planned for.

I exhaled and typed "baby" into the search bar. This sort of thing was much better suited for Julie.

Julie.

My shoulders rose in tension as I thought about my dear friend. How would I ever tell her? How could I conjure up the courage to tell my possibly barren best friend that I now had the one thing she wanted more than anything in the world? Every Sunday afternoon, we met at our favorite coffee shop, The Purple Fox. After we were fueled up on too much caffeine, we took a walk downtown where our ideas flowed like the river adjacent to us. In our uninterrupted time, we vented, made life-altering decisions, and threw our cares to the wind.

Our scheduled Sundays were precious for not only for our mental health, but for our friendship. Usually, I complained about my job and how it wasn't good for my mental health while Julie laughed and offered me sound advice. I had followed the safe path of accounting in college. At the time, it felt secure.

Orderly.

Predictable.

All things I found very important.

Yet over the last few years, I had realized it also made me feel trapped. Like a sheepdog locked up in a high-rise apartment. Julie always laughed when I said that. *"That is the weirdest analogy ever."*

And every day she told me to quit. To switch to something that I loved. It was easy for her, though. She had her dream job.

But she didn't have a baby.

My stomach flip-flopped at the idea of coffee and spending ample time with Julie. I was going to have to come up with a very good excuse to get myself out of our weekly meetup.

The app was now populated with results such as, *app baby tracker for breastfeeding, baby games, baby generator*, and *baby milestones*. This didn't seem right. Why did a baby need games? I was looking for something that would tell me about my pregnancy.

Frowning, I kept scrolling and then realized where I had gone wrong. I'd made the mistake of using the word baby when I should have typed in pregnancy. I replaced my search with the appropriate word, this time met with countless options. I clicked the first and scroll through, eventually choosing the one that showed an actual baby and not the one that showed the baby as a navel orange. What an odd thing to compare a fetus to.

The app wanted to know what the baby's name was. Seemed a bit early to be naming such a thing. Wouldn't it have been more appropriate to enter my own name? I was the one using the app, not the amorphous blob in my uterus. I put a question mark in for the name and moved through the rest of the information. The due date I knew now, thanks to the secretary and her handy chart. I clicked update, and the app sprung to life, as if it was trying to force excitement onto me.

Your baby ? is as big as a raspberry! 32 weeks to go!

There was a quaint cartoon picture of a raspberry next to a tiny fetus as if they were thick as thieves. It appeared that fruit would be used in place of a baby no matter which pregnancy app I chose. The thought of fruit really was disgusting. I would think that the designers of these apps would be more sensitive to nauseated pregnant women. Why not compare the baby to a Munchkin donut or a bite of grilled cheese? That sounded much more on brand than a healthy berry.

I scrolled through the app a bit more before tossing the phone down onto the bed. Rolling over, I stared at my nightstand. I'd deep cleaned the upstairs just a few days ago. Not a speck of dust lingered on any surface, yet there was the faint ring from a glass on the wood. Cade must have brought his nighttime beverage upstairs last night after I fell asleep. I had constantly requested that he use coasters, but he continuously ignored me. Reaching over, I rubbed the mark away with my thumb. If only it were as simple to brush away this unfortunate predicament that I was in.

Sighing, I sat up, dithering over what to do. How long could I stay in this limbo? The emotions building within my head and my heart were urging me to tell the truth. It was as though someone had my control of my thoughts, like a puppet master, leading me to the most important people in my life, asking me to share my announcement with them. There was an odd nagging feeling in my chest that would not go away. As much as this baby changed my plans, I couldn't help but wonder what life would be like as a mother.

Could it work out after all?

Becoming a mother would give me a chance to do everything differently than my parents had. Or I should say, my mother had. My father was about as useful as a wet dishrag. I shook my head. This was exactly why I didn't want to reproduce. Based on the evidence throughout my childhood, the failure rate as a parent was very high. As much as my mother fought to provide for me, she still ended up in a toxic relationship and a minimum-wage job. I wanted to give myself all the opportunities that I wasn't given as a child. That was why I had created the five-year plan.

Perhaps I would test it out for another day or two. I imagined that this was what a normal pregnant woman would do, lie around leisurely in bed scrolling through pregnancy apps while her handsome husband completed normal Saturday activities. I could have that life. It was right at my fingertips.

All I had to do was say the words out loud.

The problem was, I didn't want it.

NANCY

Nancy pulled her car into the garage and shifted it into park. Her eyes ached, begging her to shut them. Last night had been wonderful but mentally exhausting. All of those conversations with different people, it was a lot to keep track of. Names, faces, and stories she should have remembered. They seemed to slip through her grasp, sometimes all at once and other times just bit by bit. With each forgotten piece of information, she became worried someone would notice; however, she made sure to carry around a full margarita that willingly took the blame.

The garage steps loomed in front of her, reminding her she needed to get out of the car and into the house before she accidentally made an overnight out of the front seat. Blowing out a sharp breath, she reached over to grab her purse from the passenger seat. She fumbled around for it, but it wasn't sitting in its usual spot.

"Gosh darn it. Where is it?" She peered into the back seat, but it was empty. Where was her phone? Most likely in the purse. She hadn't needed to use it at the party; all the people she normally conversed with were right there with her.

Julie probably took it home with her. Nancy would just drive over to her house and grab it. Backing out of the garage, she gave her cheeks a little tap with her hands. "Time to wake up, Nancy."

Julie lived only a few blocks away, so she felt confident she could drive over despite her exhaustion; she only hoped she wouldn't be interrupting Julie's evening. She imagined Greg would be home by now, and they hadn't had a lot of time lately together. Something about a promotion at work and opposite schedules. Nancy knew that much, although many of the details had faded away already, like a cluster of fall leaves in the wind.

As Julie's house came into view, she slowed down, pulling in and parking behind Greg's

truck. He'd finally purchased one a few months ago after years of driving a sedan. Nancy always thought it was odd that such a tall man drove such a small car. She used to press Julie about it. *"Why not take Greg out car shopping for a new truck? Something with more legroom. Wouldn't it be nice to have a vehicle that you could use for yard work or to pick up a piece of furniture with?"* Julie's response had always been the same—a scowl and something about it being none of her business.

Nancy clambered out of the front seat and made her way up to the mudroom entrance. She turned the knob ever so slightly to open the door. With one foot inside, she heard raised voices coming from the kitchen. She froze, unsure of what to do. A small voice in the back of her head reminded her not to eavesdrop, demanding that she slowly back up and close the door; however, the nosy, motherly part of her wanted to listen, and that part always won. Craning her neck forward, she slowed her breathing and stayed as still as possible.

"It's constant, Julie. Every day you are obsessed with that tracker. With the goddamn research. This doctor said that, or so and so told me this. It's suffocating us. It is all you think about. All you care about is having a goddamn baby."

Nancy's shaking hand seemed to move to her mouth in slow motion in a feeble attempt to cover up her audible gasp. What doctors?

Silence.

It seemed as though a lifetime had passed before she heard her daughter's voice, much calmer than Greg's had been. "You have no idea what it is like to be in my shoes, Greg. Do you not understand what the doctors said? It's not going to happen naturally. It's not going to just work itself out. Either I become obsessed and figure this out, or we never have children. Is that what you want? It seems like you just want to throw your hands up in the air and walk away from this. If that's the case, then fine. The door is right there."

Nancy shrunk back, unsure if she should back away now before one of them noticed. But surely Greg would not walk out right at this moment.

She had to keep listening.

Greg released an exasperated sigh, and Nancy gripped the doorknob harder, waiting. "I do understand, Julie. But I also need you to understand that I am losing my wife." His voice dropped an octave, and Nancy craned her neck, trying to hear the rest. "I am not so sure I want a baby anymore, not if it means that I lose you in the process."

Nancy heard the slam of a cabinet door and the shuffle of feet heading up the stairs. She closed the door a bit more and pressed her ear to the opening to confirm what she already knew.

The only sound left was the quiet sobs coming from her daughter.

JULIE

Julie rolled over, reaching for the screeching alarm. Blindly, she tapped her phone a few times until the noise finally subdued. Groaning, she pivoted the other way, expecting to meet the warmth of Greg next to her. Instead, she was met with a heap of crumbled blankets and a deep emptiness in her gut. She sat up and looked around the room.

His phone and watch were gone.

Where was he?

A wave of anxiety washed through her. Was she really going to have to do another fertility treatment alone today? She threw the blankets off the bed and shuffled over to the window, peering out as she looked for his car.

Gone.

"Damn it." She slammed her fist down on the dresser next to the window. It was as if Greg had simply dismissed himself from their marriage overnight. In the back of her mind, though, she knew it hadn't been overnight. It had been happening more with each passing appointment. With each night he stayed late at work. With each weekend that he was out of the house longer and longer. Every time they received another round of bad news, not only did she lose a bit of her hope, but she also lost a bit of Greg.

She looked back at the bed where her phone sat. A lurch of anxiety shot through her chest and she closed her eyes, reminding herself to stay positive. They had been waiting on blood work results all week. If all went as planned and her blood work came back as they hoped, she could start another round of IVF.

She needed that to be the case

She needed something to focus on.

Something that made her feel like she was moving the needle forward.

As Greg seemed to slip away from her, Julie's primary company slowly became the shadows within her own home. They swallowed her in a deep darkness as she ventured further and further into this fertility journey completely and utterly alone. This was supposed to be an exciting day for the both of them. Right after they purchased the condo they were living in now, Greg had made it a non-negotiable that every Saturday morning they slept in together, followed by an elaborate break-fast. Despite her frustration with him, she smiled at the memory. He was her rock.

Or had been.

And he should have been there with her. He should have been there making pancakes and reassuring her that everything would be fine. Not high-tailing it out of the house before she woke up.

She couldn't even remember the last Saturday they had done that.

She couldn't remember the last time Greg had really asked her how she was feeling.

Taking another deep breath, she tried to push away the persistent anger that was always threatened to bubble up to the surface. She knew from experience that the anger usually morphed into a dark sadness, and it would not help if she turned into a blubbering mess at 8 a.m.

Julie tossed her long dark hair up into a bun and marched downstairs to the kitchen. If Greg didn't want to be on board, then she would manage it herself.

She didn't need him right now.

She had Ally.

On Sunday, when she and Ally met up for their weekly walk, she could dump the bucket and decide how she was going to handle this, but for now she just needed to get through the day. She would simply distract herself from the absence of Greg and fulfill their Saturday tradition alone. But the fact that Greg chose to leave lurked in the shadows of her morning while she made breakfast.

Local eggs with spinach.

Fresh fruit.

Chamomile tea.

She had read that one of the most important things about preparing for IVF was diet and keeping stress minimal. Since the first two rounds had failed, she was even more determined to make sure things were perfect. She was going to do everything in her power to keep her body pristine, even if that meant sacrificing coffee and avoiding the impending doom of her relationship.

She picked her phone back up and almost sent a text to Ally but stopped. As much as she wanted to vent to her best friend, she didn't want her to know that Greg had backed out, again. Instead, she moved into the mudroom to tidy up between bites of food and groaned out loud.

Her mother's purse was sitting on the bench. She had totally forgotten that her mother had left it in her car and that she had planned to drop it off this morning on her way to the doctor's office.

"No!" Julie yelled. "I don't have time for this right now."

Sinking down onto the bench, she dropped her head in her hands. It wasn't that hard. She could drop it off. Ol' Nancy would be lost without it.

For as long as Julie could remember, her mother was always

misplacing things and operated in a constant state of frantic energy. Growing up, Julie was always late for something: school, parties, playdates with friends. You name it, it got messed up. Her mother seemed to make it her personal mission to forget an item crucial to their departure. With the amount of alcohol her mother consumed in the evenings while Julie was growing up, it was never really a surprise to her. Ally and Julie had connected over their parents' relationships with alcohol, but Ally always argued that Julie got the better deal.

"Your mother is a wonderful woman! Who cares if she consumes a few drinks during the evening hours? It doesn't seem to be affecting her mothering skills or her ability to contribute to society."

Julie understood Ally's perspective. From an outsider looking in, it was harmless. A lot of parents drank alcohol. But it had always bothered Julie.

It bothered her because she could hear the slight slur in her mother's voice when she would get home from practice or come down to get a snack after doing homework.

It bothered her because her mother always had to stop at the liquor store *after* the grocery store.

It bothered when her mother shoved her hands into the fridge's ice bin and then sloppily sloshed her vodka and orange juice together, making a mess that Julie knew she would eventually have to clean.

She looked at her watch again and sighed. "Fine. I'll just get it over with right now." Grabbing the purse, she tossed it in her car and backed out of the driveway. Julie glanced at the dashboard clock as she turned off her street and onto the main road.

8:35 a.m.

If she ran into her mother when she dropped off the purse, she would most certainly get locked into a long-winded conversation and end up late to her appointment.

If Greg had been with her, she could have made him drop the purse. She mentally added that to the reasons why she currently hated him and swung a left onto her mother's street. As she approached her mother's house, she slowed down, fantasizing about tossing the purse out her car window and right into the driveway.

Pulling in, she took a deep breath. As if on cue, an obnoxious sound came booming out of her mother's purse. Her mother was probably the only woman on the planet who actually chose the dog-barking ringtone above the default options.

"All right, all right. Enough," she said to the purse, reaching inside for the persistent little device. Just as she clicked the side button to silence it, she heard the rattle and screech of her mother's garage door opening. Looking up, she waited for the door to recede into the ceiling and watched as her mother trotted down the steps, looking properly disheveled.

"What is she wearing?" Julie muttered to herself.

She had on a long night gown that was riddled with holes. It looked as though it had been pulled out of one of those free bins people put at the end of their driveway after a successful yard sale. Her mother's streaky hair sat lumped together on one side of her head while a few straggling pieces left behind a mess of frizz on the other side. She had on those new cloud-like flip-flops that all the younger TikTok kids wore.

Julie closed her eyes and pinched the bridge of her nose.

Be nice.

"Mom, I have your purse, and I'm sort of in a rush," Julie yelled, climbing out of the car and making her way into the garage where her mother was now rummaging through a plastic tote. "Mom," Julie pressed, "what are you doing?"

Her mother's head popped back up out of the tote, and she stared at Julie, a look of confusion flashing through her eyes.

"Mom? How many margaritas did you actually have last night?"

Her mother waved her hand and turned back to the bin. "Just hold on a minute, Jules, I'm looking for something."

Julie rolled her eyes right as her mother swiveled back around, her face serious. "You know I don't drink anymore, Jules."

Julie scoffed and muttered under her breath, watching as her mother dove back into the pile.

"I've got a book in here somewhere that I think you would love. It was your dad's. Let me just find it."

Julie groaned. This was exactly why she couldn't be patient with her mother, ever. "Mom. I told you. I'm in a rush, and I don't want any of Dad's things." She could feel her face growing hot with impatience. "Here." She thrust her mother's purse forward, so it was directly under her face. "You left this at the party."

Her mother stood up and snatched the purse out of her hands. "Oh! I have been looking everywhere for this!! Where was it? How wonderful! You are a saint, you know that? Always helping everyone else and working so hard."

Julie raised her eyebrows. "Mom. You are acting weird. What's up with you lately?"

Her mother placed the purse down next to her on the ground and grabbed Julie's arm, gripping her fingers into her sleeve.

Julie tensed under her mother's grasp and tried to relax.

Be nice.

Her mother's eyes flashed nervously, and she dropped Julie's arm. "Nothing is wrong with me. I am fine. I am just concerned about you. Is something wrong? Something with Greg? I know he has been working a lot, but I think you should take him out to dinner. My treat!" She let go of Julie's arm, snatching the purse back up, and began shoving things around inside it. "Here, let me get you some play money. I've got a few twenties in here somewhere."

At the mention of Greg, a pang of stress shot up through her chest, and she felt herself move back into defense mode. "I don't need any money, Mom. Greg and I are fine. Listen. I have to go, okay? I have an appointment at 9:30."

She winced. Too much information.

Her mother froze, one hand still in the purse, and met Julie's eyes. "An appointment? With a doctor?"

"What?" Julie whispered.

How did she know?

Julie hadn't told a soul except for Ally, and she knew Ally would never ever tell her mother. She shook her head, watching her mother stare back at her with a blank expression.

"Did I say something wrong?" Her mother frowned, looking down at the purse.

"No, it's fine. Listen, I have to go, okay?"

Her mother nodded and turned back to the bin full of junk. "Of course, I'm just sorting through all these items. Let me know if you want anything."

Julie turned back toward her car, grateful to have dodged the doctor question. But she couldn't let go of the nagging feeling in her chest that there was something off with her mother, more so than normal.

ALLY

Now that I was positive Cade would not follow me around for the rest of the morning, I managed to get myself properly dressed and planned a trip to the grocery store. Despite the onion bagel I had collected from the local coffee shop down the road, I still felt famished. I would need sustenance, and a lot of it, in my home no less, to keep the nausea at bay. This was what I'd learned from the pregnancy app. Small, frequent meals would help me feel better. So that was what I was after, at least for the next few days while I mapped out a plan.

As I made my way through the busy morning traffic, I made a mental list of the things I would need from the store. What troubled me the most was the issue that Cade would most certainly take notice of my new purchases. Perhaps I would have to hide some snacks in our upstairs closet, which only I frequented. I was, of course, the tidy one of the household. He never so much as opened the linen closet. An excellent spot to stow away a few bags of chips and granola bars. I would have to pick up a bag of rawhides for Archimedes to keep him distracted, so he didn't go sniffing and snuffling around in the closet.

A surge of excitement ran through me as I thought about my snacks as little stowaways. Never had I been so enthralled by the thought of keeping food all to myself.

By the time I had found a parking spot and begun the

daunting task of choosing a cart, it was apparent that the grocery store was settling into prime shopping time. I filtered through the lineup of carts, pushing aside several that had a used sanitizer wipe discarded in the bed. How disgusting and rude people were, leaving behind their crumpled-up germs to sit and fester in the morning sun. Another cart had a receipt lingering in the front section, and one even had a lonely baby's toy, still attached to the handlebar, like an afterthought in a deserted in a sea of metal.

Finally, I found a suitable cart and made my way inside. Normally, I only shopped the perimeter of the store; I had learned that from a health and wellness podcast I used to frequent. The middle aisles were all rubbish. As long as you stuck to the edges of the store, you would walk out with mostly unprocessed food and much more meat, fruit, and veggies than the lurking middle aisles provided.

Today was different, though. I had to admit it felt like a bit of a thrill to meander down the forbidden aisles, tossing boxes of white crackers and peanut butter filled pretzels into my cart. I traveled down the bread aisle, inhaling the sweet, comforting scent of the freshly baked loaves, and lingered by the English muffins. Those were a favorite from my childhood, especially with butter and a bit of jam. I could still picture my mother in the kitchen of our grungy apartment trying her best to feed me. Little had she known that I would often fill up on a huge family dinner at Julie's, then come home to pretend that I loved my mother's ketchup and American cheese pizzas on store-brand English muffins. I had always wanted to tell her the truth but never had the heart to come clean.

I tossed a pack into my cart, feeling a bit giddy at the possibility of spreading some jam on a toasted half later that evening.

By the time I was in the checkout line, I had quite the array of items. I planned to hide most of the perishables in the back of our extra refrigerator that we kept in the garage. Cade often stored beer in that fridge, but he hardly took the time to poke around at what was lurking behind his Sunday beverages.

"Ally? Is that you?"

Startled, I turned around quickly to follow the voice. *Who was it?* A flash of heat traveled up my chest and overtook my insides. I glanced at my cart, suddenly embarrassed of its contents. When I looked back up, my eyes landed on Nancy. Thank heavens, it was only her. This could have been much worse. Someone much more observant would think it was odd that I was buying junk food, but this would go right over Nancy's head.

I made a mental note to be more careful next time before I turned to acknowledge her.

"Nancy! Hello! How are you this morning? Thanks again for coming to my party last night; it was just wonderful."

Nancy beamed and pushed her cart over to my lane, tucking in behind me so we could check out together. I pushed mine up a bit, hoping Nancy wouldn't take too much notice at what I was buying, but I also understood the appeal of checking out one's purchases. One of my own favorite pastimes was seeing what other people had in their carts at the grocery store. It was much like visiting a friend's house and having an uninterrupted moment while they went to the bathroom to poke around in their fridge and see what they kept inside. I had a feeling I wasn't alone in this enjoyment.

"What are you buying, dear? Looks like you might be having a gathering? Another birthday celebration perhaps?" Nancy nodded to my cart, and I forced a smile.

Ignoring the comment, I unloaded my items onto the grocery belt.

Nancy stepped closer to me and lowered her voice. "Ally, dear, I don't mean to be secretive, but I was wondering if you knew anything about Julie? I am worried about her. I think there is something happening with her and Greg, and well, you know how she is with me. Sometimes she isn't too quick to share the details."

I shifted on my feet and tried to find something neutral to say back, but words seemed to fail me. The faint beep of my items being scanned pulled me forward in line, and I hoped this was enough to end the conversation.

Nancy looked behind her as if someone else was listening and then glanced back at me. Her eyes held a deep sadness and a whisper of confusion. I gave her an encouraging smile while I pulled out my wallet. I was never good at this type of conversation. I did not do well with the emotions of other people, aside from Julie, that is. Plus, I was starting to feel the nausea creep back in. I fought the urge to rip open a bag of chips that was still sitting on the grocery belt and shove a few in my mouth.

The grocery assistant was now bagging up some of my items, and I needed to remit payment soon.

I forced myself to say something nice before the heat and nausea got the best of me. "Oh, I think she is okay, Nancy. You probably just caught her at the end of the work week. You know how she can get a bit unsettled when too many people ask her questions."

Nancy shook her head, and I bristled. Why was this happening?

I needed to get out of the store immediately.

I started to unzip my sweatshirt; the heat was unbearable.

Nancy's brows furrowed in confusion as she watched me, and then she took yet another step closer, only increasing my feelings of suffocation.

"Ally, I think her and Greg are having problems. Fertility

problems." Nancy reached over and grabbed my arm, which was mid-transferring a rather delicious-looking frozen pizza to the belt. It hovered there while Nancy clung to my arm, threatening to unravel my neat little life.

NANCY

Nancy pulled out of the parking lot, taking an absentminded left. Her head was spinning, and she didn't know where to go or what to do. When she had seen Ally in the checkout line at the Shop Mart, she had deserted her own shopping trip halfway through, zooming her cart in behind Ally in hopes that she could get some information about Julie's situation.

Ally was a peculiar girl, always had been. Nancy thought longingly about the girls in high school. Ally always came to their house, something about a troubling home and a father who liked to dabble a bit too much in the whiskey bottle. Nancy had taken the girl under her wing, even bringing her on family outings and putting her own little section of Christmas gifts under their tree. She thought back to the first time they had taken Ally on a family trip to Bermuda. Ally had never even been on an airplane! While Julie and her older brother caused a ruckus in their seats, Ally had sat quietly, coloring in one of those adult coloring books, her perfectly sharpened pencils lined up neatly on the airplane tray.

Nancy wasn't really surprised that Ally had brushed off her question about Julie. The girls had always been thick as thieves, and despite Nancy's prying, Ally had always protected Julie, even once when they had been caught with an open beer container at a high school football game.

But this was different.

This was about Julie's dream to be a mother.

This was the type of topic you tossed the rules aside for and spilled the beans.

When Nancy had said the word fertility, something in Ally's body had shifted. Nancy saw it right before her eyes. There was something different about her.

Something off.

This was something she just knew in her gut, and she was positive that it wasn't connected to the mess of problems in her own brain.

And it was something she was going to get to the bottom of.

Suddenly, she came to the dead end of a road. Where in the world had she ended up? She pulled her car over and got out, looking around. The smell of salt air filled her lungs. A breeze lifted the collar of her shirt just enough to send a chill through her body. She hadn't remembered deciding to drive to the beach, but she was glad she had.

It was beautiful here!

Peaceful and quiet.

A perfect place to take a walk!

She headed down the path leading to the sand, where old wooden planks were sitting haphazardly, half sunken into the beach, clearly misplaced and rearranged by the latest storm. Living on the coast of New Hampshire always came with its set of weather surprises. It was one of the reasons she and Dean had settled here.

Oh, Dean, how she loved him.

He always knew how to make her happy.

She couldn't wait to get home and cook him a hearty beef stew later that evening.

As she walked along the beach, she tossed around the word infertility in her brain. Oh, how it must be crushing her daughter. As a mother, Nancy carried around the emotional pain of her daughter by default. It was sitting deep in her chest, slowly eating away at her from the inside out, much like a worm in a rotten apple.

It had to go.

There had to be a way to cut this out of Julie's life and make sure she had the baby she had always wanted.

The sun seemed to be slinking lower on the horizon, and Nancy fumbled in her pocket for her phone. Had that much time really passed since she was at the Shop Mart? The wind picked up again, pushing back against her. She checked her other pocket for her phone, but it appeared to be missing, much like her purse last night.

"Oh dagnabbit." She sighed and stopped, looking back and forth across the sand.

Which way had she been walking? Both ends of the beach looked the same.

"You can do this, Nancy. You are not lost." She spoke quietly to herself as she picked a direction, confident it was the right one, and started off toward what looked like one ending of the beach. This was one of her and Dean's favorite spots. She knew it like the back of her hand. There was no way she would get lost. Yet, as she marched forward, she had a sinking feeling that she was already more lost than she cared to admit.

JULIE

GREG WASN'T RETURNING HER TEXTS OR HER CALLS. If she were being honest with herself, there was a possibility he was cheating. It was almost as if he had moved on to a new life and forgotten to let her know. The worst part was that she couldn't talk to anyone about it. If she confided in Ally, she would immediately want to investigate. Telling her mother was off the table, and she couldn't confide in anyone at the office about it. She didn't want to give them any more cubicle content than they already had. Plus, the thought of having to emotionally process anything else right now made her want to crumble into a black hole of despair.

Sitting in the waiting room of the fertility specialist's office, she tried to kick the assumption from her brain. Every other woman around her sat next to their partner, holding hands, chatting quietly, giving each other encouraging smiles and warm glances.

And here she was.

Alone and on the verge of crumbling.

Julie straightened her spine and pushed down the feelings. She could hear her therapist's words in her head.

I know you are a very independent person, Julie. I know you are self-led and don't like to ask anyone for help. But I want you to think about your current situation. At some point, you need to ask your friends and family for support. Even the most successful people have a support team around them. You can't do this on your own. Take some time and make a list of all of your goals.

Think about what you can realistically do on your own and what requires more. Asking for help isn't a sign of weakness.

The threat of tears hit the back of her eyes, and she quickly wiped them with her sleeve.

Fuck.

She couldn't cry.

Not here.

Not now.

She focused on a painting of the ocean on the wall in front of her, willing herself to stay strong. So what if her husband wasn't with her for the appointment? She wasn't the first woman on the planet to attend a fertility appointment without a partner present. Some people had lives. Had to work. Had things to do. Not everyone had the luxury of being together for every single update that came along with this process.

Julie pulled out her phone and began scrolling through the photos from the party last night. Later, she would need to pick the best ones and upload them to Instagram. She flipped over to Facebook and exhaled with relief. Thankfully, her mother hadn't uploaded anything yet. There was nothing worse than waking up the next day after an outing with her mother. The woman took photos of you in secret and then uploaded them in a jumbled mess on Facebook, with a caption that hardly made sense and way too many, "xoxoxo, I love my family" titles.

She sent a quick text to her mother.

Reminder. Do not upload any photos until I approve them.

A ripple of guilt shot through her abdomen. There she went again, turning her sadness into anger and using her mother as a punching bag.

She promised herself that once she was positive this round of IVF would kick off, she would make a better effort to spend time with her mother. She would be patient and understanding, maybe let her take her out to lunch. Perhaps she would even tell her about the IVF. No. She definitely would not. Her mother would never let it go. She would alert half the town and start sending her articles that didn't even have a direct correlation to fertility. She could already feel the stress building in her body just thinking about it.

This was something that she would keep to herself. Only Greg and Ally knew. The more people who knew, the more questions she would have to answer. The more sympathetic looks she would have to dodge at the gym or the grocery store. Once she was safely pregnant, she could share the good news and act as if it was no big deal.

"Julie?" A nurse's voice rang through the waiting room, interrupting her thoughts. She stood up, smoothing down her sweater, and gathered her oversized tote. Smiling at the other couples, she walked confidently across the room, following the nurse through to the hallway to a patient room.

"By yourself this morning?" The nurse looked at her expectantly, giving her an encouraging smile. Julie stiffened and then forced herself to relax. The woman was just trying to make conversation, even if it was a bit condescending.

"Yes, my husband had an important work meeting."

As she followed the nurse down the hallway, she fantasized about saying, *Why yes, my husband packed a bag last night and left. No note. I think he is cheating. Everything is fine, though!*

As they turned into a treatment room, Julie placed her bag down on the posh chair next the exam table, purposely letting her hand linger to show off her enormous ring. Just so it was clear she wasn't lying.

The nurse raised her eyebrows and leaned forward, eyes flashing. "What a beautiful ring!"

Julie smiled, satisfaction landing in her chest. "Oh, thank you so much," she gushed.

The nurse smiled. "I always told my husband he better get me a redo ring on our twentieth anniversary."

Julie took a deep breath. She couldn't picture her and Greg in ten or fifteen years. The image of the family and life they were supposed to have seemed to be slipping through her fingers. She forced herself to smile back at the nurse as she continued to make light conversation while she collected all the usual information from Julie.

Height, weight, blood pressure.

She patted the exam table and beamed at Julie. "You won't be needing this today since you are just receiving your blood work results!"

Julie nodded, growing impatient with the small talk.

Finally, the nurse seemed to take the hint and gathered up her files. "The doctor should be right in."

Once the door was firmly closed behind her, Julie exhaled and collapsed into the chair. It was exhausting sometimes to be so friendly with people. She much preferred to be alone with her thoughts and skip the riffraff of bedside manner that accompanied this process. Part of her wondered if that was why she was being punished with infertility.

Was it her fault she couldn't conceive? Was her cold demeanor partly to blame? Was her body rejecting a baby because she treated her own mother badly?

Her phone buzzed, pulling her out of her spiral.

Greg's name flash across the screen.

She silenced it immediately, just like she had with the rest of their marital issues. Julie reached over to snag one of the pamphlets on the wall. A smiling couple both wearing neutral colors stared back at her. Underneath, there was a tagline that said, "Knowing both sides of the story can make all the difference."

She frowned, what was that supposed to mean?

Opening the pamphlet, she skimmed through the text and graphics. *How common is male infertility? Environmental and external factors can have an impact.*

Maybe all the alcohol Greg had been consuming was to blame, not her relationship with her mother. She made a mental note to talk to Greg about this after she figured out why he had left last night. Add it to the list, she thought. Lately, when she tried to talk to Greg about anything, he would accuse her of over reacting.

"You are making a big deal out of nothing."

"Just calm down for once."

"Why are you getting so worked up?"

"Do we really need to talk about this right now?"

Annoyance spiraled its way up her chest cavity, followed by a looming sense of dread.

She needed to fix things between them.

Plus, it wouldn't hurt to be proactive. If there was something wrong with him specifically, it would be a relief to take some of the blame off herself.

Was it wrong that she was hoping for that?

Was it wrong that she wanted him to be the problem?

Maybe this wasn't all her fault.

Maybe the combination of the two of them together was toxic.

ALLY

I had secured away all my cold snacks in the back of the garage refrigerator, confident that Cade would not notice them. My nonperishables were placed strategically underneath a pile of towels in the linen closet, and I was happily munching on a bag of potato chips, the ones with the ruffled edges to be exact. I couldn't be bothered with the thinner option. I needed the crunch and satisfaction to accompany my indulgent snack. Archimedes was going to be very excited about my new eating habits. He was like an overweight anteater, snorting and snuffling around the floor, always looking for the faintest trace of a crumb.

Luckily, I worked from home, so I would have easy access to my snacks at all times. The thought of work, of staring at a computer screen and answering panicked client emails about their accounts, made me feel like vomiting. That was certainly going to be an issue moving forward. How did pregnant women continue to work? It was as if my body had suddenly decided to be absolutely against any form of concentration.

Normally, I wouldn't be watching TV in the middle of a beautiful Saturday, but I was allowing myself this luxury given the circumstances. Cade had texted, saying that he had taken Archimedes to the dog park and then planned on making a trip to the hardware store. I smiled, picturing them sauntering around looking at the hammers and garden tools and other fix-it related items. It was a glorious message to receive. I had initially thought that I wouldn't be able to enjoy any alone time when I returned from my errands.

I pulled up my pregnancy app again and scrolled through some of the additional content. There was a link to create a baby registry. Rather early to be thinking about material items, wasn't it? I knew from attending baby showers that the gizmos and gadgets required for one mother and baby was quite astronomical, and I hadn't the slightest clue of what would be needed or why.

I closed the app.

Why was I entertaining the idea of a baby shower?

I did not want a baby.

I thought about my mother, working double shifts at the store, trying to save up money to buy the baby a gift.

No.

I couldn't do it to her, and I wouldn't do it to myself. I was not having a baby. But thinking about making that final decision soon made me feel like I was in a tug-of-war with myself. This was going to be hard enough to do alone.

If Cade were to find out about the baby, it would be ten times more difficult, as he longed for a family. I could see him now, doting on my condition. Helping me down the stairs at the end when I was as large as a small porpoise. Attending all the doctor's appointments and taking down notes when I wasn't able. Listening to my requests and making sure everything was in tip-top shape.

A small smile tugged on my lips. "No," I said out loud as I straightened out my shoulders. Glancing in the mirror, I forced my face back into its default, a slight scowl with a serious undertone.

My phone buzzed, and I looked down at the screen. My stomach dropped, and instant nausea crept up my esophagus.

Julie.

She was at the fertility specialist this morning. I had completely forgotten in my quest for snacks, followed up with the run-in with Nancy.

Ally, where are you? I need your help.

My fingers hovered over the text box. Her test must have come back badly.

What time was it? It had to have been hours since she had received the results.

What a terrible friend I had turned out to be. Throughout my whole life, Julie had been there for me. Every time my dad had ended up back in treatment. Every time I didn't have enough money to buy new clothes for school and was too afraid to ask my mother, Nancy and Julie would take me under their wing. I could still smell the Cinnabons from the mall, our shopping bags heavy with the latest jeans and layers of long sleeves.

How selfish I had been these last few days.

I should have asked her right away.

I should have been kinder to Nancy in the grocery store!

I was just not myself. It was almost as if the baby had hijacked my brain. I made a mental note to set an alarm on my phone for her next appointment so that I followed up at the appropriate hour.

I typed back a response, trying my best to act normal despite the tremendous secret that loomed in my belly.

Jules! How was the appointment? I took a catnap on the couch and lost track of time. That party got the best of me last night.

My fingers hovered over the text.

Lying to your best friend is not a good trait, Ally.

This was bad behavior.

I hit send anyway.

Oh my gosh Als, it's my mother. She is missing. Well, I think she is. She isn't returning my calls and I went to her house and her car is gone. It's not like her to not answer. I just have a bad feeling. Any chance you can meet me to help me look for her?

My heart picked up the pace in my chest as the nausea swooped back in, overtaking my senses. I stood up, and then sat back down. My hands shook against their will. Black dots swirled in front of my face, and I tried to focus on the looming texts.

Nancy was missing, and I had just seen her. Surely this was just a misunderstanding. I would make sure to calm Julie's nerves and help her locate Nancy. That I could do.

I just wasn't sure I could do it without vomiting.

"Well, this is not an ideal feeling," I muttered to myself as I typed back to Julie with my trembling fingers.

Yes, yes of course. I will help you look. Come to my house and we will go together.

Julie needed me.

Nancy needed us.

I took a few deep breaths and reached into the bag of chips, my hand disappearing into the depths as it collected a smear of grease while I continued to shovel them into my mouth like a caged animal.

This pregnancy thing was very messy.

Embarrassing even.

It was as if I had lost all control of my body.

I stood up, holding on to the side of the couch as I walked gingerly toward the kitchen. I had to pack a few snacks in my bag. Ones I could eat discreetly while we were on the search for Nancy. I also needed a drink. Orange juice sounded divine. After chugging a large glass, I felt myself stabilize, and my thoughts became a bit easier to manage.

I gathered my bag, making sure my snacks were tucked

away in the bottom, along with a large bottle of water, and headed out the door. I would wait on the front steps. The fresh air would surely give me a boost before I had to sit in a contained box of steel, hiding my looming secret next to my best friend, who wanted a baby more than anything is this world.

NANCY

"Oh dear, oh dear. I don't know how I ended up here," Nancy sang to herself. A lovely man sat next to her on a bench, overlooking the ocean. It was a beautiful evening, yet with the sun setting it was becoming rather cold. Nancy shivered and looked over at the man. He was munching on a granola bar. A steaming cup of coffee sat on the bench beside him. Nancy longed for a sip. She imagined the hot beverage traveling down her throat and warming her from the inside out. The caffeine would give her a bit of energy she needed to try to make it down the beach once again.

She watched him take another bite of his bar. A few crumbs jumbled from his lips and landed on his sweater. Brushing them off, he turned and smiled at Nancy.

He reminded her of Dean. Her sweet, sweet Dean.

Maybe she should tell him she was lost. Surely he would understand; he looked about ten years older than her. A pang of jealousy shot through her chest. How wonderful it would be to not be in her situation. She was aware things were getting worse, yet it was confusing because some days she was sharp as a whip. Ironically, at times she would forget all about her diagnosis.

That was the trouble with memory. It was a double-edged sword. Sometimes it was a luxury to forget. To be a twig in the stream and travel through life with only what was in front of you, never having to mind the past or the constant worries that usually hung suspended in the air, separating you from the things you loved and the life you wanted to live.

Other times it was a burden.

A terrible inconvenience.

To not recognize where you were or what you did the day before. To have to resort to Facebook or an address book to remember your friend's name or an event you attended. To try to keep track of what stories your children and friends have told you.

Of what you should and shouldn't know.

Nancy was thankful that at home, she had begun keeping a journal with all the important details. Just last night she had penned in the information about Julie's infertility. Right now, as she sat on the bench with no idea what direction she had come from or where her car was parked, she found it absolutely unbelievable that she would ever forget that her daughter was struggling with infertility. Yet she knew that even though this information was so important, it too could drift off with the wind, similar to a plastic bag in the park on a blustery day. No matter how fast you ran or how quick you were at changing directions, you just couldn't quite catch it.

The man finished his granola bar and tucked the wrapper into his jacket pocket. She turned to him and cleared her throat. She had to say something, because if she didn't, she might end up staying on this beach until nightfall, which would not be ideal. She needed to find her car and get home. Nancy shuddered at the thought of being stranded overnight somewhere. No one would even notice until the following day, if that!

The doctor's words nudged their way into her head.

You will have to share this with your family soon.

No.

This was just one incident, and it was still daytime!

There was no need to let her children know about the diagnosis yet.

"Excuse me, sir, ahhhh this is laughable, but I can't remember which end of the beach I came from, and I was hoping you could help me find the exit. I think it's the one with the sand dunes? I remember a bit of beach grass, too?"

The man watched her, nodding along. He raised his hands a bit, and she waited. They trembled ever so slightly, and she smiled encouragingly, giving him space to speak.

"Of course, yes, I can help. Have you been here long? I apologize, now that I am looking directly at you, you look a bit chilly. It's not particularly warm this evening. What is your name?"

Relief flooded through her. "My name is Nancy. Thank you so much. If I don't get off this beach soon, my kids might end up sending me to one of those old folks' homes." She laughed nervously at her own joke, mostly out of fear that it would actually come true.

The man chuckled and stood up, reaching for her hand to help her up. "Come on, we can walk together. I think we might have come from the same entrance, so let's give it a whirl. If not, I can give you a lift home."

She allowed him to help her off the bench, and they steadied each other as they trudged down through the deeper sand to the shore, where it was easier to walk.

"I can't tell you how much I appreciate this. You are a true hero. A knight in shining armor."

The man patted her arm. "It's my pleasure. I don't get much excitement in my life these days, and I love a good rescue story."

Nancy shivered as the strong wind pushed them along the shoreline. She just had to make it home. After that, she promised herself she would be more careful. No more afternoon adventures without her purse and phone in tow.

Suddenly, she heard her name being called.

She shook her head, trying to rattle the outside noises loose from her brain.

"I think perhaps your children might be onto you after all. Is that them coming down the beach?" The old man placed his hand on her arm. A silent gesture. One that brought her back to reality, and surprisingly, despite barely knowing him, felt very calming.

"Oh no. I think it is." She squinted as the bodies came closer and closer. "Uh-oh."

"Mom?"

Nancy winced at the accusatory tone in her daughter's voice.

"What are you doing?" Julie was marching toward them, looking livid. "Are you serious? Who is that? Why haven't you answered my calls?" Julie had reached them now and stood with her hands on her hips, slightly out of breath, with Ally at her heels.

It seemed as though Nancy's vocal cords had taken the day off, because when she opened her mouth to speak, she couldn't find the words. Nothing she could say right now would help her case.

"Who is that? Why are you not speaking?"

Nancy stood up taller and cleared her throat. "Julie, calm down now. I was just taking an evening walk, that's all. This is, uh, well, I am deeply embarrassed now. I never asked your name!"

Julie groaned and turned to Ally, mouthing the words, "Can you believe this right now?"

The man patted her arm again and turned to Julie,

outstretching his hand. "Jack. Your mother and I are beach pals. We meet here sometimes to go on evening strolls."

Julie eyed him suspiciously, and after a long moment, accepted Jack's handshake. Nancy knew he had lied to help her out, she just didn't know why; but she was very grateful. That was something Dean would do. She found comfort in it, like watching a movie you had seen a hundred times.

"Okay, well, it's weird you would meet someone to go on beach strolls when you don't even know his name."

Nancy sighed in response. Julie had done those awful quotation marks with her fingers when she said beach stroll.

"You can't just disappear all day and not answer your phone. Where is it? Why don't you have it on you?"

Nancy shifted uncomfortably on her feet and glanced at Ally, who was looking rather pale. "Well... I left it in the car." She made a mental note to write this down in her journal.

Investigate Ally.

"And where is your car?"

Her daughter's sharp voice pulled her back to present.

"I didn't see it when we parked to come down here." Julie narrowed her eyes and folded her arms.

"Well, Julie." She looked at her new friend, who smiled sympathetically at her, giving her a boost of confidence. "I actually have no idea where it is."

JULIE

JULIE KEPT GLANCING IN THE REARVIEW MIRROR
where Ally lay horizontally across the seat with one hand over
her face.

"Ally, are you sure you're okay? You're acting very strange."

Julie frowned when Ally limply lifted her hand as a
response. Ally was an odd duck, so this behavior wasn't totally
out of left field, but she seemed different in some way. Julie
craned her head to the side to make sure her mother was still
following close behind her.

It had taken almost an hour to find her mother's car, which
was parked alongside a set of bushes on a random side street a
few miles from the beach. Julie tapped the steering wheel and
wondered how she had ended up with a dingbat mother and a
neurotic weirdo for a best friend.

Why was everyone was losing it? Suddenly, her Bluetooth
rang, and when she saw it was Greg, she silenced it, jamming
her foot on the gas a little too hard, causing the car to lurch
forward.

"Julie, please! Easy on the gas. I might vomit right here and
now if you don't calm down your driving."

Julie glanced back at Ally, who was clutching the handle of
the door.

She fought back a laugh as she tried to stay focused on the
road.

"Just because I am ill, doesn't mean you will get out of this.
Tell me this instant why you ignored Greg's call. Although I

am glad you did, his voice would be too much for our fragile states right now."

Julie rolled her eyes and smiled. Even when Ally was being annoying, she still always managed to lighten the mood. "I am not talking about Greg tonight. Or tomorrow, for that matter. Do you think you have the stomach flu?" Julie peered into the back again, stifling a laugh at the sight of Ally dramatically sprawled out in the back seat.

"Yes. Yes, that is what I have. I must have gotten it from dipping my hands into the nut mix at the bar. My inhibitions got the best of me. That is why I always tell you to be careful with germs in public spaces. You can never be too cautious. Take me as an example!"

Julie giggled and slowed down as they approached her mother's street. She rolled into the driveway and threw the car into park.

Ally groaned at the abrupt stop and flopped her arm against the window. "I might be dying."

"Just stay here, you weirdo. I am going to make sure Wandering Wendy gets back inside all right."

Ally mumbled something inaudible in response; her eyes closed.

Shaking her head, Julie hopped out of the car and looked at her mother, who was still sitting in the driver's seat, staring straight ahead at the garage.

"What is going on with this woman lately?" Julie muttered to herself. "Mom? Are you okay?"

She watched as her mother cocked her head to the side and looked at Julie as though she just noticed she was there for the first time. Maybe she had been drinking nips on the beach with her new friend. Julie fought back the urge to say something bratty.

Be nice.

After her dad died, her mother had abruptly stopped drinking alcohol. Julie could still remember when she'd shared her decision with Julie, her eyes full of tears.

"Julie, I don't want to forget the rest of my life. I want to remember every single memory with crystal-clear precision. So much of your dad and I's life was—I don't know. Blurry."

At the time, it seemed intentional and positive, like this was the new Nancy. The immense relief Julie had felt that her mother was choosing her health for once had been welcomed surprise.

She stared at her mother now. Full of alcohol and irresponsible decisions.

She should have known it was all an act.

She should have known her mother would let her down.

It had always been this way. Once in high school, she had gone on a run in the dead of the summer and ran immediately to the fridge to grab a bottle of water. As she gulped down a huge sip, she was met with the sharp burn of alcohol traveling down her throat. She'd gagged and spat the liquid back out all over the inside of the fridge, disgusted and ashamed.

What kind of parents filled empty water bottles with vodka?

When she had confronted her about it, her mother had laughed and said, "It's much easier to bring a little bottle of vodka to a day at the beach than lugging around the whole handle! Plus, everyone thinks you are being healthy."

Julie looked back at her mother, still sitting there with a confused expression.

"Mom. Let's go." Julie exhaled, trying to muster up the little bit of patience she had left. She tapped on the window impatiently. "Come on. It's late."

Finally, her mother seemed to snap to it and got out of the car, breezing right past her, up the walkway and into the house without so much as a single word.

Shaking her head, Julie threw her hands up and followed her inside. "What is going on with you? Are you drunk?"

Her mother was rummaging frantically through a drawer in the kitchen. It reminded her of when she was little and they were about to head out for a day at the beach. She would always forget something, leaving Julie and Ally sitting in the car waiting for what seemed like an eternity.

A blip of guilt lodged itself in her chest as she heard her dad's voice in her head.

Be nice to your mother; she is the glue of this family. Keeping track of you, your brother, and Ally, isn't an easy feat. One day when you have kids of your own, you'll understand.

A pang of sadness hit her out of nowhere as she turned his words over in her brain. As it turned out, she wouldn't be able to ever understand, because to understand, she would need to get pregnant first.

"Just a minute, I have to find a pen."

Julie shifted on her feet as irritation climbed up her chest, threatening to create another outburst.

Her mother's head popped up, and she turned and looked at Julie with concern. "All right, got one. I am fine, Julie. Just tired and cold from that beach walk."

Julie swallowed down the anger and sadness, forcing herself to focus.

To be kind.

"Your friend Jack seemed nice."

Her mother snapped her head up and looked at Julie.

There was that blank stare again.

She had definitely been drinking.

"Yes, well, I know you must need to get home. Why don't you make Greg a nice dinner tonight? I am sure he is tired from his week at work. You both need some time together."

Julie scoffed, feeling all the kindness drain from her body.

"I am not making Greg dinner tonight. I am going to sit down and have a glass of wine by myself."

She let the door slam on her way out, wincing as a pulse of rage shot through her body. She pulled open the driver's side door and climbed in. At least she could vent to her best friend about it.

"Ally, my mother is officially losing it," she muttered as she buckled her seat belt, but when Ally didn't respond, she craned her neck around and looked in the back seat.

Ally was dead asleep.

"What is with everyone today?" Julie muttered to herself.

ALLY

I HAD REALIZED, RATHER SUDDENLY THAT BEING pregnant was utterly unbearable and very hard to manage on my own. I had bought myself a bit of time after my little stint in the back seat of Julie's car, claiming I had contracted a terrible stomach bug. This, I assumed, would keep Julie at bay and from asking too many questions. I told Julie it would be irresponsible of me to be around her, considering she was about to begin IVF. I didn't want to jeopardize her chances at having a successful round. That, it seemed, was enough to keep her away for now, but I missed her terribly! It turned out that hiding your pregnancy from your best friend was not really ideal.

Cade, on the other hand, had been a different challenge. Some days I was able to manage my condition, and on others, I was running to the toilet nonstop, completely unable to contribute to society. Thank goodness he worked out of the house and was, for the most part, oblivious to what I did on a daily basis. It was one of the reasons we had decided to make the leap and move in together shortly after we started dating.

I smiled at the memory of Cade sitting down with me to make a pros and cons list. My idea, of course.

"Okay, I know you need your own space," he'd said as he drew a line down the middle of a sheet of paper, labeling the two columns.

I'd eyed him suspiciously.

"Don't worry. I have a plan." He'd leaned over and kissed

me, then focused back on the list. "So, I figure if you are going to let me marry you one day, we should do a trial first."

"A trial? This doesn't sound very romantic," I'd teased, knowing very well I wasn't really the romantic type.

He'd laughed, that deep belly laugh that made his eyes crinkle and my heart jump. "It is my life's mission to turn you into a romantic, Ally Arlington, and might I add, soon to be Ally Webster." He'd winked at me and then tapped the paper with his pen. "Pros: Cade does all the lawn maintenance and can move heavy furniture for your weekly deep cleaning." He'd looked back at me, his eyes sparkling with excitement.

"That does sound very appealing," I'd agreed.

He'd beamed and continued on, "Another pro: I am an outstanding cook. Plus, I make pour over coffee every morning."

I'd nodded. "Both excellent points, but..." I'd paused, almost feeling bad in the moment to even bring up a con. He was so proud of himself. I'd studied his face and squeezed his hand. "Con: I will have to share my bed with you. Every night. Every single night." I'd looked at him, lowering my voice to almost a whisper. "What if I hate it?"

His hand had flown to his chest, and he'd leaned back dramatically. "Oh, you poor soul! You mean to tell me you would have to share a giant king bed with the most handsome man in the world?" He'd laughed again before kissing me. "How will you ever do it?" Then his face had become serious and he'd leaned in closer to me. "We can get one of those big body pillows and put it in between us if you want,"

His eyes had twinkled with mischief, and I'd found myself smiling back.

"That way we could move it, you know, if things got wild."

I'd laughed and pushed him away, narrowing my eyes. "Fine. I will consider it."

He'd whooped and punched the air with his fist.

I'd reached up and grabbed his hand. "But, if it feels like too much for me, will you sleep in the guest room some nights?"

His face had fallen, but only slightly.

I'd smiled apologetically. "Only to give myself a recharge, just once and while."

I'd studied him, waiting.

Hoping I hadn't pushed him too far.

He was the first man who had ever truly understood me, but sometimes I worried that all of me was too much, even for him.

Cade had put his hands on my shoulders and looked at me with admiration and love. "You, Ally Webster, have got yourself a deal."

Then he'd stuck his hand out as if it were a business transaction, which I'd appreciated.

I'd shook it, and the following day we immediately started house hunting.

Now, I was at my twelve-week appointment, and the decision about sharing a bed seemed trivial and ridiculous.

Now, I had real problems. Despite my several attempts to tell Cade about the pregnancy, I couldn't bring myself to do it. I didn't know how to make a list about this. I didn't know how to tell him, sorry, I just don't want to be a mother. As if I was turning down an invitation to a dinner party.

On top of that, I'd grown oddly attached to the small being in my stomach. Perhaps it was the documentaries I had been watching on Netflix that had changed my tune, or the incessant googling I had partaken in while lying horizontally on the couch for hours on end. I simply couldn't fathom the idea of terminating the pregnancy. Based on my research, I had about ten to twelve weeks left to decide. I had also read that most women who decide to do this definitely didn't wait that long.

I was running out of time.

I had, in a lot of ways, already ran out of time.

Yet, despite all of this, I didn't want to become a mother. I couldn't be a mother. I had no interest in staying up in the midnight hours to nurse a newborn or change countless diapers.

That was what Julie wanted.

She was so wonderful with children. It was as if a switch went off in Julie when she was around kids. With adults, she had zero patience, and frankly, a short fuse, but with kids she turned into a different person. In college, Julie had always had a nannying job in the summer, toting around the tiny little gremlins to the park and the beach with a huge smile plastered on her face.

I, on the other hand, felt very confused as to why parents would bring their small beings into a restaurant, for example. What a disaster it appeared to be.

Crayons strewn in every direction.

Crumbs mashed and smashed into the carpet.

A whirlwind of cups, wipes, small, tiny race cars.

Never mind the iPads.

I could not even begin to think about the iPads that the small, impressionable children clutched in their hands as if they were their lifelines to the only boat before the great flood.

As I sat in the waiting room, I leaned back to adjust my pants. Everything was too tight. The seam of my workout leggings dug into the inside of my thigh. It felt as though a thousand tiny needles were jamming into my skin, constantly reminding me that my body was no longer mine. As a highly sensitive person, I already had resistance to many fabrics and materials. It appeared that my condition had made this much worse. I spent most of my days changing outfits and positions, trying to find reprieve from all of the feelings, sensations, and supplements all the apps recommended I consume. The jar that the giant prenatal vitamins came in was jam-packed with the worst of them all.

Cotton.

Oh, how I loathed the feeling!

I could not even ask Cade for help because, clearly, that would give me away. Every morning, I had spent over ten minutes using a butter knife to move the cotton in the jar aside so I could fish out two of the pills. I certainty couldn't just reach my fingers in and pull out the cotton, because the feeling of it was too much to handle. How did other people touch cotton without a care in the world? I shuddered as I thought about the other morning when a snag of cotton had clung to one pill after I rescued it from the jar. I had almost put it directly into my mouth, but thankfully I'd decided to do a final inspection before I swallowed them down. Archimedes had been at my feet, his giant head cocked to one side watching me quizzically.

Even the dog understood that I had some questionable traits.

It was moments like that when I really longed for Julie. I wished so badly I could tell her about what was happening. I needed my partner in crime. I could have brought the jar of pills over to her house and had her help me with the cotton.

"Ally?"

I looked up at the nurse, who was calling my name, and forced a smile as I gathered my belongings and lumbered behind her down the hallway. I seemed to be growing more tired by the day. I could feel my agility slipping away. Glancing around, I took note of the giant photos of babies and mothers plastered all over the walls. Their gummy smiles and tired eyes seemed to follow me as I turned into the patient room where even more pictures awaited me on the walls.

It reminded me of Julie's house when we were growing up. Julie's family was the type that did seasonal photo shoots and mailed out meticulous Christmas cards. My mother always proudly hung up the one she received from Nancy, beaming as she pointed at me, nestled in between Julie and her older brother Will. "Look at you, Ally! You fit right in!"

I wondered now, with this little life growing inside me, if that had bothered my mother. At the time, I hadn't thought much about it. I would tag along for family photos, and then we would all go out to a big fancy dinner.

Never once was my mother included in any of that.

Had that been wrong of me to allow myself to become absorbed by another family while my mother worked double shifts to provide for me?

I looked back to the photos on the wall. To the other expecting mothers, it was all comforting and quite endearing to be surrounded by graphics and photos and informational packets.

To me, it was all white noise. A whirlwind of data that I did not resonate with or care to consume.

"All right, Ally! An exciting day today. You will get to hear the heartbeat, and before you know it, it will be time for the anatomy scan!"

My body stiffened. I fumbled with my purse and tried to push aside my thoughts. I wanted to explain to her I had already heard the heartbeat at the last appointment. I understood that from a medical perspective this was necessary, but surely the excitement of it would wear off on the mother's end? It reminded me of a book by your favorite author that you were awaiting the release of. Once it arrived and you had devoured the pages, you were left with a slightly empty feeling.

The thrill was gone.

The pages read.

The noise dulled.

Before I could decide what to say to the nurse, she was already on her way out. The staff here seemed a bit rushed. Certainly, they had learned about bedside manners during medical school? Where were the decency and respect for the patients? I sat there staring at the various posters on the walls. I read through all the frightening facts about what would happen if I chose not to vaccinate and the importance of seat belts for children.

Surely this was common sense?

Seat belts? Were there mothers that were against seat belts?

And then, just as I was wishing I could snap a picture of the poster and send it to Julie, there was a soft knock on the door. Before I could respond, a male doctor filled up the room.

One I did not recognize.

A male doctor!

When had they planned to alert me they had changed doctors? I sat up straighter and pulled my arms around myself. The doctor smiled and reached his hand out to shake mine. I froze, reluctant to touch his germ-infested hands.

"Great to meet you, Doctor. I typically do not shake hands in public settings." I stared with disgust at his fingers, still extended toward me. "No offense to you. This is a personal choice, of course."

He dropped his hand, looking at me oddly, which made me feel better. I was used to people giving me odd looks.

"Also," I carried on. "I am a bit perplexed. I was not notified that my doctor had changed. Has there been a switch I am not aware of?"

The doctor frowned. I watched as he quickly recovered, forcing a smile across his face. "I completely understand! On the handshake, I mean." He laughed, and then it was my turn to frown.

I didn't see anything funny about this situation.

He paused as if trying to figure out what to make of me, and then barreled on with the confidence of a typical white male. "There has not been a switch; you will have the opportunity to meet everyone on our OB and midwife team here. This way, when you go into labor, you are not surprised with a doctor you have never met before."

He tapped his clipboard with his pen, and I could see the impatience lurking in his bouncing fingers.

When I did not respond, he cleared his throat. "Since babies don't care about our schedules or follow any of the rules, we can't plan on having a specific doctor for your delivery."

I swallowed and tried to remain calm. How had I not thought about this inconvenience? Of course, logically, it made sense, but when he laid it out for me in this way, I began to feel a whisper of panic rise in my throat. I inhaled slowly, trying to force more air into the bottom of my lungs, but they simply would not fill the way I wished them to.

"Ally? Are you okay? You look rather pale."

I could hear the doctor speaking to me, but he sounded very far away. I tried hard to force more air into my lungs and thought about saying something in response, but I was so tired. Instead, I focused on the black dots swirling around in front of my face. They moved slowly, as if they had nowhere to be, and then, just as I was beginning to wonder how I would get them to stop, everything went black.

NANCY

Nancy sat up, startled by the constant ringing coming from her phone. She patted her hand around on the nightstand, trying to find the light switch. Parker, her tabby cat, meowed incessantly at the end of the bed. The meowing and continuous alarm rattled around in her brain. Panic rose in her chest.

"Enough out of everyone!" she yelled.

The cat jumped down and looked back at her, rather miffed. Finally, she located the light and spent the next two minutes trying to silence the alarm on her phone. Why had she set the alarm for 5 a.m.? She pushed herself up out of the bed and slipped on her robe. She didn't think she would be able to go back to sleep now.

As she made her way down to the kitchen, she tried hard to remember what had happened the day before. Her brain was cloudy. She knew there had been something of significance, but what had it been?

She racked her brain, trying to come up with an answer, but it kept directing her back to a few weeks ago when she had to quit her part-time job due to the diagnosis. Nancy had worked as a part-time school nurse. Hiding her illness from her family was one thing, but continuing to care for children while her brain was set on abandoning her was another.

She loved her job and the flexibility it provided her. Thank goodness it had been part-time; it had given her the opportunity to hide the fact that she quit from her children. It had not been that challenging to keep the change quiet, as her children were very self-involved. They hardly asked her how she was doing or if she was okay. Nancy knew that was partly her fault. She didn't want them to worry! Navigating your late twenties was enough of a stressor. They didn't need their wobbly mother to add more to their plates.

Whenever they asked about work, she would just wave her hand and assure them it was the same as always. *"Enough about my boring life, I want to hear about yours!"*

She stood stock still in the kitchen, thinking about her children.

About how much she loved them.

No one told you that the first time you hold your child in your arms, your soul splits in two. That half of it moves into their body and lodges itself there forever. That was how it felt to Nancy, anyway. What they also didn't tell you was that you move along through the toddler years into childhood and beyond, thinking that it will get easier. That the love will become more manageable.

But it doesn't.

It just shifts.

Into a more desperate kind of love.

A love you feel like you have to chase and balance delicately in your hand.

If you move too quickly, you could break it.

They could snatch it all away from you.

Leave you guessing and wondering if they were okay.

Her children's lives and careers were now her livelihood. They were what she looked forward to hearing about every day. That was why it pained her so much to watch Julie slip away from her. With each year that passed, the distance between Julie and Nancy seemed to double, like one of those highways that seemed just fine, but the state insisted on widening, causing a two-year long traffic jam. It forced you to reroute your life, and sometimes you never found your way back to the way things were, because they had been bulldozed over.

Nancy glanced at the clock. Only thirty minutes had passed. She thought about giving Lorrie a call, but she didn't want to be a bother. Lorrie worked so hard, and Nancy always tried to be conscientious about how different their lives were. Sometimes Nancy felt guilty that she had been able to provide so much for Ally while Lorrie continued to struggle on through life. Nancy had never wanted Lorrie to feel bad, which was why she certainly couldn't complain to Lorrie about Julie. How trivial it would sound coming from her. The woman who had all the time in the world to spend with her children, only to come out on the other side of it wanting even more.

Maybe what she should do was pay Lorrie a visit at work. That way she wouldn't be a bother but she could still say hi to her. She made her way around the house, trying to figure out what things she would need to pack in that bag that she always took with her when she left the house. She couldn't pluck from her brain what it was called, but she could picture it, sitting by the door ready to filled with all her items.

She added a package of oyster crackers, always an easy snack for on the go. Followed by a bottle of water and her notebook, just in case. Julie had always loved oyster crackers, especially as a little girl. As she'd grown older and more opinionated, Nancy had always been able to connect with her over a meal. But even that seemed to have changed over the last few years.

She tried to remind herself that Julie had always been a tough nut to crack, and despite Nancy's nurturing approach to motherhood, they never really had a close bond. Now that Julie was married with a fancy career, she didn't need Nancy. She didn't need her coddling or her advice.

It appeared that all Julie needed Nancy from was a punching bag.

Nancy stared at the clock above the stove. It was now 6 a.m., but she couldn't remember what time it had been the last time she looked. Had any time passed, or was she stuck in some odd dream? She shuffled over to the kitchen table and sat down, trying to orient herself in reality. She flipped through her address book absentmindedly and caught some of the names as the pages turned.

Debra. Alice. Alma.

All three of them often made comments to her about Julie.

How could you let your daughter treat you like that! I would never allow it!

But Nancy didn't mind. She just wanted everyone to be happy. She saw the pain hiding in Julie's eyes. The longing for things she was yet to have. That was enough to keep Nancy going. Even though Julie was somewhat of a lost cause, she still let Nancy in on her life, just not emotionally.

But physically, Nancy was still there. And that, for now, was enough for her.

Nancy knew it was partly because of Dean. She wondered sometimes if things would have been different if he were still here. Julie and Dean had such a special bond. One that Nancy longed to have, but at the same time, was grateful at least one of them had with her daughter so that she still had an in.

Now that he was gone, she never knew what Julie was thinking.

Nancy felt like she was in a life-size game of Chutes and Ladders.

Every time she made progress, Julie shot her down, and she had to start over.

Will was a few years younger than Julie, and frankly, the complete opposite. She was afraid she had coddled him too much when he was a baby. She could still hear Dean's voice in her head. *Let the boy live! He is still going to be crawling into our bed when he is fourteen if you don't stop babying him!*

Nancy hadn't listened.

As her daughter drifted away from her, becoming best friends with Ally, Nancy had clung onto Will's youth, knowing he was her last baby.

Now, he had a very important job, working for an aviation company and making quite a name for himself. If she were being honest with herself, she missed her son more than ever. He was so busy with his job and family, she hardly ever spent time with him. She was glad, though, because he would most certainly catch on to what was happening with her.

With what she was forgetting.

With what was slipping away.

As the coffee machine gurgled, she searched around for her notebook, where she kept all the important details. Where was it? This was one of the problems she had been running into. She kept misplacing the dang thing. It was not very convenient to lose the notebook that held everyone's secrets. She needed to debrief on the day and get herself up to speed so she could make sure she didn't slip up in any conversations.

Parker stood at the front door, meowing again, pushing against the frame with his head.

"All right, all right, you can go outdoors for a few hours, that is fine with me." As she opened the front door to let him out, she spotted her car, which was normally parked in the garage. Why was it in the driveway? She craned her neck out the door, squinting in the early morning light, trying to remember.

Oh yes.

The beach!

She had been to the beach.

And just like that, the previous day downloaded right into her head. Quickly, she shut the door and shuffled around to the dining room. She remembered now! The journal. She could have sworn she had tucked it in the buffet table by the fireplace. After another fifteen minutes of searching, she reluctantly gave up. It would turn up at some point. She couldn't let the notebook dictate her whole day; she had things to do!

Once she had made her way to the car, she settled her bag beside her on the passenger seat. She found herself still thinking about the notebook. All her independence and confidence seemed to have stayed back inside the house. She didn't like leaving without it. What if she needed to remember something while she was out? Or needed to record something important.

She sighed with impatience.

She could always ask Lorrie for a pen and paper. Lorrie worked just down the street as the manager of a small casino. Terrible job, in Nancy's opinion, but she understood that poor Lorrie didn't have a lot of options.

As she pulled into the parking lot, she saw a pickup truck she recognized, but she couldn't place how. The casino was in a large plaza where other bars and stores sat adjacent to it, waiting to lure people in to spend all of their money. She sat there for quite some time, watching the truck as if at any moment it was going to drive away on its own. Something told her to wait a bit before she went inside to see Lorrie.

One thing she hadn't lost yet was her intuition.

She might misplace an object or two every now and then, but she still knew when to listen to her gut.

Just as she was about to give in and head inside, she heard laughter.

A familiar voice.

She pulled her sunglasses down and sank lower into her

seat, like she was on a secret mission. It felt a bit thrilling, all of this. Then she gasped.

There was Greg.

In plain sight.

Walking several yards away from her. With another woman. Holding her hand! Completely oblivious to Nancy. That little ratfink! This would not do. The nerve he had! She leaned forward and then slouched down again.

What was she going to do? She couldn't confront him, not without speaking to Julie first. She waited until they had gotten into his truck before carefully backing out and heading straight home.

Greg was cheating.

Cheating on Julie!

Once she was home and had poured herself a cup of coffee, she scoured her brain, trying to recall where the dang journal was. Parker was back at the door, meowing to be let in.

"All right, all right, in you go." She watched Parker hop onto the thing that held other things and felt a sudden sadness. Who would take care of Parker when she was no longer able to? Her cheeks were wet with warm tears, and she wiped them away, reaching over to pet the cat. She needed him to have a good home. She would have to get her affairs in order. For the future, of course. Parker nudged her bag, causing it to tumble to the ground. Everything spilled out, a splattered a mess on the floor. She watched as a quarter rolled underneath the thing with wooden legs, and that's when she saw it.

The notebook!

"Oh, Parker, you smart little fox, you!" She carried it to the living room couch, with the cat at her heels, trying her best to pinpoint what it was that she wanted to write down.

Of course, it wouldn't come.

Instead, she settled in to read up on what she had to remember and what she could allow herself to forget.

JULIE

Ever since she was a little girl, she had always dreamed of becoming a mother. She was the first one out of her friends to start babysitting. She made her mother drive her to the local library every Saturday morning for a CPR class as soon as she turned twelve. Before that, she had been a mother's helper a few afternoons a week after school. She forced all of her friends to play MASH over and over again, just so she could see how many kids she would end up with. Then, she would name them all and envision her big family with a huge backyard and an Olympic-sized swimming pool.

Lucy was going to be her first girl's name. Henry her first boy's name. Not once in all her life had she considered the fact that she might actually not be able to get pregnant. In high school, all she heard was, *Be careful! Use contraception! You don't want to end up a teenage mother!* She had spent her college years terrified of becoming pregnant before she was ready. Saying a silent prayer every month when it was confirmed she wasn't. When she'd met Greg during her senior year, he had checked all the boxes.

He was ambitious and handsome.

He wanted the same things Julie did.

Together, they were going to build a family and a comfortable life for themselves.

After their lavish wedding, she had gotten right down to business. She had been clear with him from day one about trying for a baby right away.

"Whatever makes you happy, babe," was what he would always say when she brought up trying on their honeymoon. One of her coworkers had told her that after marriage, things changed, that her husband had balked at the whole family thing.

That wasn't Greg.

He had always been so supportive of everything she chose to do in her life.

On their honeymoon in Tulum, she remembered walking around with a content smile on her face. There very well could already have been a baby gestating inside her. She could hardly wait four weeks to see the positive line. On the plane ride back, she had made a baby shower list and jotted down a few potential venues. She couldn't wait to dart to the drugstore to buy a variety of tests. She envisioned herself in their giant master bathroom with multiple positive pregnancy tests lined up on the counter, yelling to Greg to come up and see.

She had been so naïve.

She did not know how goddamn hard it was to actually get pregnant. Why did she waste all those years taking birth control and worrying when she had been late? She could have never used a whisper of contraception and still been as sterile as an ER.

Julie sighed and tapped her fingers on the side of the arm chair. She was back at the doctor's office this morning to have a conversation about next steps. Greg had left early for work. Last night after she had gotten home from the debacle with her mother, he had been posted up on the couch watching a movie.

At least he had come back.

How pathetic it was that those were her initial thoughts when she saw him. She didn't even recognize herself anymore. They'd spoken zero words, and she'd poured herself a gigantic glass of wine, which only added to her anxiety because she was always worried that the alcohol diminished her chances of having a viable pregnancy.

But so did the stress, and the wine helped combat the stress.

She couldn't win, no matter what she did.

When she complained about this to Ally, she had replied, "Well, I think this is a simple matter of picking your poison."

Julie had laughed. "Thank god for your humor or I would be even more of a stress case."

Ally had cocked her head to the side and replied, "I do not think picking your poison is really supposed to be a funny saying."

She wished Ally was with her now. Julie had almost driven over to her house to beg her to come, but she knew she still wasn't feeling well. Plus, she had to start making some decisions on her own. She didn't need Ally for everything.

Last week, one of her coworkers, Susan, had cornered her and told her all about her friend's daughter who was struggling with infertility. She could still see Susan's excited expression and sagging sad eyes as she told Julie the story.

"As soon as Gretta had stopped trying and just lived her life, she got pregnant!"

As if Julie had never heard about this amazing concept.

As if Julie was going to give her a giant hug and thank her for solving the last two years of her infertility in thirty seconds.

"You see, dear, what Gretta realized is that once she just relaxed, her body could do its thing, and whalla! She was pregnant."

Susan had flung her hands wildly, causing Julie to flinch. At the time, Julie felt like grabbing the stapler from her desk and chucking it at Susan's fluffy head of hair.

Susan had reached out and patted Julie's arm. "Just start living your life, dear. Take that infertility savings and spend it on a trip to the Gold Coast! Trust me. You have to stop thinking about it."

At that point, Julie's rage had morphed back into sadness and she had to fight back the hot tears prickling like tiny daggers in the back of her eyes.

Of course, Susan had taken her almost tears as a sign that she was grateful. She had smothered Julie in a super awkward hug and handed her a box of tissues. "Oh, dear, I knew this would be so helpful for you. All you needed was a little inspirational pep talk and a good reminder that life is too short."

Julie squeezed her fingers into fists as hard as she could, allowing the rage to travel up her forearms and into her shoulders where it would settle and collect dust with the rest of her bottled-up emotions. She closed her eyes and inhaled for six seconds, counting down in her head, trying her best to focus on the numbers.

She hated this.

With each passing day, Julie felt like her thin grasp on reality was becoming even thinner. Becoming pregnant had turned into an obsession.

She went to bed thinking about babies.

She woke up and tested her hormone levels.

She peed on ovulation sticks and gave herself shots.

She even followed influencers on Instagram who were struggling with infertility, so she felt less alone.

She counted again, this time for ten seconds. Her therapist had told her to count to twelve, but that made her feel like she was drowning. Ten was the best she could do. Then, she exhaled for three. It was supposed to get her out of the moment. To calm her nervous system. To bring her back to center. After her therapist trained her how to do it, she had lied and said it was soooo helpful!

The fucking breathing did not make a difference.

She still felt the same, but she kept doing it in hopes that it would change something.

Just like these infertility treatments.

ALLY

"I HAVE CALLED HER EMERGENCY CONTACT, YES, that's right. He will meet us at the hospital." The sound of a pen scribbling very close to my ear made me twitch. I wanted the incessant noise to stop. Who was writing a novel by hand directly next to my head, and why was it so hot? My body felt heavy; the only thing that appeared to be moving in it was my racing heart.

"I think she is waking up, doctor. Should I get her some water or juice?"

Juice, yes. Orange juice, please. Better yet, one of those cinnamon rolls from the bakery down the road would be preferable. I wanted to say all of this to the squeaky voice who had come up with the juice idea, but when I opened my mouth, it stalled, and I was unable to put the words together.

"Yes, she is definitely waking up. Ally? Can you hear me? This is Rachel, the nurse that brought you in earlier for your appointment? You fainted. You are in the doctor's office. Ally?"

My fingers twitched, and I watched her worried face. It was very close to mine. I could see the cracks where her excessive makeup had dried around the corners of her eyes. There was glittery brown on her eyelids, and I made a mental note to let her know that she would need to have a lip waxing. For someone so worried about her appearance, she had somehow missed the fact that the start of a light mustache was settling in to stay.

My eyes moved slowly to her earlobes. The poor things! They had been stretched beyond repair and were currently holding up the weight of gigantic martini glasses, complete with a little olive in each one. The thought of olives made me gag, and I groaned, trying my best to sit up.

"Oh no you don't." Rachel leaned over and put a hand on my chest, her earring coming even closer to my face than before. I struggled under the weight of her hand and then closed my eyes again.

"We can't let you get up just yet. The EMT's are coming, and we are going to head across the street to the hospital. Just to make sure everything is all right. You had quite a fall when you fainted."

I opened my eyes again and looked away from Rachel. I could see underneath the unit where I usually sat for the appointments. There were a lone paperclip and a small toy figurine. A fine layer of dust had settled over them, as if it had laid its claim, knowing they would never be seen again. I made a mental note to let the receptionist know that some small child had lost their toy and that the janitor was doing a poor job of keeping the place clean.

The door swung open, and a large pair of boots settled a few feet away from my head. I tried to sit up again, but Rachel's hand gently pushed me down. Opening my mouth, I attempted to let her know I was fine, but still, nothing would come out. It was as if my brain and my mouth had stopped communicating. I was sure this was not a good sign. The pair of boots moved closer, and I heard the loud crackle of knees as the legs bent down.

"Ally, I'm Keith. We are going to transport you to a carrier, okay? Don't try to help us, we've got you."

How did they presume that I was going to consider helping them? I was lying on the floor, useless, like a sad little baby bird. Rachel patted my shoulder, and I watched as her martini glasses swung wildly. One stopped short, catching in a wisp of her curly hair. She didn't seem to notice, and I longed to reach up and fix it for her. I had a bad feeling she would go the rest of the day with it stuck there, only to release it much later when she returned home and was preparing for bed.

"All right, Ally. My buddy Larry is going to help me get you on the gurney. We are going to count to three and then lift you up."

As he said this, he had managed to simultaneously slip a neck brace around my head quicker than I could muster up the strength to protest. For such a creaky man, he was moving quite swiftly.

Before I knew it, he was counting down.

"Three, two, one!"

Poor Larry made a loud grunting noise as they hoisted me up and over.

"Back's not the same as it used to be," Larry muttered.

We were moving now, and I closed my eyes as they carried me through the doorway and slowly down the hall.

"Careful now, don't jostle her around the corner here. That's it. Yes, you got it."

Keith appeared to be coaching Larry through the ordeal, and I agreed that he definitely needed the encouragement. I allowed one eye to open a crack and caught sight of the nervous receptionist who was scurrying over to the front door to open it for the unit to make it through.

I heard a small child say, "Mommy, mommy! Look! A dead lady."

Before I could hear the mother's response, we were out in the bright sunshine, traveling up and into the ambulance.

"Ally, dear, it's Rachel again. I wanted to see you out. You are going to be in good hands, and lucky for you it's a quick trip! The hospital is just across the street."

Rachel clasped her hands together excitedly, as if she had just told me that I had won a giveaway. I stared at her, trying to decide if I should let her know about the mustache. It was probably best to keep quiet, plus I couldn't talk properly at the moment anyway. Perhaps I'd mail in a letter or leave an anonymous voicemail on the following business day.

Rachel reached out and patted me knee, as if I were a five-year-old. "Don't you worry. I called Cade right after you fell. He is meeting you at the hospital."

My heart dropped.

Cade?

No. No. No.

Rachel you bad, bad lady! I wanted to scream.

What happened to patient privacy? I opened my mouth again to tell Rachel, NO!

Do not call Cade.

Call him back and tell him it was a mistake.

Cade could not meet me at the hospital because that would mean he knew.

I could feel tears pooling in my eyes, and I fought the urge to bring my hands up to them. It wouldn't be sanitary to be wiping at my face after all this commotion.

Cade could not know. It would break his heart. Plus, my five-year plan was dwindling by the day. I had worked so hard to line everything up. To make my exit without hurting too many people.

What would I say to Cade now?

The worst part of all of this was that I knew Cade would understand. He would engulf me in a giant hug, questioning the doctors and making sure I was comfortable. He would do everything right while in my brain I would swirl around in the idea of skipping out on all of this.

I couldn't bear to do that to him.

He didn't deserve it.

A small squeak managed to escape my mouth, but no one seemed to hear. Rachel was already marching back to the building, one of her martini glass earrings shimmering and swaying in the sunlight, the other still caught in her hair, trapped.

Just like I was on this stretcher.

With these people who didn't understand.

I tried to lift my hand to get Larry or Keith's attention, but an oxygen mask was promptly placed over my face.

"Ally, your blood pressure is dropping, and your oxygen isn't where we would like it to be. This will help."

The doors to the back of the ambulance slammed shut, and I lay there, staring at the ceiling, completely frozen and unable to stop what was about to come.

NANCY

NOW THAT SHE HAD ALL HER DUCKS IN A ROW, SHE
dialed up Julie's number and waited for her daughter to
answer. Her plan was to invite Julie out to lunch and see if she
could get her to admit she was struggling with Greg. Nancy
could fix this for her! She knew how to patch up a marriage like
the best of them. Her husband Dean had been a complicated
man but a wonderful father, bless his heart.

He had passed away five years ago.

A sudden heart attack.

As she made her way through her house after almost
visiting Lorrie, she couldn't help but think about how lucky
she was, despite everything. Lorrie had gone through so much
hardship. She had never had the support Nancy had. She had
never had the luxury of leaning on a partner. Having a best
friend to talk to. Someone who understood you inside and out.

Oh, how she missed him!

What would happen when she started to forget him?

She didn't want to think about that.

She needed to be grateful and cherish each day while she
still had the chance.

Thankfully, today, she was able to remember every detail
about him. About their conversations. What they wanted for
the second half of their life together. She wondered now
what would be different in her life, with her diagnosis, if
Dean were still alive. What would have been different for
Julie had Dean still been alive? For Will? Those were the

things you wondered after someone you loved left you unexpectedly.

Would you have made different decisions if they were still around?

Would your life have taken a different turn?

Or would you still feel just as lonely? Just as lost?

The call went right to voicemail, which was atypical. Usually, Julie silenced her when she called or left her texts on read, but it never went right to voicemail. Nancy sighed audibly and decided she would just go out and find Julie after she brushed up on all her notes.

A few months after Dean had died, Nancy had overheard Julie and Will talking about her. They had just finished Christmas dinner, and Nancy was cleaning up the dishes. Julie and Will had retreated to the family room to relax by the fire.

Nancy, like any mother to children in their twenties, loved a good eavesdropping session. If she were being honest, she had been doing it since they were little. Each year as they got older, she felt them pull away from her, slowly, like a catch of a thread on a favorite sweater. At first, you could still get on with wearing it, but as the months and years wore on, the thread unraveled until it turned into a hole that could not be repaired.

She wanted to know what they were thinking. How they were feeling. Who they were dating! What they thought about their friends or what happened at the latest high school party. One of the hardest parts about being a parent was the sudden switch in what your children share with you. One minute they were in your lap, babbling on while you wished for just a few minutes of peace and quiet. The next they were locked away in their rooms, and you were hovering there, fishing for a few overheard words.

Anything that would allow you to feel close to them again.

To know what was going on and what they were thinking.

To make sure they were still okay.

"It's weird here without dad, huh? Every year I think it will get easier, but it doesn't."

Nancy had stilled, lurking right behind the living room swinging door. She'd waited for Will's reply. He had always been a slow processor, despite his brilliant brain.

"Yeah. It doesn't feel right. I keep expecting him to march through the front door with a load of wood for the fire or to yell to Mom for a nightcap."

Nancy had smiled; that was Dean in a nutshell.

Julie had laughed and then lowered her voice. Nancy had to crane to hear the next part.

"I am just so glad he went before Mom. Is that bad to say? I just think he would be so heartbroken without her, like a big sad lost puppy. Mom is resilient and strong. She will figure things out and stay tough."

More silence.

Nancy had been aware of her own breathing and forced the tears to remain behind her eyelids.

She'd wanted to run in the room and yell, "I'm not fine! I am crumbling! I wish it had been me first! I hate it here without him!" But instead, she'd waited, slowing her breathing the best she could, swallowing down the grief and sadness that had nowhere else to go. She'd reached over and held on to the wall to steady herself.

"No, it's not weird. I get what you are saying. Totally. Mom can handle anything. Plus, she has Lorrie and all her friends at work."

Nancy had clutched the wall with her fingers so hard a few chips of paint settled underneath her nails.

I don't have anyone!

She'd wanted to yell and scream at her children for being so unsupportive and unaware. Julie lived a mile away from her, but she may as well have lived in Japan. Attempting to connect with her daughter was like trying to tap into Fort Knox. It was nearly impossible to get anywhere with her emotionally. Will was easier to connect with, but he was busy with his job, and let's face it, there was only so much you can talk about with your grown male son.

Sometimes, Nancy yearned for her daughter.

The one she never really had.

Sure, Lorrie was around, but she worked overtime almost every night, and they had grown distant over the last few years. Nancy wasn't sure if it was because Lorrie didn't know how to act after Dean passed away or if it was just age.

If this was what happened when you got older.

If Dean were still here, she could have leaned on him. He had always been there to listen. To console her. To remind her that it was normal for their children to grow up and distance themselves from the nest. What he hadn't thought about was the fact that he might not be there either.

That she would be left all alone to figure this out on her own.

That she might forget who she was entirely.

That their children would be left with one dead parent and one unsound parent whose brain had gone to mush.

She shook her head, trying to pull herself back into the present. Looking down at her notebook, she wrote *kids were glad that Dean went first.*

She wasn't, though. She was so lost without him! She needed him.

I am strong and resilient.

Dean is no longer alive.

It is just me.

Frowning, she tapped her pencil against the paper. There was something else she was forgetting to write. This was always how it started, her memory would be right there, right around the corner in her brain, but when she went to reach out for it, it would shift ever so slightly, just like she had that Christmas night, making sure she was never seen or noticed, just so she could remain close to them.

The memory was gone now. Perhaps it would come back another time. At least she had the information she needed from the last few days. Julie needed to repair her relationship with Greg, and Ally was acting strange.

It was her job now to figure out why.

JULIE

J ULIE HAD BEEN SITTING IN THIS DOCTOR'S OFFICE,
as well as many others, for over two and a half years. But she
would never get used to it. She would never forget all the
desperate women sitting near her, all wanting the same thing,
but for some reason, unable to get it. It was so hard to stay
hopeful waiting for your appointment when you had to watch
the gauntlet of couples walk out, often with silent tears
streaming down their faces.

And what was worse was watching the ones walk out that
had smiles. That were jumping for joy because it had worked.
Those were the ones that made her sick to her stomach.

The first year of appointments, Greg had been by her side.
Squeezing her hand or challenging her to a crossword puzzle to
distract her from the reality of the waiting room. Afterward,
they would go out to lunch at her favorite seafood place down
by the water. They would eat way too many oysters and sip on
hot and dirty martinis, talking about the future. Coming up
with nursery ideas and making a list of places they would take
their baby to see before they grew up.

That all felt so far away now.

She wasn't sure what had happened along the way or where
she had lost him.

Had she pushed him one too many times to discuss baby
room colors or middle names?

Had he watched her slowly unravel over the last year and

decided that he didn't want to be married to an unsound woman who couldn't give him a baby?

That was what gutted her the most. The fact that Greg had opted into a marriage with her, assuming they would be able to have a family.

Did he regret choosing her?

She wouldn't really blame him if he did.

"Julie?" A nurse appeared in the doorway, and Julie stood up, walking silently over to her. She hoped that today the small talk would be minimal. She just wanted to wallow in the reality of her situation.

As Julie followed the nurse, she already knew today wasn't going to be good because the doctor had asked her to come in to talk. Her last round of IVF had just failed. She was looking forward to trying once more, even though it was grueling. Even though she knew it probably wouldn't work.

It was the fact that it might work that kept her coming back.

She shook her head, thinking about how extremely taxing each round had been.

Mentally. Physically. Emotionally.

It was such a waiting game. You were continually pummeled with bad news, and then just when everyone was ready to give up, you would get one sliver of hope. One thing would go right, and you would pretend that this was it.

All the shots.

All the appointments.

All the ultrasounds with an empty uterus.

Only to be told the procedure had failed or the only egg you had didn't make it.

During their first ever appointment, her doctor was sitting behind his desk, a wall full of baby photos behind him. "These are all of my success stories," he had exclaimed. "Hopefully within a year your baby will be up there, too!"

Julie had been so full of hope then.

And she'd also been so naïve.

Now she was sitting in that same spot, full of defeat.

"Julie, nice to see you." He stood up, shifting a few files on his desk. "No Greg today?"

She lifted her chin. "No, he had an important meeting at work."

She wondered if her doctor knew. If he could see through her little façade. If he secretly hated his job because not only did he have to tell couples they still didn't have a baby, but also because he had to watch their relationships teeter on the edge of collapse, just like their dreams of starting a family.

"All right, well. I would have liked for him to be here." Her doctor cleared his throat and set his hands on the table.

You and me both, pal.

"I know you are determined, Julie, and I admire that, but I want to be very honest with you. After three failed attempts at IVF and the diagnosis you have, at this point, it is extremely unlikely that you will ever be able to get pregnant naturally."

Julie's breath caught in her throat, and she tried to push down the instant threat of tears. She leaned forward, trying to move away from the dull ache in her heart. Even though she knew this news was coming, it still felt like everything around her was going dark. But she refused to allow herself to crumble here.

Sitting up, she forced herself to advocate for the baby she didn't have.

"So, what do you suggest I do now? What are the next steps?"

Her doctor looked at her for what felt like an eternity. "I

don't know how else to help you, Julie. Personally, if I were in your position, I would consider other options."

She narrowed her eyes, staring at the large coffee cup sitting next to him. She thought about grabbing it and throwing it against the wall.

She thought about watching it shatter into a million little pieces, just like her heart.

"What do you mean, other options?" She was daring him to say it.

He accepted the challenge without missing a beat. "Adoption. I think it's time to start considering other ways that you could become a mother. We have a great adoption counselor I could recommend."

Julie stared at him, and without speaking another word, she got up and left. She pushed past the reception desk, fully aware that now she was just another one of them. The women who left this place with nothing but tears streaming down their faces and a sadness that knew no bounds.

Once she was in her car, she sat there for a long time trying to subdue the sobs that continuously rippled out of her body, one after the other. Each one hitting her like a wave of disappointment and grief for everything she had planned for and everything she would never get. Her phone buzzed repeatedly in the cup holder, causing some loose change to make an obnoxious rattling noise.

"If that's Greg calling me, I'll throw this phone out the window." Julie screamed, slamming her hand so hard on the center console that a woman a few cars down looked over at her and raised her eyebrows.

Julie sank lower in her seat, trying to disappear entirely. Tears streamed down her face, and she hastily wiped them away with the back of her hand.

"I just can't do this anymore. I don't want to. I am all done.

If this is how it is going to go, then I don't want to do it." She was whispering to herself now. In her car. Alone in a fertility clinic parking lot without her husband.

Without any support.

Without any answers.

Without a sliver of hope.

Completely aware she was losing it. That she had turned into a volatile person in the process. She couldn't adopt a baby if she was a single parent. If she didn't have a goddamn husband who wanted to participate.

Finally, she picked up her phone. Her heart sank even deeper into her chest. Eleven missed calls from her mother. Panicked, she called her back, sitting up straighter in her seat and checking the mirror. She wiped the running mascara and reapplied a bit of foundation under her eyes as she listened to the phone ring.

The other day, Greg had told her she looked like shit. *"You've got dark circles under your eyes. Are you even sleeping anymore?"*

Finally, just as she was about to throw the car into drive and head to her mother's house, she answered.

"Jules? Why haven't you answered my calls! I must have called you a dozen times."

Relief swept through Julie's chest, and she exhaled. "Eleven times, to be exact. I was at an appointment." She sniffled and swallowed hard, forcing the permanent lump in her throat back down into her chest with the rest of her feelings.

"Well, I need to talk to you. Can you meet me for lunch?"

Julie looked down at her phone. Technically, she was supposed to be back at work in thirty minutes, but she couldn't face everyone's expectant faces and prodding questions. Lunch with her nosy mother didn't sound much better, yet she was hungry and the idea of a mid-day martini wasn't so bad. Plus, she didn't want to go home sober and face Greg either.

"I guess I could meet you." She sighed, partially mad at herself for giving in to this trap.

"Wonderful!"

The excitement in her mother's voice ignited a slight whisper of rage in her chest, followed by immediate guilt.

Why was she such an awful person?

This was probably why she couldn't get pregnant.

She was actually irritated by the sound of her mother's happiness.

"I'll meet you at Killian's?"

Julie was already driving in that direction. Killian's was the only place her mother would go because it reminded her of Dean. It had been her father's favorite place to grab a few beers and a meal for as long as she could remember.

The servers knew all the regulars' orders by heart. The menu always stayed the same. It was a constant place of familiarity when everything around you changed. When Julie was in high school, she had worked there during the summer. There were people who came in for dinner every single night of the week.

They ordered the same drinks.

Ate the same meals.

Had the same conversations.

She could still remember one couple vividly. The woman would have two dragon slayer martinis and a French dip. Her husband would have about six Bacardi and diets with a tuna sandwich and a salad to start. After her shifts, she would come home and tell her dad about what people ordered, which customers got too drunk, and what the chefs were mad about.

Her father would laugh and say, *best place to work while you are young. It will give you an excellent work ethic and people skills. Plus, now you will be a good tipper for the rest of your life. And, Jules, when you become a mom and your kids destroy the table when you are out to dinner, you'll be sure to clean up after them and appreciate the waitress. Trust me.*

Another layer of sadness solidified itself in her chest as she thought about her father. Right on top of the reality that she wouldn't become a mother.

At the time, she hadn't minded working there, except when her parents would come out to dinner. Her mother would have a few cocktails and then start telling whoever was nearby that Julie was her daughter.

"Isn't she beautiful! She could have been a model, but she didn't have any interest."

Julie could still feel the heat rise in her chest fifteen years later. There was nothing worse than watching your parents get drunk and make a fool of themselves. But now, she would give anything to go back and have one more night with her father sitting at the bar.

With her family intact.

Without the knowledge that she was walking around infertile.

That was why she had gravitated toward Greg when they first started dating. He didn't even drink when they had first met. It was refreshing to be around someone who didn't care about alcohol. Who was more focused on advancing his career and taking care of his body.

Together, they were great. An unstoppable team. Julie's career in interior design had skyrocketed, and she had been making a name for herself. He was well known at the capital, making friends with the right people and establishing a career in politics for himself.

Now, she wanted to scream at him.

For leaving her when she needed him most.

For being so confident that she would become a mother when in fact he had absolutely no idea.

As Julie pulled into the parking lot, she looked around for her mother's car. Checking to confirm her makeup was still halfway decent, she grabbed her bag and headed inside. She could snag a table and wait for her mother.

Once she was settled at one of her mother's favorite booths, she pulled out her phone and started drafting a long-winded text to Greg. This was something her therapist had suggested she do. Whenever she was feeling a lot of rage, she could write it all out either in an email or a text.

Get it all out. Feel the feelings of the emotions leaving your body as you type.

But the catch was, once she had said everything she needed to say, she had to delete it.

"Never respond to someone when you are in an active rage response," her therapist had said. "Sit with those feelings instead. Say what you need to say, but keep it for yourself. Afterwards, if you still have something you feel that you need to say, you can say it from a grounded place, rather than from a reactive place."

Julie sighed and threw the phone down onto the table. What she really wanted to say to Greg was a big fuck you! She was beginning to fear that he no longer wanted to have a baby with her. That he no longer wanted to be married to her.

She could do all the fertility treatments in the world.

She could fly to the Middle East and try that new procedure Ally had found.

She could even consider adoption, but if Greg was unwilling to participate, how was she supposed to have a baby?

ALLY

An incessant beeping was the first thing I heard. It was quite obnoxious. Couldn't someone turn it down? Or better yet, turn the retched thing off. It was extremely hard to focus on any additional sounds as the beeping continued its desperate attempt for attention. I forced my mind to separate the sound out as I opened my eyes and pulled the room into focus.

There was also a steady hum coming from somewhere close by, and I heard the faint shuffle of shoes and the rattles of a medicine carts traveling outside of my door.

I turned my head, bracing myself for impact.

Cade.

He was sitting crumpled in a hard plastic chair. His body hunched over his phone like a question mark. He didn't notice that I was awake, so I took the opportunity to enjoy a few moments of silence to plan out what I was going to say. I knew that it was probably time to tell him everything.

That there was no going back from this moment.

Cade would want to have the baby. He knew that I was very resistant to the idea, and for good reason, might I add, but I hadn't told him the details of my five-year plan yet. I had been planning on revealing that information soon.

To break it to him gently.

Explain why I had to go and what I needed to do.

One of the reasons I had been putting off telling him was

because I knew he thought I had been warming up to the idea of a family. He had assumed that I would soften over time. That I would come around. That I would begin to see my friends have children and long for my own. I knew it troubled him, watching Julie and Greg go through their fertility hurdles.

When Cade and I first met, I had to tried to explain to him a bit about my upbringing. He'd tried his best to understand, and he'd listened intently as I told him about my alcoholic father and meek mother. Cade had come from a very normal family, but I thought he understood what I was trying to convey. He had lost both his parents to separate illnesses in his mid-twenties, so he understood having to be independent, but perhaps not in the same way I did.

I'd told Cade that I had plans to travel and see the world. That I wanted to do all the things that I was unable to do when I was younger. That my parents were never able to do.

Cade had spent summer vacations on gorgeous lakes and winter vacations exploring islands. His parents had even taken him to Australia during his senior year. In college, he had studied abroad. His travel itch had been scratched, while mine was left festering. Cade had assured me we would have plenty of time to travel. I had leaned into that idea. Perhaps we could explore the world together. It seemed, though, after we were married and living our domestic lives, the idea of travel faded, and the idea of a baby became the focus point.

I had spent my childhood pouring over books about the ancient pyramids in Egypt. Trying to uncover who had built Stonehenge and how. Wondering what it would have been like to live in Scotland in the late 1600s. The library was my source of travel, and I dreamed of the day when I was old enough to take matters into my own hands and see the world.

I wasn't sure how I ended up in this predicament with

Cade. It was why I had been slowly forming my five-year plan without his knowledge. Sometimes when you really wanted something, it was best to keep it to yourself for a while. At least until it was too late for others to try to stop you.

I closed my eyes again. Perhaps I could just pretend to stay asleep. This way I could avoid the conversation with Cade and pretend none of this was actually happening. This seemed like a much better plan. I wondered briefly if I should send a thank-you card to Keith and Larry. They had done all the heavy lifting, and I got the sense that they were often left in the dust and forgotten. I made a mental note to add that to my to-do list.

Voices lingered in close proximity to my door. Fighting my curiosity, I forced my eyes to stay closed. It was much harder to fake sleeping when you wanted to see what was going on. The door opened, and I heard Cade shuffle in his chair. I imagined him sitting up straighter, adjusting his shirt and tucking his phone away in his pocket.

"How is she?" It was a woman's voice. Quiet and welcoming. I wanted desperately to see what her appearance was like, but I did not want to speak with Cade at this time. I had to wait until he left.

"She hasn't woken up yet. How long do you think she will sleep for?" The question was coated in desperation. A small part of me disintegrated. It was quite unfair of me to be keeping him in the dark, but this wasn't Cade's decision.

This was mine.

"She was extremely dehydrated. Due to the concussion, she will be very tired for a few days."

The nurse was at my side now. I could smell her perfume. Had she used half the bottle just this morning? She smelled like the fragrance department at Macy's. I pictured her walking around at each of the different stations, trying out the sample bottles. Spritzing more and more on until she was toxic enough to take out a small army of men. I fought the urge to cover my nostrils. Someone needed to open a window! I would have to request a nurse change. Could Cade smell it? Surely, he could. If the circumstances were different, I would give him an earful as soon as she left the room.

"We actually need to wake her up. It isn't good for patients with concussions to sleep too much."

Oh splendid, I thought. Someone should let her know there was no need to wake me or any patient on this floor up due to her perfume violation. She could probably pull someone out of a coma with the amount of poison she was carrying around on her clothing. I could only imagine that her hair must smell for weeks on end! Even the chairs she occupied in the break room probably held her scent long after she left. How atrocious.

I always told Julie that if I ever became president, the first two items that I would implement would be banning fragrances and motorcycles. The fragrance, for obvious reasons, and the motorcycles, also obvious, for their horrific assault on innocent citizen's ears.

My stomach lurched. There was that feeling again. The nausea. It came on quickly, like a silent attacker. I groaned, rolling over, grasping the side of the bed rail. The black dots were back. I could see the nurse's shoes. Well, I wouldn't call them shoes, actually. They were the dreadful Crocs. Tie-dye ones no less! With little trinkets tucked into some of the holes. A small replica of a frog looked up at me. There was also a mini microphone, and what was that? A golf club. How odd. I disliked golf. Too much standing around. I wondered if they smelled like her perfume, too.

"Ally? Can you hear me? Ally, are you going to be sick?"

The Crocs disappeared, and just as the contents of my

stomach came up and out, a small pink bucket shaped like a kidney appeared in their place.

Cade was up now and rubbing my back. I felt an incredible sense of annoyance toward my body as it began to shake without my permission. I needed this nurse and her perfume to leave the room.

I needed a window open.

I needed all of this to stop.

The overheating began to set in. My pregnancy app had forgotten to alert me that hot flashes were part of the deal. Wasn't that more suited for later in life? I glanced around, looking for a thermostat. Perhaps I could just get up once everyone was gone and adjust the temperature myself.

I rolled back into the middle of the bed and looked up at Cade. He nodded encouragingly. Making eye contact with him now caused me to relax slightly. I forgot how much I loved him. He squeezed my hand, and I felt the hot prick of tears gather in the back of my eyelids. Despite my strong internal protest, the tears trickled down the sides of my face, gathering at my ears. I wiped them away quickly with my other hand.

"Als? I am so glad you are okay. You fell at the doctor's office and hit your head. Don't worry. The baby is fine."

The nausea whirled in my stomach.

He knew.

He knew about the baby.

They told him.

Wasn't there some sort of medical code of conduct to prevent this type of thing? I made a mental note to write a letter to the board of the hospital. I opened my mouth to say something, but once again, I was at a loss for words. As if he could read my mind, Cade leaned over and kissed my forehead.

"We can talk later. Don't stress right now about any of it.

Let's just see what the doctors say and focus on getting you home."

I couldn't imagine that kissing my sweaty forehead had been a pleasurable experience. The thought made my stomach churn, and I shifted my body, trying to move away from the feeling.

"Alrighty! All cleaned up!" The smell perpetrator was back, happy as ever to report the update. "Ally, let's see if you can eat something. You hit your head pretty good, and I think some of the nausea is from the concussion, but I am also guessing it's just from morning sickness. Have you had a lot of nausea so far?"

This felt like a very personal question, and I was quite irritated with her. It only highlighted the fact that I had kept this from Cade. I looked away from him and stared at the nurse. I nodded as subtly as possible, hoping Cade wouldn't notice.

The nurse seemed satisfied with my response and kept on with her little spiel. "Lots of small, frequent meals will help keep the nausea at bay. Keep some crackers with you, you know that sort of thing."

I wanted to tell her that, obviously, I had already learned that information. One Google search for morning sickness gave you about thirty-seven articles, all highlighting the same advice.

"Anyhoo!" she sang. "We need to monitor your blood pressure, and the doctor wants to do an ultrasound of the baby to make sure everything is A-OK!"

Did she always talk to her patients like they were in preschool?

As soon as she was gone, Cade pulled the chair up closer to my bedside. "She was a bit much, huh?"

I smiled for the first time in a few days. Cade always knew exactly what I was thinking. Even when I didn't want to share it.

That was the problem, though.

I was sure that, deep in the back of pocket of his mind, he knew how I felt about the baby.

I could see it in his eyes.

Cade knew what I had planned to do, and I was afraid there was no going back from that.

NANCY

SHE TALKED TO HERSELF THE ENTIRE DRIVE OVER TO the restaurant. "Greg and Julie are at a crossroads. They are fighting over fertility issues. Ally is acting weird." She said it over and over again, hoping it would stick in her brain and stay there.

If she was going to make any progress today, it was imperative that she show up sharp as a whip to this lunch with Julie. It may be one of her only chances to really get to the bottom of what was going on. The days when Nancy had all her ducks in a row were becoming sparser, and the days when she struggled to remember where she was going or where she used to work were becoming more frequent.

Nancy recognized that this was precisely what the doctor had been talking about when he told her that she would need the support of her friends and family.

"It will become too much for you to handle on your own. It's a matter of safety, Nancy. You have to tell them. Soon."

Nancy slapped the steering wheel. The hell with the doctor. She had a plan. She could manage on her own for now. Plus, her children needed her! Everything would be fine. She just had to stay consistent.

Although Nancy had to admit, it took a lot of effort to remember everything. Her mind wanted to wander and wonder. As she drove by a gated community, she saw a swan in the man-made pond. Dean had loved birds. Once the kids were old enough to talk, he had spent a small fortune on every children's book about birds he could get his hands on. It seemed like every other weekend he was hauling the kids to the local tractor supply store to get a new bird feeder or bird bath. He knew the best place to get the "good" bird seed that would attract certain kinds of birds. Bluebirds. Not blue jays, he had corrected the kids. There was a difference.

Every morning after the kids went off to school, Dean and Nancy would take a walk around the neighborhood. He would name each bird and point them out. The black-capped chickadee. Sparrows and warblers and the red-bellied woodpecker. American goldfinch. Mourning doves.

She wondered now if he had reincarnated into a bird. Maybe that swan was Dean, watching her from a distance and worrying that she was losing it.

She was losing it, but only a bit. Nothing she couldn't handle. She was at a set of lights now, and as they turned green, she tried hard to remember where she was going. How was it that she could still remember all those birds but not what she was supposed to be doing?

Think, think, think, Nancy. Think!

As if on cue, her Bluetooth rang. Julie was calling.

Oh yes! Lunch with Julie.

She shook her head. Taking a left, she took a side road that brought her right out to the restaurant. She chose to ignore the call since she was only a block away. She didn't need to be scolded by her daughter right now. Once Julie saw Nancy walking toward her, she would relax and forget that her mother had shown up thirty minutes late.

To be honest, she was always late. It was one of her imperfections. She tried hard to be on time; she really did! Yet something always derailed her, and she just couldn't ever seem to get her act together to arrive anywhere on time. Once she had over-heard Julie and Will talking about how whenever they needed her to be somewhere on time, they told her a time that was thirty minutes earlier! Just so she would show up on time. Well, little did they know that she was in on their little game. So now, when she was supposed to meet them for something, she never stressed because she knew the time that they told her was fabricated.

She hurried up to the door of Killian's and paused to let her eyes adjust to the dark setting of the bar. Killian's original bar was made up of old dark wood from a real ship that had docked at the harbor in town in the early 1900s. Instead of windows, there were portholes. It was the perfect place to forget about everything else in your life and allow yourself to be swallowed up by the darkness. Nancy used to love that part of the restaurant, but now she felt resistant to it. She didn't need any help in that department.

Her mind was already doing that for her.

Instead, she focused on the giant mural of the ocean behind her favorite booth, which was where Julie was sitting now. She had an almost empty martini and an untouched salad sitting in front of her. She was typing furiously on her phone and looked, quite frankly, very on edge.

Nancy braced herself and squared her shoulders. She never knew what version of Julie she was going to get, but today she had a feeling it was going to be the Julie with a short fuse. Her daughter looked up, her face stoic and strong, yet Nancy could see right through it. She saw the pain and deep sadness that sat there, unnoticed by everyone else.

Julie's beauty still stopped Nancy in her tracks. She watched her daughter for a minute, taking her in. If only she weren't so angry all the time. When Julie was a teenager, they often got stopped by modeling scouts when shopping at the mall or at an amusement park. Julie wanted no part in such nonsense, much to Nancy's dismay. Lorrie would always pull Ally in close to her, as if they were in danger, and tsk her lips at the situation. Nancy couldn't understand it! Why did they all want to turn down the opportunity to become a famous model!

Boys and grown men alike had always gawked at Julie. She was the type of person who looked flawless in every single photo ever taken. She didn't have to try to look pretty with makeup or anything special. She just was beautiful without effort. Nancy's heart swelled with pride and love for her daughter, even if she did often treat her like a pebble in her shoe.

Nancy plopped her pocketbook down onto the table and sat across from Julie, her body sighing as she settled into the well-worn leather of the booth. She was so happy to have made it here with all her notes still in her brain; she didn't even care if Julie said something snarky. "So," she said. "How are you?"

She watched her daughter mumble, "I'm fine," and take a long sip of her martini.

Nancy reached into her purse and pulled out her phone. "Have you talked to Ally lately? I saw her at the grocery store, and she was acting strange." Nancy leaned forward, waiting for Julie to respond.

Julie shrugged and took another sip. "She's sick, has the flu or something. You know how she acts about germs. I haven't really talked to her for a few days."

Nancy frowned. She supposed this made sense about Ally, but there was still something she was missing. She would have to try her hardest to remember to write that down in her notebook. She eyed the cocktail napkin Julie had rested her martini on. Perhaps she could grab that and write down some notes if Julie went to the bathroom.

"Well, how are you doing otherwise? You know, I can help

with anything. What is going on with Greg? You two seem distant lately. Is everything all right?"

Julie narrowed her eyes, and Nancy sat up taller. She wasn't going to let this go. She wasn't going to let her daughter scare her out of receiving information. Her daughter needed her. She could help!

"Greg left for a work trip. Everything is fine."

Liar! Nancy shifted in her seat, leaning forward a bit. Whenever her daughter lied, her eyes got slightly rounder. She could still see her little face as a three-year-old when Nancy asked her if she had dumped out the entire bag of dog food.

No, mama. I didn't.

She could still see her face as a twelve-year-old when Nancy asked her about finishing her book report.

All done.

She could still see her face as a junior in high school when Nancy asked her if the lighter that she had found in her car was hers.

I don't know what you are talking about.

Julie thought she was good at lying, but she wasn't. She was only good at lying to herself. Those who were close to her could see right through her, but they didn't dare to challenge her. Instead, they smiled and nodded along. Nancy included.

Up until now.

That was the tricky thing for people who had a short fuse. You could see each and every emotion play out on their face right in front of you. You started to become aware of their reactions to things. You started to brace yourself for impact, because you knew that the emotion they were carrying is much deeper than what is shown on the surface.

Which was why, when Nancy's phone buzzed and they both looked down at it at the same time, reading the caller ID, Nancy froze.

Terrified of her daughter's reaction.
Terrified of what this meant for Nancy.
For their future.
Everything was about to change.

JULIE

Julie stared at her mother's phone, which was buzzing wildly on the table in front of them. Neither of them said a word. They watched it in silence. Julie was trying to make sense of what she was seeing.

Bright Side Memory Clinic flashed across the screen over and over again.

Memory clinic, but why? The buzzing stopped, and she looked at her mother's face. Her mother's eyes were wide and panicked, and her mouth was pursed shut.

Fuck.

The phone buzzed again, and the screen lit up.

One new voicemail.

Just as Julie was about to open her mouth, the server appeared.

"How are we doing over here! Ready to order some lunch?"

Her mother scrambled, jumping into action. She grabbed the phone and shoved it back into her purse. A menu plopped in its place, and her mother held it up, like a small child handing back something they were not supposed to have.

"I know what I want, no need for this!" she sang, pushing the menu back at the server. "I'll have the Caesar salad wrap." She smiled and looked to Julie.

Julie raised her eyebrows but said nothing. She was never rude to her mother in front of other people.

"I am okay with this salad, but I will have another dirty

martini." She narrowed her eyes at her mother and waited for the server to whisk away their menus and disappear into the kitchen.

"I saw your phone. We both did. Why is the Bright Side Memory Clinic calling you?"

Her mother waved her hand, taking a long sip of her water. A little bit dribbled down her chin, and Julie closed her eyes briefly, taking a deep breath.

She is not doing anything wrong.

Julie repeated this in her head, coaching herself to stay present and not spiral into unnecessary rage.

"I am part of a study! Isn't that wonderful? The clinic reached out to a variety of medical professionals in their sixties. You see, they want to study the brain and how it changes with age. They are studying two different groups. One group, that's me and some of my nurse friends."

Her mother took another sip of her water, this time clunking it back onto the table so that half the water sloshed over the side.

Julie exhaled.

Count to ten.

"Alice is doing it, too! We are all still actively working. Then, there is another group, retired nurses." Her mother paused and stared at Julie, as if she lost her train of thought.

Just as Julie was about to cut her off, she kept going.

"It's a shame, all those retired nurses with not much to do. They were happy to volunteer. As was I! But you see, it does require a bit of commitment. The bonus is I get to take time off from work to participate in the study. I'll call them back later; don't worry for one minute about me."

"Why are you just telling me now? When did you start this?" Julie was becoming bored with her mother, and irritated. If she wanted to do some insane medical study, then fine.

"It just started, Jules. That is why they were calling me, to get the rest of my information and set up a time to meet. I'll call Will later and tell him, too, so he isn't in the dark."

Julie frowned and took another sip of her martini. Whatever. Maybe it was good for her mother to have something to focus on. She knew it had been a challenging couple of years for her, losing Dad. She glanced back up at her mother, who was now deeply engrossed in her phone; her smudged glasses sitting crooked on her face.

For a minute, Julie had been so wrapped up in her mother, she had forgotten all about her own mess of problems, but now they were back, hitting her like a sledgehammer.

The devastating appointment.

Greg.

Front and center, haunting her every waking moment.

As if on cue, her mother flung her head up and stared directly at Julie. "Tell me what is going on with Greg? I know something is up. You're my daughter, after all. I can read you like a book." Her mother leaned forward, putting her hand on top of Julie's. Instinctively, Julie pulled her hand back and tucked it into her lap.

"I don't want to talk about it." Julie took a deep breath, resisting the urge to make a comment about her mother's disheveled glasses.

If her mother was hurt by Julie pulling her hand away, she didn't show it. Instead, she barreled on.

"Well, I do want to talk about it. I'm not leaving this table until you tell me what is going on." Her mother sat up taller, clearly proud of herself for pushing back.

The second martini was affecting Julie's ability to control her anger. Her guard was slipping by the second.

Maybe it would be easier to just tell her mother what is going on with Greg.

Maybe she would feel less alone.

Maybe it would be helpful to have someone who was angry at Greg too.

Her therapist was constantly encouraging Julie to talk about her experience with friends and family. That the more she bottled it up, the harder it would be to navigate.

"It's similar to shame, the more you hold in, the bigger and more anxiety-producing it becomes. When you talk about it openly, then you don't have to hide anymore. You have outed your infertility. How great is that?"

Julie could still remember trying to not roll her eyes right there in front of her therapist. Of course, that all made sense. But how did you deal with everyone knowing? How did you deal with the constant questions and reminders? How did you keep answering questions and pretending to be optimistic when deep down all you really felt like was a failure?

Her body had failed her, and she had failed as a wife.

Sometimes she lay awake at night consumed with guilt.

Guilt that Greg had entered a marriage with a woman who was unable to give him a baby.

Guilt that she had used up all their savings trying to create a baby.

Guilt that she was so goddamn angry all the time.

Guilt that she resented pregnant women.

"Julie. What is it? Tell me. I can help."

She looked back at her mother, who was shoving her Ceaser wrap into her mouth. A piece of lettuce hung out the side of her lip as she chewed, and Julie fought the urge to get up and leave. She watched as the lettuce continued to dangle, her mother completely oblivious to food cascading out of her mouth. Why couldn't her mother just act normal? Heat rose in her chest, and she exhaled, counting to ten as her mother chewed loudly.

"Julie, please."

You know what? Fuck it. Let's go.

"Greg doesn't want to have a baby anymore. In fact, I don't think he wants to stay married to me."

Julie watched as her mother's mouth opened, the lettuce flopping down into her lap, still unnoticed. Julie could see a bit of the wrap still sitting inside her mouth.

She was pretty sure that if someone took her blood pressure right now, it would be through the roof. Picking up her martini glass, she drained the rest of it in one sip.

If she was going to deal with the fallout of losing everything she had ever wanted and her mother at the same time, she was going to need a lot more fucking alcohol.

ALLY

Cade was asleep in the chair again. He was sleeping more than I was, and I was the one lying in a hospital bed with a concussion. It wasn't as though he had been woken up in the middle of the night to dart off and care for me. It was only mid-afternoon! On a weekday, no less. That was always the thing I found intriguing about men. They could sleep anywhere and at any time. I knew this to be true for multiple men because Julie had confirmed that Greg did the same thing. Plus, I had seen it on various TV shows.

It had only been about thirty minutes since I had vomited, and the nurse I had nicknamed *Toxlicious* had finally left. Now we were waiting for the ultrasound technician to make the rounds and check in on the baby.

"Don't worry, dear," the smell perpetrator had told me. "Your baby is just fine. We heard the heartbeat, and your blood sugar is back up where we would like it. It's just protocol after a fall to do an ultrasound check."

Cade had smiled at me encouragingly, and I could see the relief settle over his face as he watched the nurse shuffle out of the room in her tie-dye Crocs. Of course, I did not wish ill will toward the baby, and I felt genuinely torn with my emotions. It was almost as if I was becoming attached to the tiny being in my belly, but I also resented it for throwing a huge wrench in my plans.

For giving Cade hope for the future.

A future I did not want.

I was well aware that my time to make a decision was running out. If only I had made an appointment and taken care of it directly after the surprise party, I wouldn't be sitting here now in this predicament. The problem was, I had made an appointment. Several of them, in fact. Yet every time, on the day of, I woke up in a sheer panic, unable to physically get myself into the car and to the clinic. It was as if something had taken over my logical brain and replaced it with a gigantic marshmallow.

I had gone soft.

I lacked judgment and reason.

Instead of being proactive, I spent my days reading online reviews about the best slice of pizza in town or the latest trick to keep nausea at bay. Just yesterday, I had found myself scrolling through the best of Amazon baby registry items.

If I was being honest with myself, I didn't know if I could make the decision I had originally set out to make. Yet, I could not imagine myself a doting mother.

Surely, I would be a failure. Surely, I would regret having to care for a tiny little human that did not understand how to be a civilized person and follow the rules of society. Surely, I would mess everything up.

The world was quite cruel, putting me between a rock and a hard place with a baby I did not want while Julie was fighting tooth and nail for the very same thing.

There was a soft knock on the door, which was already ajar. I did not understand why these medical professionals insisted on knocking. We, the patients, were at their disposal. There was no form of privacy here. There was no schedule or plan. It was a free for all. They breezed in and out as they pleased. Some left the door open. Some closed it. Some spoke to you; others spoke about you. I wondered if they were trained in medical school about bedside manner. I would hope there was at least one course provided. I made a mental note to ask later about the prerequisites.

"Ally? I'm Dawn, the ultrasound technician."

I sat up in my bed, peering out. I did not see a face; all I saw was a giant cart with a large screen wheeling toward me.

"How are you feeling?"

I jumped, taken aback by the woman who popped out from behind the cart. She was exceptionally short. Like a little quiet mouse. She wore round spectacles, and her brown hair was cut in a bob, hugging her cheeks on either side. I couldn't decide if her haircut made her look shorter or if it was giving her a leg up. How did she perform ultrasounds with that height? She would definitely need a stool to reach the buttons on the machine.

"I am quite all right, thank you," I replied after I remembered my manners.

Cade was stirring in his seat, and Dawn turned to look at him, as if she had just noticed him for the first time. If I still wasn't digesting her height or lack thereof, I would have missed what happened next. She gave him the slightest shake of the head, as if she was disgusted with his decision to take a nap.

I decided in that moment that I liked her.

She kept her gaze on Cade while she pushed the cart up closer to the side of the bed. "Will you be joining us?"

It took Cade a minute to realize she was talking to him, and I felt a bit of pity. He was only just waking up and a bit disheveled. I watched with a scowl as he stretched out his arms and glanced quickly at me before answering.

"Yes, yes of course! I can't wait to see the baby. This is my first time!"

Dawn blinked slowly at him before she turned back toward me. "All right, Ally, I am going to lower this bed a bit so I can reach better." She smiled at me, an unspoken nod to her height, I presumed. "We are going to look at the baby, take a few measurements, and then we will call the doctor in so he can have a look too."

Cade had made his way to the other side of the bed now. He smelled of sleep and stale coffee. "Will we be able to find out the sex of the baby today?"

I could see the eagerness plastered all over his face. His eyes wide and inquisitive, a small smile playing at the corner of his mouth.

His excitement caused me to retreat, even though I was still in a hospital bed. My brain clouded over, and the dull headache I had seemed to intensify, turning into a persistent pulse, as if the marshmallow thoughts were trying to break their way out. Cade squeezed my hand and looked at me, his eyes searching for answers that I could not give him.

Dawn continued to unravel her equipment, and I watched as she pressed a button on the side of the cart so that the base the machine was sitting on moved down to her level. She tapped a few buttons on the screen and grabbed a tube of that awful jelly. I did not like the feeling on my skin and made a mental note to request a shower afterward.

"We rarely look for the gender in these circumstances. The most important thing right now is making sure your baby is healthy. Plus, at twelve weeks, it is very hard to determine the sex. A sixteen-week ultrasound will be much more successful. Were you not offered the blood test at ten weeks?"

I inhaled sharply and tried to lean into the pounding in my head. Of course, I had been offered it; I had just simply declined.

Why would I want to know the sex of a baby I was not keeping?

Cade shifted uncomfortably on his feet. "Well, I am not... I only just found out about the baby today."

Dawn paused ever so slightly and glanced at me. I waited for her to say something, but thankfully she carried on, opening the tube and preparing the ultrasound wand in her other hand. I was correct in my character judgment. Dawn was a good egg.

"Let's just focus on making sure the baby is okay, and then we can discuss the gender afterwards. Ally, can you scoot down a bit and pull your shirt up?"

I shimmied my body down and reluctantly pulled my shirt up so that my stomach was exposed. It was embarrassing, all of this.

I did not like being on display.

I did not enjoy being the center of attention.

I wanted to be alone. In my body and in my mind.

Cade leaned closer over the bed and squinted expectantly at the blank screen. I winced as Dawn squeezed an alarming amount of the gel onto my stomach.

Before I could gather my thoughts, she pressed the wand down onto my stomach, swirling it around on the gel, making a giant mess. She was pushing down rather hard; surely this wasn't ideal for the baby, but I assumed she knew what she was doing.

She reached up with her short little arm and pointed to the screen. Her fingers matched her height. Short and stubby, as if one day they forgot to continue growing. It took me a minute to stop focusing on her fingers and focus instead on the words she was saying.

"There is the head, you see, and here are the feet and hands." She moved the wand around to a different part of my stomach, clicking a button repeatedly on the machine. In addition to the clicks, there was a printing noise coming from somewhere, and I realized she was preparing more images for me.

I thought about that first one I had received and how I had thrown it into the trash. Hopefully Cade would never ask me about that. I wouldn't have the heart to tell him what I had done.

What I had been thinking.

What my plan had been.

I watched as the baby did a flip and reached its arm out, closing and opening its little, tiny fingers. It was quite a wonder.

Cade laughed and squeezed my hand again. "That's our baby, Als!"

Dawn continued moving the wand around, taking a few measurements with a line on the screen, and just as I started to enjoy watching the show, she pulled the wand off and grabbed a tissue from the box near the bed.

"The baby looks just fine, but I'll have the doctor come in and take a look just to sign off on it. Here is a tissue to clean up the gel," she said cheerily, placing it in my hand.

This was what she expected me to use to soak up all that liquid? Surely it was a joke. I took the tissue and started at one side, trying to collect the remaining gel in an organized fashion. The tissue was soaked in a matter of seconds, and I looked around for a towel or something larger. I would need a proper shower as soon as possible.

Cade seemed to be in a bit of a daze; I didn't blame him to be honest. This was probably a lot to process. I'd spent weeks with this information, and he had only had two hours to process it. Finally, he looked at me holding the saturated tissue, and I watched with slight irritation as his brain snapped back into action.

"Here, let me take that. There must be a towel or something else to clean the rest of that up." He hurried over to a cabinet in the corner of the room and opened it up to find a few clean folded white towels. "Perfect!"

He tossed one over to me, and I caught it, glad to have a proper fabric to clean up with. As I started to wipe off the remaining gel, I watched out of the corner of my eye as Cade shifted on his feet. He looked at me with a sadness in his eyes that I did not want to face.

"Als." He lowered his voice a notch as if he was unsure if he should keep talking.

I nodded, even though I didn't want him to continue.

He smiled sadly. "I know I said we could talk about this later, but I don't think I can wait. I need to know now."

I knew this was the moment when I should say something, but all I could think about was that I did not want what he wanted. His giant puppy-dog eyes stared back at me, wondering how I could be so heartless.

So self-involved.

So cruel.

He was still standing over by the towel cabinet. If the circumstances were different, I would have reminded him to close the cabinet door. He'd left it open, his body already turning from it, leaving a huge gaping hole where the contents should have remained tucked away, invisible to everyone.

NANCY

Greg doesn't want a baby anymore.

What kind of man suddenly decides he is going to just throw in the towel on trying for a baby while his wife is actively going through fertility treatments? She couldn't imagine Dean ever doing something like this. Sometimes she had to remind herself to stop and think about how much she forgot to teach Julie about. What a terrible mother she had been! She had been so busy trying to win her love and approval that she neglected to make sure Julie understood how a man should treat her. At the time, Nancy assumed that seeing her and Dean's loving and supportive relationship would be enough. That they were modeling it for their children in real time.

That was one of the sneaky things about parenting; often you didn't realize the big life lesson you were supposed to teach them until it was way too late. At first, it was just small things, like teaching your seven-year-old that they should hold the door for people. Then, when they were suddenly twelve and slamming the door in your face, you realized the mistake you made. And by that time, there was sass and eye rolls and a mentality that they knew more than you did.

Then, it morphed into bigger issues, like forgetting to teach your children the importance of time management, so they didn't end up procrastinating every single project all four years of high school. And finally, it was realizing you forgot to teach your daughter about self-worth, because you were too busy worrying about whether she still loved you. Maybe she didn't have to blame it on bad parenting, maybe it was just her darn memory. Already short-circuiting decades before anyone noticed.

Now, she didn't know what to say to her daughter, which was a first. What she wanted to do was go find Greg and talk some sense into him. It was clear he was just under a lot of stress. He would probably come around. Julie wasn't particularly easy to deal with, and Nancy could only assume that there was quite a lot of tension between the two of them.

The more Nancy thought about it, the more she saw Greg's side of the situation. She was sure Julie was being hard on him, and frankly she was afraid to bring up the subject of fertility or anything baby related to Julie, ever. It had to be challenging living with that huge elephant in the room day in and day out all while Julie marched on, determined to make a baby whether Greg was on board or not.

Nancy was still sitting in the booth. Julie had left over twenty minutes ago, claiming she had to get back to work. Nancy wasn't sure how work would feel about their employee being half in the bag after two very strong, lunchtime dirty martinis, but she certainly hadn't been about to offer up her opinion on the matter.

Finally, the waitress showed up with the coffee she had ordered.

She stared at it with a sinking feeling.

Did she take cream and sugar?

Or did she like it black?

Perhaps the server had already added the sugar. She poured a generous amount of the cream into the cup, watching as the thick liquid swirled and twirled into the black coffee. Much like her brain, it began to blend together, but she could still see where the black wanted to hold on. Like the memories she was still grasping onto.

One mix with a spoon and they would all turn to white. Gone forever.

Nancy suddenly remembered her phone, and the missed call. She had completely forgotten about it after Julie had dropped the news about Greg. What a close one it had been! She would need to be more careful. Despite her deteriorating brain, she was quite impressed with herself and the lie she had spun out of thin air. Julie had almost uncovered her secret. Twice now. She was going to have to be more careful. She was going to have to move more quickly if she wanted to save Julie's marriage and get to the bottom of what was going on with Ally.

Ally! That was it. Nancy needed to talk to Ally. Ally would have better insight on both Greg and Julie. The girl had a practical brain, and you could always count on her to leave the emotions out of the equation. When the girls were in high school, Nancy found herself relying more and more on Ally for information about Julie. Ally was a straight shooter, different from her daughter and practically every other high school girl Nancy had ever met.

She could still hear Dean's words in her head.

"It's her upbringing, Nancy. She didn't have the opportunity to be a little kid like the rest of them. She's had enough chaos in her life. She tells it how it is and doesn't let anyone mess with her."

Nancy loved that about Ally. She knew her daughter did too. It was one of the reasons they were best friends. Both outspoken and driven, yet so completely opposite at the same time. One wanted a family more than anything in the world, and the other wanted to see the world for herself.

She would drive over to Ally's right now, straight from the restaurant, and see what she had to say about Greg. That would also give Nancy a chance to see what was really going on with Ally as well. Sure, Julie had said she was sick with the flu, but Nancy wasn't afraid of a little flu virus. She could sit on the opposite couch and ask Ally a few questions.

As Nancy made her way out to her car, she talked to herself out loud to be sure she wouldn't forget.

"Heading to Ally's house to ask about Greg."

"Heading to Ally's house to ask about Greg."

"Heading to Ally's house to ask about Greg."

The problem was that by the time she got to Ally's house, she couldn't remember what it was that she had wanted to ask Ally about Greg.

JULIE

IT WAS TRUE THAT GREG NO LONGER WANTED TO have a baby, but the part Julie didn't tell her mother was that he had said he didn't want to have a baby with *her*.

He didn't say ever.

He didn't say with someone else.

He had said, "I don't want to have a baby with *you*."

How could you want to stay married to someone after you admitted that you no longer wanted a child with them? That with all the words you didn't say, you had said everything.

She could still remember the way her whole body had frozen at the words. They'd been driving home from dinner, the silence between them the whole evening had been so thick, so heavy, so final.

She'd tried one more time to talk to him about it. He'd rolled through a stop sign, tapping his fingers impatiently on the steering wheel. "Julie. Can you just drop it?"

She'd tensed up even more as anger slowly spread from her chest. "Just drop having a baby? You want me to simply say fuck it! Never mind! Forget I mentioned it!"

Greg had sighed and hit the gas. "I'd actually like to forget it."

Julie had spun her body towards him, watching the trees whiz past behind his head. She looked at him. At her husband. At the man who was supposed to be her best friend. The man who was supposed to love and support her. Who was supposed to be there for her no matter what.

And she dared him to say it. "Forget what, Greg?"

His fingers tightened on the steering wheel. "I don't want to have a baby with you anymore."

That was the moment Julie had gone numb. The moment she had known that her marriage would never be the same. But she hadn't stopped obsessing. She'd just kept moving forward, determined to have the baby they were supposed to have.

While Julie was at her appointment, Greg had gone to the house and packed a bag, *again*. She knew because his closet had been ruffled through and his suitcase was missing. The clean pile of laundry she had folded the evening before had dwindled substantially in size. A few pair of his shoes were gone, and his office upstairs had been cleared of his work essentials.

What Greg didn't realize was that it didn't matter to her anymore that he didn't want to have a baby. She couldn't have one even if he wanted to. Her body simply couldn't provide her with the one thing she really wanted in this life.

The one thing she wanted, if she was being honest, more than love.

More than a happy marriage.

More than a loving relationship or a best friend.

She just wanted to be a mother.

What did you do when you couldn't have the one thing you wanted more than anything in life?

Up until this point, Julie had always gotten whatever she wanted.

When she wanted a new outfit from the mall in high school, her mother bought it for her.

When she was in college and she wanted to switch her degree to interior design midway through her sophomore year, she didn't waver. She just marched over to admissions and made the switch.

When she wanted to find the love of her life, she set out one weekend and found him.

When she wanted to land her dream job at the best design agency in the state, she had applied and it was hers. Now she was leading her own projects and working on a plan to branch out on her own. She had been featured in countless magazines and was beginning to pick up more well-known clients.

She knew this was a privileged way to move through life, but she also knew that she had something a lot of her friends didn't have, confidence.

She never doubted herself. She simply decided and the thing was hers.

When she was ready to be engaged to Greg, she casually sent him links to her favorite diamonds. Her friends had always laughed at her, saying things like, *You can't just tell him to ask you to marry him and pick out the ring! That's not how it works!*

"Why not?" Julie had asked. "That's what I want. I don't need a big charade and surprise. I just want to be engaged."

Looking back, maybe this was where she went wrong. Maybe she should have listened to her friends and allowed fate to hop into the driver's seat for once. But it didn't seem like fate was on her side anyway, because the one time in her life where she had to rely on fate, it had proven to be one gigantic bust.

The first year they started trying was right after her dad had died. Losing him had been so unexpected. Amid planning a wedding, she was attending a funeral. She was coming to terms with the fact that he would not be there to walk her down the aisle. That her future kids wouldn't have a grandfather.

After his death, she had become hyper-fixated on a baby. Looking back, it had probably been a way to cope with the loss. A way to override the sadness and loss of control. And at the time, she had thought that a grandchild would help her mother find happiness. If Julie couldn't connect with her mother, then maybe her having a baby would bring them closer together.

After a few months of trying, she could still remember where she had been sitting when she had googled infertility for the first time. On their front porch right after sunrise. Greg had just left for a morning run and Julie had walked out from the bathroom, a negative pregnancy test sitting neglected on the counter. She'd read articles and downloaded apps. She'd looked up specialists and read reviews. She'd ordered supplements and started meditations.

Slowly, it started to consume her.

Julie knew that infertility happened to people, but she never thought it would happen to her. As each month of negative pregnancy tests passed, she lost a little more of herself. When she had hit the year mark, she was weirdly excited because then she was allowed to take next steps with her doctor.

At that point, Greg had been fully supportive and on board. He gave her shots during the first IUI procedure. He cheered her on and whispered to her belly, telling her eggs to grow and grow. When the IUI procedure had failed, he had booked them a surprise trip to California for a few days. They went wine tasting and hiking. They made a new plan and talked about options while they sat overlooking a vineyard.

"I wish I had a time machine so I could go forward and find out if all of this was worth it," she'd mumbled, swirling the wine around in her glass.

Greg had leaned over, kissing her on the cheek. "It's going to be worth it, babe. I can feel it."

She felt like calling him right now and screaming at him. *"Was it worth it? Huh? So worth it that you up and left your wife?"*

After the first failed round of IVF, her therapist gently

pointed out that perhaps she was too focused on controlling the outcome of her life. That maybe Julie was bypassing the grief of losing her dad. But Julie didn't understand was why was that such a bad thing. Why was it frowned upon to want to have complete control over your life? Was it even your life if you were not able to make decisions for yourself that made you happy?

The women who decided to have a baby and then got pregnant on their first try weren't labeled as controlling. They weren't asked to slow down or to take a step back and think about what they might be avoiding. They were celebrated and oooo'd and awed over. Sprinkled with elaborate gifts and smiles from strangers in the grocery store.

They were allowed to be happy.

Julie's chest tightened. She'd become so bitter and she hated herself for it. The other day she had seen a super pregnant woman waddling down the aisle at Target, her cart filled with newborn essentials. Julie had scoffed and rolled her eyes. At a sweet pregnant woman shopping in the middle of the day.

Then she went to her car and cried.

Cried about how badly she wanted a baby and about how terrible of a person she was becoming. How had she become someone who was resentful of people she didn't even know?

And now here she was, sitting at the kitchen table with a pounding headache. As it turned out, drinking two martinis at lunch mid-day didn't set you up for a good evening.

Julie picked up her phone, clicking Greg's name on the screen.

She would try to contact him one more time, and then she was done.

As the phone rang and rang, she paced back and forth in her kitchen; the anger building up in her chest with every step.

She envisioned him seeing her name on the screen and silencing the call. She pictured him sitting there with someone else.

Someone who was capable of having children.

Someone who wasn't her, while she sat at home, alone, with the weight of their marriage and its failures on her shoulders.

She slammed the phone down onto the counter and yelled at the top of her lungs.

She yelled at the injustice. The unfairness. The perpetual disappointment.

Greg was gone. Her fertility journey was over. Her boss was probably pissed at her.

Everything was falling apart. In the back of her mind, she had always thought about what would happen if the fertility treatments didn't work, but what she hadn't considered was what would happen if her husband just gave up and left her to figure it out on her own.

There was no Google search for that scenario.

That, no one could prepare you for that.

ALLY

CADE WAS STILL STANDING BY THE TOWEL CABINET, and I could tell by his facial expressions that he was upset with me. Which I did agree was warranted given the information I had withheld from him.

"When were you planning on telling me? Because I don't want to think about the other option. The one where you planned on not telling me."

His nostrils flared slightly, and I sighed internally.

He didn't understand.

I hadn't even had a chance to let him know about my five-year plan. That everything had changed. That I no longer wanted to be married. That I had to make a new choice for myself. How did I tell him that what I felt before was no longer what I felt now? That sometimes you went through the motions and said yes to huge life events, only to realize later that it was all wrong. That there was something more out there for you. That sometimes in life you outgrew the people around you, and once that happened, the only way to stay was to go dark on yourself.

And that I was unwilling to do.

I was trapped like a rat in a cage. I did not respect him for this. For a moment, I considered using the special call button for the nurse. Certainly, this would count as an emergency. I imagined the smell perpetrator racing into my room, her Crocs making that awful rubber sound on the tiled hospital floor. Where was my undying nausea when I actually needed it? This would be a wonderful time to retch into the kidney-shaped container. Perhaps I could fake a version of narcolepsy, due to my concussion.

As I stared back at Cade, my brain began to feel foggy again. As if I couldn't think straight. As if all my usual direct communication skills and confident decisions had up and left me.

This was the worst possible outcome. I had not imagined what a pickle I would end up in if I needed to be hospitalized. In my marshmallow haze, I had only been focused on my imminent survival, in the short-term vision of my life. Naïvely, I had assumed that I still had time to sort out my predicament. I thought I could make a sound decision and get on with my life without Cade ever suspecting a thing. Breaking up a marriage sounded like a walk in the park now that I was facing the reality that I would also have to break his heart and take away his unborn child.

It was unfortunate across the board for everyone involved.

For myself.

For Cade.

For the baby.

What was I going to do about the baby? With every passing second, my chances of unbecoming a mother were slipping away. Cade would not understand this decision, especially now, when so much time had passed. When the idea of starting a family was hypothetical, he had been more understanding because it was not our lives that were at stake. It was not our baby's life that was on the line. It was a made-up baby. A potential down the road circumstance.

He had been willing to wait.

He had been hopeful I would come around.

He had been patient.

His love had been everlasting.

It was me who had been deceiving. I had always known deep down I would not change my mind. That I had been brewing up a plan to move away from him. I allowed him to think that perhaps with time, I would view the idea of a family in a new light. That I would come around. That my maternal clock would finally set off into the sunset and I would be forever changed.

When you love someone, you are willing to overlook certain aspects of their character. You think to yourself, I know this may be true about them now, but they will change in time.

We can make this work.

I can change his mind.

I had been guilty of this. I had decided that Cade would meet me where I was at in time. That he would realize having a family wasn't everything. That he would see that I was not meant to be a mother. That I loved our life the way it was. That maybe he would even want to travel with me!

We both had entered this partnership with assumptions that the other one would bend. That there would be a way to fill in the cracks in our foundation.

I realized now how naïve that thinking had been.

You could not expect another person to morph into someone you wished for them to be.

You could not ask someone to change their standards.

To want something more out of life or simply something different.

Instead, you had to do the very hard thing of saying, this isn't working for me. I have to set you free, so I can be free. But how did you do that? How did you tell your very loving, supportive, outstanding husband that the marriage was over simply because you did not want to be a mother?

I stared past Cade, avoiding his eyes. Knowing all of this, I still could not imagine a reality without Cade. I was confused about so much, but there was one thing I had clarity on in this moment. I simply could not break his heart.

Heat began to rise in my body as this realization settled in my chest. I tucked my hair behind my ears; it was bothering me much more than usual. The single strands that escaped the rest felt like slivers of imposters on my skin. I would need to keep it up in a high bun from now on, especially with this nausea.

I cleared my throat, and before I could stop myself, I began saying words that I knew he wanted to hear.

"I was planning to tell you, after this appointment. I wanted to make sure the baby was healthy. That this was really happening, before I got your hopes up."

Cade froze, halfway between the bed and that annoying towel cabinet that still had the door open. "Ally. Are you saying you will keep the baby? Are you saying you are willing to do this? For real?"

I swallowed hard and tried to act excited. "Yes. I mean, I am not saying this will be easy, but I am willing to give it a go." I forced a smile and sat up straighter. This was a giant mistake that I would certainly pay many consequences for, but what was I to do?

Cade rushed over to the bed, as if what I was saying had finally caught up to his sweet, slow-moving brain. Men always moved like molasses in that regard. You had to give them time to process emotions. Often times, they were nonverbal when it came to the department of expressing feelings. I had never understood this. Why not voice what was bothering you? Why not tell the person of interest that you had an opinion about their actions? Why not lay it all out on the table so that nothing was left uncovered.

But I understood now. This was something that I simply couldn't speak out loud to Cade. I could never look at him, the man I loved, and break his heart in two, which was precisely why I had moved forward with pretending to want to have this baby. The question I now had lingering in my brain amidst the marshmallow and nausea was this:

What was a person to do next when they broke their own heart, just so they wouldn't break the heart of the person they loved?

NANCY

T‍HERE APPEARED TO BE NO ONE HOME AT ALLY'S house, which was just as well since she couldn't quite remember what she had wanted to ask Ally about anyway. She was still sitting in Ally's driveway when a truck pulled in behind her. She glanced in the rearview mirror and racked her brain, searching for the piece of information that was just on the other side. Whose truck was that? Nancy knew she recognized it, but who was the owner? She waited patiently until the truck turned off and the man stepped out.

It was Cade! Of course. He lived here too; how silly of her. Nancy smiled in the rearview mirror and watched him as he frowned, looking at her car in front of his. It seemed that across the board, everyone had been really grumpy lately.

"Nancy?" Cade's voice traveled into her passenger seat, and she searched the side of the door for that button that she would need to press so they could have a conversation.

She decided she would just stay sitting here in her car, no need to get out and have an awkward conversation in the driveway. Finally, she found the thing and pressed it. Rolling down the window, she stuck her hand out and waved him over. He walked slowly toward her car. His body looked crumpled, like it needed ironing out.

Nancy thought about her own children and how hard it was to see them looking like they had been run over by a truck. You wanted to reach out and hold them, like you used to when they were five years old, but you couldn't. So instead, you offered to make them dinner or pressed a twenty-dollar bill in their hand when no one was looking. Nancy would do anything to make sure her kids didn't suffer, and that included getting to the bottom of what was going on in their lives, even if she hadn't been asked.

"Nancy? Ahhhh, is everything all right?"

She smiled at Cade. "Yes, of course! Sorry!" She waved her hand to act like it wasn't a big deal, because it wasn't. "I had just stopped by to talk to Ally, but it doesn't look like she is home right now." She faltered, because she didn't have much else to say after that. She didn't even know why she wanted to talk to Ally!

It was all becoming very confusing.

Something in Cade shifted. She saw a flicker in his eyes. It was as if she had unlocked something inside of his brain. She wished the same had happened in hers! She had the feeling there were two people here who didn't know what to say next.

"Ah, well. Yeah, she isn't home right now. Did Julie tell you to stop by? I'm sure she was worried about her when she didn't hear from her after her appointment."

Nancy nodded. Yes, this made sense. Julie did send her here; she just didn't know she had.

"Yes! Julie was busy at work, and she wanted to make sure Ally was okay. So, I am just doing what a mother does best, answering the ever-demanding requests of her children."

Cade seemed to relax a bit at this. His shoulders dropped, and he let out a long sigh. Looking around, almost as if he was making sure no one else was listening, he took a step closer "I am so glad Julie told you. I really need someone to talk to about this, but is Julie okay? You know...with everything? I am sure it is hard for her to take in."

Nancy had no idea what Cade was talking about, but that was becoming the norm for her these days. Clearly, this was a topic she should already be well versed in. The good news was that she was getting much better at playing along in conversations. Without missing a beat, she followed Cades body language and leaned in a bit closer.

"Julie will survive. You know how she is, just a little bit of frost around her heart, but once she warms up to the idea, she will soften."

Cade's frown slowly dissipated, and she saw the prospect of a smile.

He nodded. "You're right. They're best friends. I can't imagine Julie would ever be angry at Ally, plus it's not like she has any control over what happened anyway. I'm really hoping she will come around. I think it will be good for her, you know, in the long run."

Nancy still had no idea what they were talking about, but goodness did she really want to know! She racked her brain, trying to find something to say to keep Cade talking longer. "Julie would never be angry with Ally; she loves her more than anything."

Cade glanced toward the house and back to his truck. "Yeah, well, that is true. Hopefully it won't be too hard for her as things progress. I know she is strong, but I can't imagine seeing her best friend pregnant will be an easy thing to watch... you know, with how badly she wants a baby of her own."

Nancy's mouth opened, but there were no words that followed. She closed it again and forced a smile. *Don't let him see you flounder*, she repeated to herself. Reaching out, she patted his arm.

Cade looked at her with an odd expression and then glanced toward the house again. "Well, don't tell Ally or Julie we talked; I don't want them thinking we are making a big deal out of this."

Nancy sat up straighter and put her car into reverse. "I

won't say a thing. Our little chat never happened." She didn't hear what Cade said next because she was too busy repeating in her brain

Ally is pregnant.
Ally is pregnant.
Ally is pregnant.

She needed to get home and put it in her notebook before the information was lost forever. That was just what she intended to do until she heard the heavy thud of her car smashing into something behind her.

JULIE

Ally hadn't returned her texts. It had been a
few days since she had come down with the flu. She knew Ally
had been trying to protect her by staying away, but it wasn't
like Julie was going to be trying for a baby this weekend. What
did it matter?

She needed her best friend.

She needed her direct, odd commentary and practical
thinking.

Maybe Ally would have an idea of how to get Greg to
change his mind. Or present a new update about infertility to
make Julie feel better.

When Julie first realized that she might have fertility issues,
Ally had poured over hours of research on her own time,
without Julie asking. She simply showed up at Julie's house a
few days later with a mountain full of articles, the names of the
best doctors in the state, links to blogs and success stories.

"The first step to hitting a goal is to do research. You know,
continuing education. You must get familiar with the field,"
Ally had said confidently.

Julie had laughed. "Is it kind of weird that you are putting
having a human baby in the same category as goal setting?"

Ally had blinked back at her. "I am not sure why you think
that is weird? Your goal is to have a family. You have hit an
obstacle. All you need to do is pivot and try a new way, but
researching is imperative if you want to hit the goal."

Julie had shaken her head and shrugged. "All right, you are in charge of this ship. Let's set sail."

Ally had nodded. "Excellent. Now, I have highlighted the top three doctors that I think would be the best fit for you..."

Julie smiled at the memory.

A few months later, after nothing had worked, Ally had even presented Julie with a special fertility doctor in Dubai. "I have heard he is one of the best in the world. I think you might want to keep him in your wheelhouse." She had also taken Julie to acupuncture and even found her a personal trainer that specialized in "toning and priming" the body. She had researched fertility meal plans and convinced Julie to get an energy reading.

Ally's support had always been unwavering, ever since they were little girls. When Julie had trouble with the spelling bee in seventh grade, Ally had shown up at her doorstep with a stack of index cards. "The best way to commit something to memory is repetition. I have drawn up these index cards for you. I want you to go over them during breakfast, lunch, and dinner."

"Where did you get these?" Julie had asked, knowing very well that Ally's mom didn't just have extra school supplies lying around.

"I purchased them at the store, of course."

Later, Julie had found out that Ally had used money out of her savings that she kept neatly tucked away in the top drawer of her dresser at Julie's.

"I can't keep the money at my house, you see, because there is a high probability that my dad would steal it to buy alcohol."

Julie had nodded, as if this was a normal problem for most kids.

It was easier for Ally to look at Julie's infertility as a minor hiccup, something that would just take a bit more time. Something that Julie could strategize her way out of. Plus, Ally had no interest in having a family. She thought children were hostile, sticky, little creatures that sucked the life out of you.

Julie picked up her phone and dialed Ally's number. She needed her help. The phone rang and rang as Julie picked at a piece of thread on her sweater, unwilling to accept the fact that Ally was not answering. Sighing, she finally let it ring all the way through to voicemail.

"Thank you so much for reaching out, unfortunately, our schedules have not aligned, and I am unable to be present for a phone call at this time. Please leave your detailed contact information, and I will be sure to get back to you in a timely manner. If you are a telemarketer, please delete my number from your list. This is a violation of my privacy, and if you call again, I will report you to the authorities."

Julie burst out laughing. When she finally caught her breath, she giggled into the phone.

"Ally, that is the weirdest voicemail greeting ever. Call me back. Text me. Something. I need you!"

She sighed, leaning her head back against the couch. Leave it to Ally to be able to make her laugh during one of the worst weeks of her life.

Her thoughts traveled back to Greg. Could he really just up and leave their marriage without so much as a conversation? It had been almost three full days since they'd spoken. She tried to go back to the other night when he ignored her from the couch.

Should she have tried harder then?

Had she done everything she could?

He could only sleep at his office for so long. Was he just planning on never talking to her again? They had a home together. A joint bank account. Plans and dreams and memories. If he was really done with her, they had a whole life to divide between them. She tried pushing away the thought that kept trying to move to the front of her brain. But it kept coming back.

Was he cheating?

He had to face her at some point. She picked up the phone again and called him. This was ridiculous. Her husband didn't just get to opt out of their problems. That wasn't how life worked. He needed to be held accountable. Plus, Julie had his frozen sperm. Well, technically the fertility clinic did, but if Greg didn't want to partake in this anymore, that was fine. His sperm didn't have an opinion or a pressing timeline.

And that was all the hope Julie needed.

ALLY

Cade had left the hospital for a few hours to
go home to feed Archimedes and take him for a short walk,
thank the heavens above. I smiled thinking about Archimedes
waddling down the street. As a bulldog, he didn't need much
exercise, only cuddling and lots of snacks. It would be good for
Cade to get some fresh air and for the both of us to have a
break from each other.

I needed an abundance of alone time. We had received the
news that I would stay in the hospital overnight for observa-
tion. If all went well, I would be discharged tomorrow mid-
morning. I did not feel keen on the idea of staying overnight in
this very loud, intrusive building. I wasn't sure what the
evening would bring, but I was hopeful the hustling and
bustling outside my door would calm down significantly.

Surely, the nurses would need to go home and sleep. I imagined the night nurses would be calmer personalities. That the
person in HR arranging the nurses' schedule placed the quiet
souls on night duty and secured the ones like the smell perpetrator for the day shift.

Cade had plugged my phone in right next to my bed so that
I could access it at any time. It had low battery before my
appointment, which now seemed like days and days ago. I had
a rule with my phone: I charged it once every twenty-four
hours, and if it ran out of battery before then, then I was not
allowed to continue using it until the next day.

This kept me from falling into an addictive pattern. You

wouldn't believe what those social media apps were up to behind the scenes. Last year I had learned that they actually had teams of neuroscientists working with the marketing departments to create a user experience that was addictive on purpose. Our brains were trained to crave more and more from the apps. That was something I refused to conform to. How vulnerable our poor society had become. We were all running on our own individual hamster wheels, hardly noticing when the wheel had been replaced with one that was rigged to keep us locked in a loop for the rest of our life.

Today was an exception to my rule. Technically since my phone had died mid-morning, I shouldn't allow myself to use it until tomorrow, but I was stuck in a hospital bed and in need of Google. I also was unsure what else I would do to pass the time without a phone. I wondered briefly if the hospital had a library. I would imagine so. I made a mental note to ask the next nurse who came in if she could wheel me down to check out the selection. I had been instructed by the last nurse to not get up and walk without help, so I assumed a wheelchair would be required to take any trips down the halls.

"Just hit the button love if you need to use the bathroom or need anything else at all!"

I never understood people who referred to strangers as love. What an intimate word to paste onto just anyone. I had immediately written her off as untrustworthy. As the type of person who most likely said whatever you wanted to hear, just to keep you happy.

I reached for my phone and startled a bit as I took in all the notifications.

My heart sank.

Poor Julie.

I had completely forgotten about her as the events of the last few hours had unfolded. What an inconsiderate friend I was. There were multiple texts and a missed call from her. I began to overheat as I thought about calling her back. What would I say? How would I explain this?

When we were younger and my poor mother had been working overtime, I would often spend several nights in a row at Julie's house. One weekend I had gone home to check on my mother, and she had expressed to me that it felt so lonely to come home to an empty house after work. I had promised her right then and there that I would be sure to balance my time better, even though I preferred Julie's home with a fully stocked kitchen and abundant warmth. That weekend our electricity had been shut off because my mother didn't have enough to pay the bill, which meant my phone had died. Julie had been unable to reach me and I certainly wasn't going to leave my mother in the dark, literally. After I had told Julie the story the next day at school, she had made me promise to always find a way to contact her, even if my phone died.

"I don't care! Borrow someone else's phone! We were worried about you! Plus, I need you, Ally."

I remembered protesting that it wasn't sanitary to use a stranger's phone. Think about all of the objects a person touched on a given day. Smudging their grimy little fingers all over the screen. Holding the phone up to their ear. Placing it down on dirty surfaces! It was a hard no from me.

Julie had laughed out loud. "This is why I love you the most. You always know how to make me laugh."

I still didn't understand what about that was funny, but I think that was why we had always been thick as thieves. We balanced each other out. She was the yin to my yang, as they say.

How was I going to tell her that I was pregnant? Would we be able to come back from that? Would Julie be able to look at me and still love me the way she always had? Would I always remind her of everything she couldn't have? Just as I used to look at her and be reminded of everything that I wasn't able to have growing up?

Yet this was different.

Julie had shared everything she had with me.

And here I was, hiding the one thing she wanted so badly, right in front of her.

The machine next to my bed started to beep, and I glanced at it, watching the numbers flash and increase in the computerized version of sheer panic. I tried slowing my breath, watching the screen to see if it would adjust. It was not happy with me; I could tell that much. Just as I decided that perhaps I should wait until later to reach out to Julie, a nurse swiftly appeared at my bedside.

"Ally? Is everything all right? Looks like your blood pressure has shot up." She was clicking buttons on the screen and then turned back to look at me. Concern swept over her face, and she frowned. "You look rather pale. Do you feel nauseous?"

I didn't know what I felt. The marshmallow in my brain had taken over again, and I couldn't focus. "I, I am, I don't…" The black dots were back again. This time they moved faster. Were they faster, or was I just better at recognizing them now?"

"Ally? Can you hear me? I need some help in here!"

The nurse was so close to my face. Why was she yelling? I wanted to tell her to stop yelling. It was making me sick. But as I tried to form the words to do just that, everything went black.

Again.

NANCY

Shortly after Dean had passed away a doctor at Bright Side Memory Clinic explained to her that the amnestic MCI, short for mild cognitive impairment, would start to affect her memory. At first, Nancy had been ecstatic. Here she was thinking she was doomed, but the doctor had diagnosed her with something that had the word mild in it! A walk in the park. It didn't sound so bad. Yet, he had gone on to explain that in many cases, those living with MCI can develop dementia.

She refused to be one of those.

After she had left the doctors, his words rang in her head.

"You will start to forget important information, such as appointments or specific conversations. You may not remember recent events and start to feel foggy on a regular basis. Right now, you can carry on with your everyday activities, but, Nancy, you need to alert your family. It will be hard to keep track of every-thing, and if your symptoms progress, we will need to have addi-tional conversations."

Nancy had smiled and nodded, pretending that she was taking in everything he said. The irony wasn't lost on her in that moment. Here was the doctor feeding her a boatload of facts, expecting her to file it all away into her deteriorating brain.

This was where she probably had made it really difficult for herself by not allowing any family members to know what was going on.

Someone could have been there to take notes.

To follow up with her nightly on the phone.

To make sure she didn't drive alone or get lost somewhere.

However, this was the reason she hadn't told a soul. She didn't want to be treated as an inept, confused woman. She didn't want to be told she wasn't allowed to drive anymore or to be hovered around during family events. Nancy could already see her children making eye contact behind her back, worried and stressed over her inability to keep up mentally.

She wanted to keep her freedom for as long as possible. The doctors had explained that for the timing being, it could be manageable, but in a majority of cases it would advance.

And then a few weeks ago she had met with the doctor again and he'd used the phrase, "early onset dementia."

Nancy wasn't available for that diagnosis. No, thank you! She had told herself that as long as she had her notebook, she could keep track of anything and everything. What she hadn't anticipated was that her notebook couldn't protect her from the physical world.

Like this moment for instance.

Backing into Cade's truck and creating a huge scene.

"Nancy!"

Cade was still talking to her, and she wished he would stop. She was trying to remember something really important, but it was slipping away.

Ally was what?

Ally.

Something about Ally.

God dammit! How was she going to explain this mishap to Julie? She would be irate. It would have to wait, as the memories often did. That was the special catch to this slow downward spiral. For every memory she lost, another seemed to resurface, causing her even more confusion.

Nancy was beginning to trust that the memory would come back at some point, although never when she needed it most. And always at an inconvenient time. Slowly, she opened her car door and stepped out onto the driveway. Anger bubbled up inside her, threatening to spill over as Cade's voice continued to hammer away on the outskirts of her brain.

She spun around toward him and heard the panic in her own voice. "Why did you park your truck behind me when you knew I was leaving?" She winced, immediately feeling guilty for snapping at him. She was beginning to lose her patience with other people. Poor Cade happened to be in the wrong place at the wrong time.

Cade stopped short a few feet from her. He was frowning again. "Nancy, are you all right?"

"I am fine, I just really wish this hadn't happened. Can we not tell Julie about this?"

"Ahhhh, I'm sure she will find out. Won't she see your car? Why don't we check out the damage and go from there?" Cade shuffled toward his truck.

Nancy wanted to go home. Who cared if there was a little bang up in the metal? If the vehicle still drove around fine, what did it matter?

She hurried behind him, shivering in the cold air. She hadn't even worn a jacket, but then again, she hadn't planned to be out hitting cars in driveways. Cade was running his hand along the front of his truck. Nancy could see a small pile of headlight crystals on the pavement in between the cars. She shifted impatiently on her feet. What had she been trying to remember about Ally?

Cade stood up and brushed his hands off on his jeans. "It's minor. Your taillight is crushed, though, you will need to get it fixed before you drive at night."

Nancy waved her hand. "Phew! That's no problem. I'll call

my mechanic..." She trailed off. She couldn't remember what his name was. She snapped her fingers, as if that would conjure it. "What's his name, over in the center of town." She started backing up away from Cade. "Doesn't matter, you know who I mean!"

Cade watched her; the frown plastered back on his face. "Right, okay, well. Let me move my truck and then you can back out."

Bless his heart for reminding her that he needed to move his truck before she attempted to leave again. She was afraid if he hadn't, she would have just repeated the same collision. Nancy clambered back into her car and leaned her head back. She closed her eyes, trying so hard to remember what they had talked about.

Nothing.

There was nothing there.

She heard the rumble of Cade's engine, and while she waited, she picked up her phone. There was another missed call from Bright Side Memory Clinic. Sighing, she shoved the phone into the bottom of her purse. Apparently, they called a lot when you ignored them, probably because they assumed their patients had forgotten about them.

Nancy backed out cautiously, being careful to avoid any object that could cause a problem. What a stressful morning.

That was it!

A stressful morning with Ally.

Ally and Julie.

Julie and Ally.

Was there a fight? No, that wasn't it. There was something else. She slowed as she got to the intersection at the center of town. She watched as a group of pedestrians crossed in a cluster. Bringing up the rear of the group was a mother pushing a baby stroller. She seemed busy. On a mission. Nancy could see that the baby was happy to be out on a walk. Its little hands flung from side to side, legs kicking with delight. Her heart sank as she thought about Julie and how badly she wanted that very thing. A baby to push hurriedly across the street in a stroller.

A baby.

A baby!

Nancy shrieked out loud as the light turned green, gunning it across the road.

Ally was having a baby.

Nancy kept her hands clutched to the steering wheel the whole ride home. She didn't stop driving until she had reached her house, even though she had run two stop signs and received the middle finger from a jogger.

She slid her car into park and ran inside as fast as she could, pulling out her journal from the drawer by the hutch in the dining room. She flipped to a clean page and wrote in capital letters: ALLY IS PREGNANT.

Then she turned and looked at the calendar hanging on the wall by the entrance to the kitchen. She jotted down the date next to the words and collapsed into one of the chairs at the kitchen table. She was so happy to have gotten that detail down onto the page that she didn't even realize she had left her car running in the driveway.

JULIE

Greg had sent her right to voicemail, and Ally
still hadn't responded. Why was everyone ignoring her except
for her mother? She had been acting so odd at lunch; maybe
Julie should have been worried.

She needed to tell Ally that her mother had volunteered for
the memory clinic study. Ally would certainly have a mouthful
of comments about that. Julie sighed and checked her phone
again. She needed someone to unpack this with. The last few
days had been depressing, and she was actually beginning to
miss interacting with people.

She glanced at her watch; it wasn't even 4 p.m. yet. Cade
worked until about 5 p.m. every day, and Ally normally worked
from home. If she wanted to talk to her in private without
Cade hovering, she needed to do it now.

As she drove over to Ally's house, she thought about what
it would mean logistically to use Greg's sperm. Would she need
his permission? Had he already signed off on it somewhere
along the line? One of things no one told you about the infertility journey was the amount of prep and paperwork it
requires. Freezing sperm, creating embryos, the whole lot
wasn't exactly a quick and dirty activity. There were rules and
regulations.

She pushed her doctor's voice out of her head. She wasn't
going to accept the fact that one person's opinion meant the
end of her journey. He could suggest adoption all he wanted.
She wasn't going to buy into it.

She wondered if that was where she had lost Greg. Looking back now, he had never been overly excited sitting in the doctor's office listening to them go over the process. Julie had been so engaged, so excited, taking notes and hanging on every word spoken by every medical professional, she hadn't even stopped to observe how Greg was taking it all in. She just assumed he shared her level of enthusiasm.

When you were locked into a goal, as Ally put it, you didn't see what was happening on the peripheral. You only saw one thing. The thing you wanted more than anything else in the world. It was easy to slap on a pair of rose-colored glasses and expect that everyone else was just as invested as you were.

There should have been a guidebook that came along with all the happy smiling pamphlets they handed you. Sure, there was a pamphlet on what to do if the first treatment didn't work, resources for couples, etc...but there was never anything that lent a hand to what would happen if your partner decided to opt out. If you were left without any options and a shitty husband.

Where was the rule book for that?

She hit the gas, speeding down through the intersection toward Ally's neighborhood. First, she just needed to unpack all of this with her best friend, then she could decide what to do next. As she pulled into the quiet development where Ally lived, she checked her phone once more.

Nothing.

Her heart sank as Ally's house came into view. Cade was home. She groaned out loud. He was never home at this hour. She assumed Ally's car was in the garage since it wasn't out front. As she pulled into the driveway and shut off her ignition, she paused. What if Cade and Ally were having a romantic afternoon?

She shook her head. No. That wouldn't happen. Ally didn't do things like that, plus she was getting over the flu.

She opened the mud room door slowly, knocking softly as she did. "Als? Are you awake?"

She waited, listening for a response.

Nothing.

Archimedes, their super old bulldog, was asleep sprawled out on the kitchen floor. She took a wide step over him. He opened one eye, glancing up at her. Satisfied, he closed it again and continued snoring. Julie smiled, still in disbelief that Ally had a dog. When Ally had told her they were adopting him, Julie had been surprised.

"But you hate pet hair?"

"I know, it is rather unfortunate, but Cade really wants to have something to care for and you know how I feel about starting a family." Ally had shuddered, making a repulsed expression. "This is a great way to hold him off and give him something to focus on instead. Plus, I have always wanted to name a dog Archimedes."

Julie had laughed. "Do I even want to know why?"

Ally's mouth had fallen open, and she pretended to look utterly shocked. "Excuse me, please tell me you remember *The Sword and The Stone*?"

Julie laughed. "I think maybe I do?"

Ally had brought her hand to her chest. "You think you do? Please tell me this is a joke. It is only one of the greatest movies from my childhood. You don't remember the owl? Archimedes?"

"You are one of kind, Ally, you know that?"

"I do know that, and you know what else is one of a kind? That movie. Don't worry, once your future child is old enough to watch movies, I will make sure they see it about fifteen times."

Back then, it had been so easy for them to think about her future child like it was no big deal. Like she could snap her fingers and be a mother. She closed her eyes, trying to push the sadness out of her brain.

Julie had understood the reasoning behind Ally's decision, but she still didn't think it was the best idea to replace Cade's longing for a baby with a senile bulldog. That was a few years ago, right after Julie and Greg had gotten engaged. She hadn't anticipated at that time what would follow.

Now, looking back, she understood Ally's decision.

Sometimes you had to do something for yourself, even if it wasn't the best choice for the other person. Sometimes you had to be selfish, because the alternative was much too hard to face. The one where you actually saw the flaws in your significant other. The one where you acknowledged the stark differences in what you wanted and what you expected to happen. The ones that, when avoided, would cause a whole crumbling of your intricate systems.

She needed to talk with her best friend. Who knew the ins and outs of her marriage to Greg. The only person who could make her laugh no matter what was going on. There was nothing more healing than having an in-depth conversation with your best friend about your relationship struggles. To have someone who knew every single part of you discuss and analyze and commiserate with you. To have someone who also told it to you straight. Who would push you when she knew you could handle it, and pull back in areas when she knew you couldn't. Julie needed that today. More than ever. She breezed past the dog and made her way to the bottom of the stairs.

"Ally!" she yelled, opening the baby gate at the bottom of the stairs. She didn't really understand why it was there; she highly doubted that Archimedes would be able to climb all the up to the second floor.

"Hello? Nancy? I thought you left." Cade's voice cascaded around her, and she froze. Nancy? Why was he asking for Nancy?

"Oh, Julie. Hi." Cade ran his hand through his hair. "What are you doing here?" He looked confused and, frankly, exhausted.

Where was Ally?

"Umm. I came by to see Ally, but why did you say Nancy? As in Nancy, my mother?" Julie felt the threat of tears. All she wanted to do was talk to Ally.

Cade looked at her quizzically. "But Ally is—I mean, hold on." He shook his head. "Sorry, it's been a crazy day. Your mom just showed up here, and I had parked my truck behind her and she, aahhh, she backed into it."

"*What?*" Julie spun around. "Is she okay?" She shook her head, trying to hold in the tears. Why was she going to start crying? Why was her fucking mother hitting cars in her best friend's driveway? "I am sorry, I have to go. I need to—"

"No, no. It's okay. Your mom is fine. I mean, she was acting a little odd but, you know..."

Julie threw up her hands. "Oh, I know. No need to explain. So, she is fine? What about the cars? Where did she go?"

Cade sighed and turned to the fridge, grabbing himself a beer. He cracked it open and guzzled a huge sip. "She went home. Her taillight was smashed in. I told her to make sure she got it fixed before she drove around at night. My truck is fine. Listen, I-I am sorry about Ally. Are you..."

Julie shook her head. "Don't be sorry, is she okay?" She was already heading back out through the mudroom.

Cade was saying something in response, but she would worry about Ally later. Right now, she needed to check on her mom.

She had a bad feeling.

Something wasn't right.

Well, nothing was right anymore, but this was different.

ALLY

THE DOCTOR'S VOICE FELT LIKE IT WAS JACK hammering into my brain.

"I want to order another MRI immediately. Yes, it's fine."

There were other voices, a woman and a man. I tried hard to push through the fog that circled my vision.

"Let's take her up right now. I want to make sure we didn't miss anything. She shouldn't be continuously losing consciousness like this."

I tried to speak, but once again, nothing would come out. It was becoming very frustrating. This whole marshmallow brain, seeing spots and black dots, not being able to articulate properly. I needed to know what was happening.

As if the woman's voice could read my mind, she appeared at my side. "Ally, you fainted again. We are going to take you up to get a few more images, just to make sure everything is all right. Squeeze my hand if you can hear me."

Squeeze her hand? Had she washed it properly? Where was her hand? I didn't feel it in mine, which I was glad about. Just as I was planning to object to the nurse's request, her hand landed in mine. It was softer than I had expected. Slightly squishy. As if it were retaining water. I suspected she had consumed too many cocktails and slices of cheesecake over the holidays. That would have done it. I felt a few rings. They were exceptionally tight on her swollen fingers. She would need to take those off immediately before there was an issue with circulation. I myself was against wearing any rings on my fingers.

The thin metal felt like it was purposefully suffocating my digits. Once, I had tried my hardest to wear the engagement ring Cade had gotten me, but no matter what I did, I could feel its hard surface rubbing against my other fingers. I did not like the feeling it created. A foreign imposter taking up space on my hands. Restricting me from using my fingers freely, in the way they were meant to be used.

"Ally? Can you squeeze my hand?"

I could, but I didn't want to. Was there a way to tell her this?

"Ally, I need to know if you can hear me. Give my hand a light squeeze if you can."

Oh, for fuck's sake, fine. I curled my fingers into her hand ever so slightly, giving the squishy part of her hand a little pinch, and then released them, moving my hand away from hers as quickly as possible.

That was all she was getting.

A deep, throttled laugh bubbled out of her throat that sounded like she had smoked a whole pack of Parliament Lights during her break. Absolutely repulsive. Wasn't there a policy against nurses being allowed to smoke as a recreational hobby? It seemed quite counterintuitive to their job at hand. I wondered what her name was. If I wasn't feeling so awful, I would have made an attempt to figure it out. I imagined it was something like Wanda or Deb.

Another nurse had entered the room. I could hear her squeaky sneakers on the tiled floor. "Where is her husband? He was here a bit ago."

Wanda was shuffling around right next to me, moving wires and fidgeting with blood pressure cuffs. She turned and looked at me again. I could see more clearly now. Her hair was just as I imagined it would look. Slicked back with too much product, with the exception of one long strand on either side, strategically straightened to be hanging there. I fantasized about cutting them clean off of her head. Didn't she feel upset always having them in her peripheral vision? Small hoop earrings traveled all the way up and down both ears. How did she lay her head down comfortably at night? I shuddered at the thought of those pesky fake gold pieces invading my own ears.

"Ally? Is your husband still here?" She leaned over, getting much too close to my face. The long stands threatened to graze my skin. I pulled my head back as far into the pillow as I could.

"No," I managed to croak. My voice sounded foreign, as if someone had reached in while I was asleep and given it a rebrand.

Wanda's eyes lit up, and I took note that she most definitely had drawn on her eyebrows with a color that did not entirely match up with her skin tone. I did not understand why a human would draw on their face with a pencil. Certainly, that would seep into your skin and cause an issue. What if one day they woke up and forgot to pencil in their eyebrow imposters? Did they just show up to work and pretend that everyone didn't notice their eyebrows had suddenly disappeared overnight?

"You are talking! Good girl." She patted my arm approvingly. I bristled. I was not a dog. This was not the veterinarian's office. Unfortunately, Wanda's communication skills matched up with her appearance. A bit rough around the edges. It was probably not her fault. She was doing the best she could. I decided to cut her some slack, mostly because I was too weak to argue with anyone.

"Do you want me to call your husband? The MRI might take a while, and it's helpful to have a support person."

I hadn't considered the logistics of the MRI given the fact that I was still seeing black dots when that had been mentioned. Would I be placed in a long tube? I did not like being in enclosed spaces. Were there safety precautions imple-mented for the baby? I knew I should have been asking these things, but my marshmallow brain made it hard to get every-thing out. Perhaps I would like to have Cade present. He was very good at calming me down.

Once we had gone to Boston to spend a day visiting the Museum of Fine Arts and to have a proper dinner at Capital Grill. Cade had wanted to make a weekend of it, and after much convincing, I agreed to stay at an exquisite hotel for the evening. I was not fond of hotels. Who in their right mind would sleep on a mattress slept on by strangers? Thousands upon thousands of foreign bodies farting and rustling around on the fabric. Cade had laughed out loud when I told him my predicament with the mattress.

"They use sheets, silly! They wash them and sanitize them. It is perfectly safe to sleep on a hotel mattress. What about waiting room chairs? You sit in those!"

At the time, I did not have the heart to tell him that I certainly did not sit in a waiting room chair that resembled a couch. I preferred something harder and plastic. If that was not available, I brought a jacket or sweatshirt to sit down on top of. Perhaps I could bring my own sheets to the hotel.

After dinner, we'd had a nightcap in the lobby. Usually, I avoided drinking alcohol because I did not resonate with the feeling of losing control. But, on special occasions, I would entertain Cade and sip a glass of red. And sometimes, for Julie's sake, I would partake in a single margarita. Just like I had at my birthday. As we'd prepared to head back up to our room, Cade had strode confidently toward the elevator. I'd stopped in the opening right before everyone congregated to hop on the jostling contraption that kept people from getting in a few extra steps in their evening.

"I will not be getting on the elevator. I will take the stairs."

Cade had frowned, and I could see a whisper of agitation on his face. "But, Als, we are on the fortieth floor. You surely don't want to go up forty flights of stairs, do you?"

I had to admit, it did seem like a lot. "You know I don't have much faith in elevators. What if there is a malfunction?"

Cade had smiled and stepped forward, embracing me. I thought he did the hugging gesture on purpose to calm my nervous system down. I saw it once on a television special, and I had to admit; it did the trick.

"Just trust me. It will be very fast, and we will be in our room before we know it."

As I'd stepped onto the elevator, I had the sinking feeling it was a mistake. Cade had squeezed my shoulders after he hit the buttons to direct us to the fortieth floor. As we started to ascend, there was a jolt. A shudder. And then nothing. We had stopped moving. Cade had glanced at me and then hit the buttons again, but nothing happened.

"I would like to get off the elevator now," I'd said, in a slightly alarmed tone. I could feel the panic rising in my chest. How would the elevator resume its climb? How would we get out?

"Don't worry. It's just jammed. Let's focus on something else. What did you think of your dinner tonight? Tell me about it."

I had stared at him for a long beat. He wanted to talk about our dinner while we were stuck in an unresponsive elevator? I did not think this was an appropriate time for a Yelp dining review. He'd continued to look at me expectantly, waiting for my answer. Sighing, I gave him a recap of my mediocre filet. I had asked for medium, but it was a bit charred for my liking. The hot buttered dinner rolls were exquisite, though. I had thought highly of our waiter, who maintained a very professional and educated conversation throughout the length of our meal. By the time I was about to discuss the dessert portion of the dinner, there was a humming sound, followed by a ding. Suddenly, we were moving again.

I'd exhaled, relief crashing through my tense body.

Cade had stepped forward and embraced me again. "See?" he had whispered in my ear, "nothing to stress about."

NANCY

When Dean had asked her to marry him, she had known it was coming. He had been nervous for weeks on end. Extra jumpy. It didn't take a rocket scientist to know what he was up to. Men were simple like that. Multiple times a day for over a month he would retreat to their bedroom while she was cooking dinner or watching a television show in the living room and fidget around. She could hear him open and close the engagement ring box.

Snap.

Snap.

Snap.

When he finally worked up the courage to propose, she had heard the snap first. She wondered at the time why he opened the box so much. Was he worried someone had stolen the ring? Or was he afraid it was the wrong choice?

She had been in the kitchen cooking lasagna; an array of noodles lined the counter; pasta sauce smeared on her shirt. She hadn't exactly looked her personal best. As he walked down the hallway toward the kitchen, she heard again.

Snap.

Snap.

Snap.

She bristled at the stove, watching the water start to form little bubbles as it boiled, just like her nerves in that very moment. Nancy had tried to act natural when Dean called her name softly to get her to turn around. She had tried to act surprised when she saw him kneeling down on one knee in the middle of their humble kitchen. For Dean's sake, she had tried. He had been so proud of himself in that moment, she couldn't bear to crush his excitement.

Afterward, when they sat together on the couch admiring the ring, Dean had asked if she had any idea he was going to propose.

"Not even the slightest! I was completely in the dark."

That was how she felt now, as she sat in her armchair in the living room.

She was in the dark, and she was afraid she didn't know how to get herself back to the light.

Snap.

Snap.

Snap.

Went her memories.

She looked down at her ring and twirled it around her finger. Dean loved that story of their engagement. The kids had heard it a thousand times. Nancy had never told him about the box. That she had known weeks before what was coming.

Was that wrong of her? To lie to him?

Was it wrong of her to lie to her family now? About her condition?

No.

It wasn't.

Sometimes people were better off not knowing the truth. Sometimes it was best if you just played along. Sometimes it was easier for everyone involved if the people you loved believed something completely different because there was no harm in what they were believing.

There was more harm in the truth.

Suddenly, there was a loud knock on her door. She clutched her chest; the noise had almost given her a heart attack! The knocking barreled through her brain again and again. With her heart still pounding, she stared into the abyss of her living room.

Someone was at the door.

She pushed herself up and out of the chair, walking slowly into the dining room. "I'm coming, I'm coming."

The knocking continued. Did people have any respect? It was irritating, the incessant noise. Each one seemed to land inside her brain and jar her thoughts loose. Looser than they already were. Who was visiting her at this hour, anyway? She glanced at the dining room clock. Admittedly, she didn't even know what hour it was. Nearly dinner time.

As she unlocked the door, it swung open. A blast of cold air stung her face, and she backed up away from the entrance.

"Mom? What the heck? What are you doing?"

Her daughter threw her hands up as she barreled into the house, as if that helped Nancy understand what she was referring to. It didn't.

Nancy stared at her. She looked like she had been crying. Why was she so infuriated with Nancy all of the time? She had just been sitting here having a rest for herself, doing no harm to anyone.

"Julie. Why don't you sit down? You looked stressed."

"*Oh*, great. Thanks so much for the kind gesture. That will solve all my problems."

Nancy winced as Julie slowed the words down as if she were a toddler who couldn't understand everything.

Julie kept going, her eyes flashing. "Just have a little sit-down, Julie! That will fix everything right up."

Nancy said nothing. She waited, as she always did with her daughter. The more you pushed her, the more she shut down. If you remained quiet, she would talk. Much like a first grader after school. Pepper them with questions, you would get nothing. But wait until they were ready, and you'd get the whole play-by-play of the day.

"You left your car running with the door open." Julie jutted her finger toward the driveway.

Nancy's heart skipped a beat at the volume of her words, and she looked cautiously out the large dining room window. "I don't think so, see? All the doors are closed and it's clearly off."

Julie scoffed. "Yes, Mother. Because I turned off the ignition and shut the door."

There she went again, sounding out the words as if Nancy were decrepit.

"Right, well. I had intended to go back outside to shut it off, but I sat down for a moment to check my phone, and whoops! I fell asleep." She settled into a nearby chair. She was so tired of arguing with Julie. "I've had a busy day. Thank you for checking on me."

Julie started pacing back and forth and then turned to Nancy. "You expect me to believe that? I just went over to Ally's house to check on her, and I ran into Cade. Ally's husband? He said you backed into his truck in his fucking driveway! Why were you sitting in Ally and Cade's driveway? Do you know your taillight is smashed? I mean. What is going on with you?"

The words hit Nancy like tiny bullets, all at once, hammering little holes in her brain.

The overwhelm she felt when someone was talking to her was constant. Combine that with someone yelling, and it was a miracle Nancy remembered who she was. Honestly, Nancy had forgotten all about the incident with Cade. She racked her brain, trying to remember why she had been there in the first place. She shook her head, trying to jostle it loose.

Julie was still pacing the room and then, all of a sudden, she stopped short. Right in front of Nancy's notebook. Nancy could see the explosive energy ripple through Julie before she said another word.

She held her breath, waiting.

"What is this?" Julie reached over and picked up the notebook off the dining room table. She clutched it with a shaking hand and looked at Nancy, deep disappointment and utter hatred flashing in her beautiful eyes. But Nancy also saw a sadness there, underneath all that anger; and it broke her heart.

Nancy wasn't sure why she was so upset, but she knew that her own cover might have been blown in that moment. If Julie had read through the notebook, she would know Nancy's secret.

Nancy eyed her daughter carefully and whispered, "That's my journal where I write down important information that I don't want to forget."

JULIE

"Please tell me this isn't true." Julie was grasping onto the shitty dollar store notebook with one shaking hand, staring at her mother who looked bored with the whole thing. Her mother's lack of reaction only increased the rage pulsing through her body. She could feel her arms and chest radiate with tension.

She could feel the tears coming.

God damn it, how many times was she going to cry this week?

"Mom?" She took a step toward her mother, who blinked rapidly and looked out the window at her car. "Answer me!"

She could see the slightest hitch in her mother's shoulders as her voice landed in between them, but she couldn't stop the rage pulsing through her body.

"Why are you ignoring me?"

Her mother turned back toward Julie and frowned. "Can I see the notebook?" Her mother sat down at the end of the table, choosing the seat farthest away from where Julie was standing.

Julie threw up her hands and, in the same motion, tossed the notebook across the table, forcing it to slide in her mother's direction. It went flying past her mother and landed on the floor near her feet. Julie let out a breath. Why was she like this? She was low-key abusing people now. She couldn't help it, though. With each passing month that she didn't get pregnant, she seemed to adopt another layer of built-in rage, like the metaphor of peeling an onion, only backward.

And that was before she had come to terms with the fact that her marriage was dissolving and she might never have a baby of her own.

She just couldn't take it anymore.

Her mother sighed and looked at Julie for a long moment before she leaned over and picked up the notebook. Its pages flapped and protested as she smoothed them out and closed the cover. Julie could see the hurt in her eyes, and she hated herself for it.

She was a monster.

"Mom, I'm…"

Her mother shook her head. "Julie, I don't think this is a good time to chat. You seem awfully on edge. Why don't you go home and get some rest? Give me a call later and we can talk. You don't look well."

Julie clenched her fists and took a deep breath. "Mom. I am not going anywhere until you tell me why your goddamn weird notebook says that my best friend Ally is fucking pregnant."

Her mother jumped a little in her seat and looked at Julie. "Ally is pregnant? Where does it say that?" She flipped frantically through the notebook, muttering to herself.

Julie winced, her chest deflating. Her mother's hands were shaking slightly, and she looked like she'd seen a ghost. Her emotions toward her mother were ping-ponging around in her brain. It felt good to yell, to direct her anger toward someone safe. She could feel that some of the tension had left her body. Yet, what immediately stepped in and took its place was a deep sadness.

A sadness she didn't want to face.

A sadness that was trapped.

That was continuously pushed down, moving around in her chest, only allowed to escape through short bursts of shouting and the slamming of fists on steering wheels. During her last therapy appointment, her therapist had recommended that the next time she felt out of control or angry to try punching pillows.

"It might feel silly at first, but would it be worth it if you felt better afterwards? Just give it a try. Most of my clients find that all it takes is a few punches before the tears come."

Julie had nodded eagerly in agreement, mostly just to get her therapist to stop talking about it. Sitting here now, with the possibility that Ally was pregnant and her mother had been hiding it from her would be the thing that sent her over the edge.

It might be time to start punching pillows.

"Mom?" Julie said quietly, a stark juxtaposition to her previous outburst ten seconds earlier. She could feel the tears building, as usual. "I just really need to know. Is Ally pregnant? Please tell me it is some sort of sick joke. I just saw Cade; he would have told me!"

Would he have, though? Or would he be hiding it from her because Ally told him not to tell a soul, especially not Julie. She retraced her conversation with him. He was really stressed because her own mother had just hit his car. Then she thought about how she didn't really hear the last thing he said because she was hurrying out the door.

Fuck.

Ally couldn't be pregnant.

No. Julie thought back to the last few days.

Ally lying horizontal in the back seat of the car. Claiming to have the flu. Sleeping at 4 p.m. Ignoring her calls. Acting super weird at her birthday dinner.

She felt like she couldn't take a full breath.

Every time she inhaled, it felt shallow.

Like there wasn't enough room for all her emotions to land.

White-hot tears seared the back of her eyes.

No.

No.

No.

This couldn't be real. She shook her head and inhaled, trying to hold the tears in. If there was anything she was good at, it was stopping tears. She'd had a lot of practice. Or she used to be. She didn't even know anymore. Lately, it seemed like she was losing a grasp on that too.

"Julie, dear. Are you all right? Why don't you sit down?" Her mother was standing now, busily trying to shove the notebook into an overstuffed drawer of the large hutch.

"Mom." Her voice shook as she spoke. "Tell me right now. Is it true?"

Her mother sighed and abandoned the drawer. She looked at Julie with sad eyes. "I think it is," she whispered.

There was something about the way her mother said it, the delicacy of it, maybe, that cracked something open in Julie. A sob ripped its way up and out of her chest, and she collapsed to the floor.

She was so tired.

She was so tired of fighting for a baby.

She was so tired of being angry.

She was so goddamn tired of being disappointed.

She was so tired of trying not to cry.

"Julie? Oh, Julie. I am so sorry," her mother whispered, sitting down on the floor next to her.

She could feel the light touch of her mother's hand on her back. She winced, feeling her body resist the support. The last time her mother had rubbed her back, she had probably been nine years old. She wanted to move away from her, to keep herself locked up from feeling anything at all, but for some reason, she stayed put, letting her disheveled mother console her while she wept for everything she would never have.

ALLY

Cade was not answering his phone. The nurses sighed and shuffled around my room, preparing to take me up to the MRI. Wanda was still here, and I was afraid I would be stuck with her for the remainder of the day.

"We don't want to wait much longer there, girlie. Unfortunately, you will have to get started without him, but no need to worry. I'll be right there with ya!"

Wanda said this as if I were happy to relinquish all my faith in humanity to her. She would not be my first choice for a partner if the world was ending or if we had to compete in one of those survival TV shows together. I imagined her making bad choices. She would probably prioritize packing hostess cupcakes and cigarettes while I was making sure we had extra batteries and a warming blanket.

Perhaps she would be called into another room, and I would receive a nurse who was more my speed.

Proper and put together.

Quiet and diligent.

No long strands of hair slicked down in front of the face.

Wanda was still talking, and I wanted her to be quiet. I wasn't sure how much more of it I could take. It felt as though my head was floating around the room and I was trying to catch up with it. I tried to focus on the positives. In my preparation for all the traveling I planned on doing, I had taken into consideration that I would be exposed to a lot of noises.

People.

Germs.

Unexpected situations.

I was aware that all those things were not moments I typically enjoyed. In my research I had come across the idea of exposure therapy. The more I put myself in these types of situations, the more I could train my nervous system to adjust accordingly. This was a great opportunity for me to chip away at that concept. I would have to keep that top of mind today.

Wanda barreled on, cutting through my thoughts. "You'd think that you'd be able to listen to book on tape or your own playlist during the MRI, but don't worry, we've got a few popular satellite stations you can pick from! Do you have anything you would like to listen to?" She was typing into the screen next to my bed and paused as if she was waiting for my encouragement to continue her spiel.

I considered pointing out that a "book on tape" was an outdated term. However, I knew better than to egg on her kind. If you gave her an inch, she would take a mile. Normally, I would entertain the idea of a podcast, yet lately listening to anything made me feel extremely nauseous, and it was off the table anyway.

She kept typing in the computer and looked over at me, her gums flapping. "If you don't want to listen to anything, you could meditate! A lot of patients find that helps! Are you good at mediating?!"

I could tell she had been waiting to say this bit the whole time. She was proud to share this fact as if she was the next Gabrielle Bernstein. I could not imagine Wanda meditating. If I was in better spirits, I would have asked her if she meditated herself just so I could watch her flounder.

I continued to look at her, purposely not providing her with any answers. I knew I was being a bit of a brat, but I was the patient here and I had been left to my own devices without my husband and without any idea of what was going to happen to me in that god-awful tube.

"All right, Ally, I understand you are not feeling great and it's okay if you don't want to respond. I am going to wheel you up to the MRI imaging center now. We have left your husband a few voicemails, and I am sure he will be right along as soon as he gets the messages."

How did she know he would be right along? She hadn't even met him yet. He could be a psychopath for all she knew. It wasn't healthy to make assumptions about people without having all the information. Wanda propped up the sides of the hospital bed and kicked the locks on the bottom, swinging it around so it was facing the exit of the room. There was a small thrill in getting to travel somewhere new. I was looking forward to sightseeing as we traveled through the hallways.

"Once we get up there, we will get you prepped. You are going to be just fine! Have you thought of names for the baby? That's always my favorite part, hearing the names people choose! You wouldn't believe some of the ones I have heard. You get to hear a lot at the hospital. Always been a bit jealous of the labor and delivery nurses, they get a first-hand pick at all the names!

I wished Wanda would stop talking for just a moment so I could take in my surroundings in peace. I wanted to scream, *Silence! Shut your mouth and zip it up. Lock it up. Throw away the key, Wanda.*

A name for the baby.

Of course, the pregnancy app had been hinting at it and sharing external links to lists like "The top 100 baby names of all time!" Yet, I hadn't even considered clicking them. Instead, I had been considering how to backtrack out of this predicament and move on with my life the way I had intended.

All of that was null and void now. Cade would never

recover if I chose not to have the baby. Yet, I wondered as I watched nurses' stations and waiting rooms and way too many bright ceiling lights whiz by, would I ever recover if I did have the baby? Would Julie ever forgive me?

We stopped abruptly, and I heard the familiar ding of an elevator. I inhaled sharply. Wanda frowned and looked down at me. No, I did not want to go on the elevator.

"You all right, love? We are almost there."

I shook my head. No, I was not all right.

I needed Cade.

I needed to not go on the elevator.

I needed to not be pregnant.

I needed a meal that involved a cheese quesadilla and orange juice over lots of ice. I needed a side of hot buttered rolls. I needed quiet. I needed to rewind and go back to a few weeks ago when I was putting the finishing touches on my five-year plan.

When I had no idea any of this was about to happen.

NANCY

Nancy stood in the middle of the kitchen staring at the kettle on the stove. It was heating up water, that she knew. But why? What was she supposed to do with the water? That she did not know. She opened a few cabinets, staring at the dishes. Plates and the things that held liquid. She couldn't remember the name of them. Tall ones and round stunted ones. She turned and looked around the corner at her daughter who was sitting in the large armchair in the living room.

She hadn't seen Julie cry like that in decades. The last time had been when she was a little girl. When she hit her knee on the edge of the table or when Nancy told her no, she couldn't dump the dog's water all over the floor. Nancy could still remember the soft smell of Julie's hair and how she curled up in her lap, trying to get as close as possible. So why couldn't she remember how to follow through with a simple kitchen task?

She thought about asking Julie what she was supposed to do with the hot water, but she didn't want to draw attention to her problem. So far, Julie hadn't asked about her memory issues. Nancy assumed it was because she was so self-consumed regarding the news she had just received.

She knew the questions would come. Most likely today or tomorrow. Would she call Will? Would her children send her to one of those old folks' homes where she would be left to rot, ironically forgotten by everyone in her family. Her mind wandered back to before Dean had died. What would he have done if he were still here?

They had always had a running joke between the two of them. She would say to him, "If I ever lose my mind, just take me out back in the woods and put me out of my misery. I don't want to be dropped off and left to perish in one of those rancid nursing homes."

Dean would smile and take a sip of his drink. "Don't worry, babe. I wouldn't allow it. We can go out together. Just take a long, long walk in the woods, and that will be that."

She shook her head. The kids always hated when they said things like that, but as you aged, you had to plan ahead. She had never planned on losing him first and then actually losing her mind as well. What would Dean have said if she had presented that scenario to him? Why hadn't they considered that this was a possibility?

Suddenly, there was a loud screeching sound. She jumped up, spinning around in a circle frantically. "Make it stop!" she yelled, covering her ears.

"Mom? What are you doing?" Julie gave her an exasperated look and then walked over to the stove, pulling the thing that had the hot water in it off the burner. The sound subdued to a low-grade whistle. Nancy pulled her hands away from her ears. Thank goodness. Who would make such a contraption that made such a horrid noise?

"Do you have a headache?" Julie frowned at her. "Why were you covering your ears? Where are the teacups?"

Teacups! That was what those round things that held liquid were called! She moved swiftly to the cupboard she had opened a few moments before and pulled two down. Julie opened another drawer and pulled out two bags of tea, placing one in each cup and giving Nancy a weary look.

Nancy watched as she poured the piping hot water over the

bags. A small gasping sound escaped from the cups as the water stilled. This felt very calming. A slow, steady steam rose from inside each cup, and she felt herself relax just a little bit. Julie placed the water holder back on the stove and turned back to Nancy.

"It wasn't a study, was it?" Julie stated, her eyes glassy with tears.

Nancy blinked at her daughter. What was she talking about now?

"The memory clinic that called you the other day. It wasn't for a study, was it?" Julie ran her hands down her face and sat down at the kitchen table. "You didn't volunteer to let them test your memory," she whispered, leaning forward. "You are a patient there. Aren't you?"

Nancy shifted on her feet and glanced out the kitchen window.

This was it.

The end of her freedom.

Maybe she could still downplay it.

"It's not as bad as you think. I just didn't want to worry you, Julie. You are going through so much."

"Mom," Julie said carefully. "What is going on?"

"I have something. A condition. I can't remember what it's called." She smiled and shrugged. "That's why I have the notebook, so I can write down important things."

"The beach," Julie said slowly, picking up her mug and then putting it down.

Again, Nancy had no idea what her daughter was talking about. Maybe neither of them were all right. She frowned. "It's a bit cold today for the beach. Maybe another day."

"Mom. Are you serious? No. I am not inviting you to go to the beach. You got lost at the beach the other day. Remember?"

There she went again, spelling it out. Nancy didn't remember. She was becoming irritated now with her daughter. At this point, she could be a bit nicer considering the circumstances.

"You parked your car down that weird side street and got lost. You told Ally and I that you had a new friend. Plus, you forgot Ally's birthday. You have been doing a bunch of insane stuff." Julie stood up, pushing the chair back.

Nancy felt herself shrink down, like a turtle going into its shell.

"Then the memory clinic called you, and I believed your weird story! Gosh, how could I be so stupid?" Julie was pacing now, muttering under her breath and glancing back at Nancy as if she didn't recognize her. "I'm sorry. I just, I don't... I am so mad at myself for not noticing." Julie leaned forward onto the kitchen counter and then straightened back out.

"I am going to have to tell Will, okay? We need to meet with your doctor. We need to figure out what is going on with you. This is not okay. You could hurt someone or yourself! You can't just pretend this isn't happening and wing it through town. You hit someone's car today!"

Nancy sighed. She supposed Julie was right. It wasn't really safe of her to be hiding this secret. Plus, she was tired of hiding other people's secrets for them.

Like Ally and Greg.

JULIE

As she drove away from her mother's house her head was spinning.

Ally was pregnant.

Ally, who didn't even like children.

Ally, who said she would never want to be pregnant.

Ally, who was the most unmotherly person she knew.

Ally, her best friend.

She clutched the steering wheel so hard that her knuckles started to ache. She had no idea what to do. Maybe she would just quit her job and move to Bali. She could start over as a bartender on some beautiful beach and buy a little hut. Make necklaces and sell them to tourists. At least she wouldn't be constantly reminded of all the things she would never be able to have.

Yesterday she had been utterly consumed with what to do next about her infertility. She had planned to ask Ally for her opinion! She was going to use Greg's sperm without his consent! And now Greg was God knew where. Ally was pregnant, and her mother was actually losing her mind.

Julie sniffled and wiped her nose with the back of her hand. She didn't have a single tissue in this car, because she was determined to never cry. Greg always referred to her as a robot. If only he could see her now.

A complete, blubbering mess.

Her mother was sick. Her best friend was pregnant, and her whole persona had been ripped out from underneath her.

That was the thing about infertility. It stripped you raw. It made you look at all of your brokenness. It forced you to really evaluate what you wanted out of life. It slowly sucked the life out of you, procedure by procedure, injection by injection, loss by loss.

It turned you into someone you didn't even recognize.

It was as if someone was moving you through the motions like one of those little puppeteers. Before you knew it, you were choosing a home that had two extra bedrooms. Bedrooms that you kept mostly empty, save for the quiet baby items you sometimes purchased and hid in the back of the closet.

It ramped up anxiety and sent you into stress spirals.

It turned you into a monster.

It robbed you of your joy.

It took a toll on your body and made you question your sanity. It turned your life upside down to the point where you didn't know which way was right side up.

By the time she got home, it was dark outside. The whole day had been one disappointment after another. A small voice in the back of her head told her to call Ally again. She thought about sending her a text and saying, *Hey! Heard you are expecting—congrats! When were you going to tell me?*

Was she supposed to act happy for her when they both knew that there was no way in hell either of them were happy about it? Julie didn't know if she had the strength to support Ally through this. How could she watch her best friend carry a baby when it was all she wanted more than anything in this world.

How could she keep moving through life this devastated?

How was she going to deal with her mother?

She ran through what would need to happen next as she rifled through the pile of clothes on top of their dresser. She had just carried all the laundry upstairs that morning. Everything was folded perfectly, unlike her life. Pulling out the jeans she was looking for, something solid dropped to her feet.

Fuck.

Greg's wedding ring.

Her stomach dropped and she grabbed onto the dresser to ground herself. She took a deep breath and picked it up, fumbling it between her fingers for a few moments. He never took his ring off.

Ever.

Her throat felt tight, as if all the things she wanted to scream about were trying to come up and out, but she couldn't find the words. Like she couldn't take a deep breath. Like she was trapped here, stuck in a perpetual cycle of bad news. Tears hit the corner of her eyes, and she shook her head.

Julie looked back down at the ring.

At the sleek edges.

At the way it continued to loop, just like her problems.

She took the ring and chucked it as hard as she could at the dresser mirror. It pinged off the corner and landed with an unsatisfying thud back into the open drawer. There was a small crack though, where it had hit the mirror. She reached out with her finger and pushed against it, tiny pieces of glass sticking to her finger, like all the setbacks of her infertility and disappointments from her marriage.

Each their own separate smattering of what she had thought was the perfect life

She slammed the dresser drawer shut. Everyone could wait until the morning. She reached to Greg's side of the bed and pulled open the drawer where he kept his nighttime CBD. She pulled two gummies out of the bottle and popped them in her mouth. The only thing she was opting into tonight was the kind of sleep where she felt nothing.

ALLY

I SURVIVED THE ELEVATOR TRIP.

Apparently, when you are held hostage in a traveling hospital bed with an impending brain injury while pregnant, you didn't get much choice in the matter.

Now we were in the MRI imaging center, and there is still no word from Cade. I was beginning to worry he had found out more than he should. That somehow, he had hacked into my computer and uncovered all my travel plans. That he had found out who I really was; a woman of childbearing age that did not want to have a child. A woman who knew exactly what she wanted but was also afraid to say it aloud; in fear that no one would understand.

I tried to remind myself that Cade wasn't the type to go snooping around. He certainly wouldn't be in contact with the cell phone company to review my messages. If he had, he would have seen my calls. Unless he was just seeing them now, which could be a possibility. I was told I had to leave my cell phone behind in my room. I certainly didn't think the hospital would put him on speed dial with my new best friend Wanda.

She had moved on from Cade and had sprung into action, chatting with the MRI technicians. One of the technicians had moved over to my bedside, with Wanda as her shadow. Didn't Wanda need to take a break soon? Surely there were rules and regulations about how many hours you could work before taking a break. I did recall watching a documentary a few years ago about nurses. Often, they did not have the appropriate amount time to pee or eat a proper meal. Perhaps they were exempt from taking normal breaks.

I thought back to college when Julie and I would gather at a Starbucks to get our work done. The baristas there were very serious about their breaks. They would announce, "I am taking my break now!" Then they would ring themselves up a fancy latte and a snack box and post up at a table on their phone for a prompt fifteen minutes. Even if the line was out the door, the barista on break would not falter. It always amazed me.

This was not the case here with Wanda. She didn't care about taking a break. All she cared about was pestering me with her long strands of gelled hair and raspy cough. And now she had a partner in crime.

"Ally, my name is Carol, and I am one of the MRI technicians here at Central West. I am going to give you the rundown on what to expect, and then we will get you ready to go."

My ears perked up. I immediately liked this woman. She was all business. No small talk. Normal appearance. Small studded diamond earrings. An organized ponytail. Manicured nails in a nice neutral tone. She had kind eyes and a no-nonsense face. Finally, someone to put me at ease!

"An MRI is essentially a strong magnet that takes detailed images of your body. Now, some MRI's require contrast, which is administered through an IV. This helps us see the images more clearly. Normally we would use contrast for an MRI like yours today, however the safety for your baby is our top priority, so the doctors have opted out of using the contrast."

I exhaled.

I did not enjoy needles. I had never been one to give blood, even though I empathized deeply with those who needed it. It always made me feel lightheaded and unable to function to my highest standard for much too long. I was happy that I felt confident enough that the hospital was taking proper measures to ensure that a fetus was safe in any procedures conducted on the premises. Surely, I was not the first pregnant person to receive an MRI.

"Now, I am specially trained to guide you through the exam, and I will be communicating with you. I will ask you to do things like hold your breath or count to ten. This helps me to make sure we get the clearest images possible. The MRI machine makes loud noises, and you may feel warm, which is completely normal. If you feel uncomfortable at any point during the exam, please let me know right away. There will be a button you can hold in your hand. and you can press it at any time if you need me. I am not the person who reads the scans, so I cannot give you any information about what comes up. After the exam, a radiologist will meet with your doctor to discuss your results."

I took all of this in and nodded in approval. Bless up to Carol for keeping things matter-of-fact. I wanted to tell Wanda to take notes on how Carol was handling things, but I held back, mostly because I did not want to give her the satisfaction of hearing me speak.

"We will transfer you to this special bed here that is attached the machine. Once you are settled, we will raise the bed and slide your body into the tube. The tube is open on both ends. It does not spin or move in any way. You can wear special headphones, and we do provide music if you would like."

I bristled. I did not want to be subjected to a playlist I had not approved of.

Carol seemed to notice my change in body language. "The sounds the MRI machine makes can be very loud, so if you opt out of the headphones that is perfectly fine but just be prepared for the noise. We will provide you with earplugs." She nodded at me and then turned to gather a few things from the tray nearby.

I would most certainly be opting out of the music. Not only was I against someone else choosing a playlist for me, I also wanted to make sure that I was fully present to listen to any chatter between the technicians. Plus, I had to keep tabs on Wanda. Surely, she would linger during the exam.

"Okay, Ally, nod your head if you are ready to start."

I nodded.

I was ready.

What I wasn't ready for, I realized, was the assault on my ears.

NANCY

Nancy was grateful that Julie had not asked to look through the rest of her notebook. Although Nancy had no idea what else was written in it, she knew there were things that Julie shouldn't see. Luckily, Julie was too self-consumed to think that anything else aside from the news about Ally would be of importance in the notebook.

Julie had just left a few minutes ago, making Nancy promise not to leave the house for the rest of the day. She said she needed time to process things and talk to Will. Tomorrow they would talk with her about what the plan was.

Nancy scoffed. "The plan." She didn't need her children making a plan for her. She was perfectly fine, just a few hiccups now and then. A fender bender and a day at the beach. She didn't see what the big deal was. As long as she stayed local and kept to herself, she would be perfectly fine. Julie had her own issues to worry about, like saving her marriage and figuring out how she was going to have a baby of her own! Will was busy with his career and family life. Nancy could manage just fine. She would promise them that she would keep up with her doctor's appointments and only drive during the day.

She wasn't about to give up her freedom just because of one minor incident.

As she gathered her purse and slipped on those things that go on your feet, she turned and double-checked that the stove was off. Julie had been very adamant about the stove.

"What if you left the stove on all night! Or one of the burners?"

That was the thing about losing your memory; everyone had all these fears of the things that could go wrong, but if you asked the person with the memory problem, they would tell you that some of their biggest fears had already happened.

Their freedom had been robbed from them, and they were living between two worlds.

The one where they were aware their memory was deteriorating and the one where it already had.

She stopped and looked out at the driveway. Once when Julie had been a newborn, there had been a freak blizzard in late April. They barely had two pennies to rub together, and at the time, Dean had been plowing for extra cash. Nancy was beside herself with anxiety, trying to navigate motherhood.

She'd felt so isolated and alone.

The nights long and unbearable.

Lying awake just to make sure her daughter was still breathing.

Never putting her down.

Pacing back and forth in their small apartment, wondering how she would ever feel normal again.

So, when Dean announced he was going out plowing for the evening, Nancy had almost burst into tears.

"Don't worry," Dean had assured her. "I will be close, just doing a few driveways nearby. I'll come back and check on you in between rounds."

Shortly after Dean had left, she had fallen asleep with Julie nestled next to her. While they were asleep the power had gone out, and with it, the heat.

When Julie had woken her up to nurse, it had been pitch black and freezing.

Quickly, their house had become an icebox.

At that time, there were no cell phones, and Nancy hadn't been able to call Dean. In her postpartum haze, she'd lugged an armchair into the kitchen and turned on the oven, which was gas. Propping open the oven door, she set up in front of it to nurse Julie so they could stay warm. She remembered being so tired.

Trying her best to keep her eyes open.

To stay vigilant.

To keep her baby warm and fed.

She must have dozed off, because suddenly Dean was shaking her and Julie was crying.

"Nancy!" he'd yelled, sheer panic radiating around them. "What in the hell are you doing? You could have killed both of you."

She had stared up at him, completely confused; and frankly angry. "What are you talking about?"

Dean's eyes flashed in the dark. "The oven! You have just been sitting here, breathing in fumes. Luckily our windows are shit, so there was enough of a draft to keep you from dying."

Nancy remembered feeling so ashamed. How was she fit to be a mother when she had put herself and her child at such risk? What had she been thinking?

She shook her head, thinking about it now. Had that been a sign all those years ago that her brain had already started to deteriorate? Had her mind been betraying her for decades and she'd been oblivious to it?

She had never told Julie this story because she would never hear the end of it, but now she wished she could have because then Julie would understand.

Nancy would never forget to turn the oven off.

Ever.

She skimmed through the notebook now, feverishly looking for something that she couldn't quite place. She knew it was in here. Something else. She stopped flipping the pages abruptly when she saw it.

One sentence.

Greg is cheating.

She snapped the notebook shut and shoved it into her bag, hurrying toward her car.

She had to get there before she forgot.

She had to do something before it was too late for Julie.

She couldn't let her poor, fragile daughter stay with a man like that. Who would she turn to once Nancy was no longer coherent? Once she was a bump on a log at an old folks' home?

As she backed her car out of the driveway, she repeated her monologue out loud. Just in case anyone saw her while she was out, or if she got pulled over due to the broken taillight.

"Oh, I am just on my way over to the mechanic to get this darn taillight fixed. It's been such a task, trying to get in for an appointment!"

No one would question that. She was sure of it.

She didn't go to the mechanic, though. She kept on driving. Right out of town and all the way to the highway, where she planned to drive straight to Greg's work to confront him while she still had half a mind. If he didn't want to tell Julie the truth, that was fine. Nancy had no problem doing it herself. Her daughter already hated her, and as of today, officially thought she was crazy.

She had nothing left to lose.

But she figured she would give him one last chance to make things right.

JULIE

THE FIRST THING SHE NOTICED BEFORE EVEN opening her eyes was that her heart rate was out of control. Sheer panic radiated through her chest and up into her brain. It was just a nightmare. Her heart continued to hammer through the quiet.

She hated this.

She inhaled for ten seconds and tried to pause there. She needed to do that annoying box breathing her therapist had recommended. Why did it feel so hard to hold her breath for that long? After exhaling, she tried to force herself back into the pattern of inhaling. She barely made it through three rounds before she sat up.

"Fuck this," she muttered, reaching over and turning on the bedside lamp. Every time she took one of those gummies, she regretted it the next day. Was she the only person on the planet where they actually created more anxiety instead of their intended purpose?

Glancing at her phone, she took in the string of notifications and gasped. Ally had called her. Six times! She scrolled through, looking for a text or a voicemail.

Nothing.

She tossed the phone away from her, she couldn't deal with this yet. She needed to play dumb for a few more weeks and do what she was best at; avoiding the reality of her crumbling relationships while the anger and resentment snowballed into something she couldn't manage.

She wanted Ally to tell her the truth when it was way too late.

When their friendship simply couldn't be repaired.

Then she could easily excuse herself from the life she had built and dip out. Bali was sounding more and more appealing.

She couldn't caretake Ally through a pregnancy.

She couldn't face everyone and admit that her marriage was falling apart.

Maybe it was better to just leave today.

She threw open her closet doors and kicked shoes and bags and more shoes aside. Last year she had forced Greg to knock out the small hallway closet and connect it to their closet in their bedroom so it was a miniature walk-in closet. She had complained that she didn't have enough closet space, when she had just wanted a distraction.

Something to focus on instead of her empty womb.

She dropped to her knees, searching around for her suitcase. If Greg could leave, so could she. Moving quickly, she pulled a few pairs of jeans off the shelf. Reaching up, she ripped down a few of her capsule wardrobe shirts she had purchased last year with the help of a stylist. Maybe she would go to Europe for a few weeks first.

Something like an *Eat Pray Love* situation.

Dragging her suitcase out of the closet, she turned around, thinking about what else she needed.

Always pack an extra outfit, underwear included, for your carry on. Just in case your luggage gets lost.

Her mother.

"Damn it!!!!!" Julie screamed.

She sank to the floor right next to her suitcase and began punching the top of its hard shell.

She couldn't go anywhere because her mother had to go

and start losing her mind. This was supposed to be her crisis, not her mother's.

There she went again, turning into a monster.

Turning into the type of person who resented pregnant woman and now her own mother for developing a memory issue.

"I don't have time for this!" she screamed into the abyss of her designer clothes and perfectly organized shelves. Immediate rage pulsed up through her body and into her throat. Crawling over to her bed, she reached up and felt blindly for her phone. Her therapist's voice rang clear in the back of her head.

"Try not to reach right for your phone first thing in the morning. Do something calming or creative! You can meditate, set intentions for the day. Listen to music while you make breakfast. Go on a walk! Don't dive right into the world. Slow down and ground yourself first."

To hell with her therapist. She didn't have time to slow down. She needed to form a plan for her mother so that she could then form one for herself. She knew she was being heartless, but she couldn't just leave on a soul-searching trip while her mother was actively losing her marbles.

There was only one person left to call at this point.

It was time to call her brother.

ALLY

"All done!"

The machine groaned and creaked as it slid forward. My logical brain knew that the technician had turned off the sound, but I could still hear the aftermath of it pulsing in my ears. Perhaps it was aftershock. A dull humming lingered in my brain, and I felt on edge. My nervous system was frazzled, and I wanted to be in the comfort of my own home.

Away from all the strangers and the sounds and the smells. My nostrils were on overdrive. They twitched and protested as the smells continued to pummel into my personal space. I felt like Nicole Kidman in that movie *Bewitched*, but without the special powers.

It reminded me of the time when I was a child and my father had thought it would be fun to take a four-year-old little girl to a monster truck show without proper ear muffs. I had cried the whole way home, clutching my ears and begging the vibrating sound to stop. That was one of the last memories I had of him. He wasn't very good at being a father, but he was very good at drinking Budweiser. It was because of him that I never had interest in developing a drinking habit. That I was repulsed by the smell of stale alcohol and loud noises.

This was why I avoided bars and large crowds of people. As an adult, I took extra precautions to avoid loud talkers. Nothing ignited my frustration more than a motorcycle revving its engine or a lawn mower driving too close to me on a morning run.

"Ally? How ya doing?"

Wanda.

Of course she was still here. Didn't this woman ever take a break? I kept my gaze steady, refusing to turn my head to look at her.

She barreled on despite my lack of participation. "You did great. I'll take you back up now and the docs will meet with you once they go over the results."

I already knew all of this because my delightful friend Carol had told me before the MRI started. I fought the urge to remind Wanda of this. Sighing, I nodded ever so slightly so she would keep the process moving.

I wanted to ask if Cade had contacted anyone, but I assumed if he had, they would have alerted me. As Wanda and Carol transferred me back to my bed on wheels, I pondered on the results of the MRI.

Would I have a life-threatening tumor? A blot clot? Perhaps there was an issue with a nerve. It would be an easy way to dip out of motherhood and dance around Cade's disappointment with the whole matter. He could not be angry if my body was unable to carry a baby to term.

My chest tightened at the thought of telling him it wouldn't be possible to keep the baby.

I shook my head.

No.

I had to remind myself that I did not want a baby. I decided to blame this whirlwind of emotions on my body. Biologically speaking, it was designed to yearn for a baby. This was an impulse that was simply out of my control. Yet what was in my control was what I was to do about it.

"Here we are! Home sweet home!" Wanda's husky voice cut my thoughts short and ignited my blood pressure. I made a grumbling noise in my throat and stared straight ahead, careful not to engage too much with her chatter. "You must be starv-ing! Let's get you the menu and you can use the phone to call the kitchen."

My body stiffened. A hospital kitchen? Surely this woman was certifiably insane.

"Ahhh, weary of the hospital food?" Wanda reached over and patted my knee. "Most people don't know this, but our kitchen was voted best in the state for hospital food! Three years in a row." Wanda stood up a little straighter and beamed at me. "My boyfriend loves the food so much he often comes here to have lunch, even when I am not working! Did you know you can do that? Anyone can walk into the hospital cafe-teria and order lunch if they want. Cheap too. Plus, they have a great salad bar!"

I stared at Wanda, appalled. People actually did that? Drove around to hospitals to have lunch? I was becoming more and more disgusted with the human race each year. If I was speaking to Wanda, which I certainly wasn't, I would tell her to keep that information to herself. It wasn't something to brag about.

"You really need to eat, dear. Think about the menu and give a call down. They are very efficient." She pulled the monitor away from the bed and adjusted a few wires. "I think we should hear from the doctor within the hour and hopefully you will be able to get out of here later this evening if every-thing checks out okay."

My ears perked up at that. I longed for a good night's sleep and my secret stash of snacks. Those would come at an expense, though. Now that Cade knew about my pregnancy, I wouldn't be able to enjoy them freely with him hovering around and peppering me with questions about what I was snacking on. I could see him getting excited about a certain craving and showing up the following day with an overflow of the product. Which, of course, would be very sweet; but I enjoyed the thrill of keeping the snacks private. Like it was my own little rebellious act.

I sighed heavily.

If I had been honest with Cade from the beginning, I probably wouldn't even be in this situation right now.

But I had to ask myself, was that what I really wanted?

NANCY

This time she had brought her notebook along for the ride. She wasn't going to risk forgetting what she was up to. She didn't have much time left before Julie moved forward with an intervention and she was shipped off to a home.

If she wanted to save her daughter's marriage, she had to do it now.

Nancy had never really loved Greg. He wasn't easy to please. He carried an air of confidence that was distasteful. The first time she had met him he had given her a smile that didn't quite reach the eyes. Constantly checking his phone, he was distracted and gave off the impression he always had somewhere better to be. The type of person who walked into a room and expected everyone to be enamored with his presence. Nancy had brushed it off because Julie seemed happy, and well, because Julie was a hard one to please as it was. She had thought that maybe what her daughter needed was a bit of a snooty man. Someone who could keep up with her attitude. They seemed like a good fit for each other. Both committed to growth at their jobs and living a posh lifestyle.

It was a hard pill to swallow, watching your daughter have different dreams than you. Nancy had always wanted to be the best mother she could be. She knew that Julie wanted that as well, but she also wanted a career.

A fancy home and a flashy car.

She wanted to have the highlight reel that all the kids talked about. Nancy had Instagram, but she didn't understand how to use it! Why did her children post those videos at the top only to take them away after twenty-four hours? Didn't they want to have them later to go back and reminiscence on?

She had noticed her daughter soften slowly over this last year, but somehow at the same time she had hardened too. The look on her daughter's face when she saw a baby at a restaurant or when her nieces and nephews clambered into her lap at holiday parties. Nancy felt that pain deep in her own heart. How badly she wanted her daughter to have children of her own!

It was in the fleeting moments afterward that her expression would harden. When someone caught her staring at the baby or made a comment like, "You are so great with kids!" She saw the darkness in Julie's eyes. The resentment. The drive to become a mother that was all-consuming.

The IVF treatments were going to work soon, though. Nancy could feel it! What was even worse, was thinking about Greg ruining all of it right behind her back.

No.

Nancy would not allow it.

She would not stand by and witness Greg single handedly take down Julie's life bit by bit.

Pulling up to the rather gorgeous state building, Nancy crept into a parking spot near the front. She reached for the door handle and then, having second thoughts, pulled her hand back, resting it on the steering wheel. She flipped down the visor to inspect her complexion in the tiny mirror. Her skin seemed to have drooped overnight. She studied the crinkles and deep lines that had settled on either side of her eyes. Her hair had lost its oomph. Single strands stuck to the side of her face and other pieces whisked in the wind. She tried tucking the loose strands behind her ears, wishing she had remembered to get it dyed again.

Nancy rummaged around in her pocketbook, fishing for her lipstick. That always brightened things up. She opened it, slapped some on, and snapped the cap back on, shoving it back into the endless abyss of her bag.

What was she going to say when she marched inside? Enough of this lollygagging. She needed to act quickly while she still had her wits about her.

"Just do it," she whispered to herself. Nodding, she opened the door and stepped out into the parking lot. She marched quickly up to the front door and tucked inside.

Nancy peered up at the high ceilings and gold trimmings that ran along the perimeter of the room. She exhaled and took a step forward. There was a large antique desk at the other end of the lobby where a woman sat chatting with what appeared to be a security guard. Nancy glanced left and then right. She assumed she would have to ask permission to see Greg, which might be a problem, but she saw no other option. Surely, they would ask her where she was going if she simply marched by them. She glanced again to the right and noticed a stairwell. When she looked back at the desk, the woman and the guard were still deep in conversation and hadn't even glanced up at her. She made a quick decision to dip into the stairwell.

Once she was alone, she wished she had paid more attention last time when she had come here with Julie. It had been when Greg and Julie first started dating. Julie had surprisingly invited Nancy out to lunch and to see Greg's office because she had to drop something off to him. Had they gone up multiple flights of stairs? She tapped the side of her head, trying to summon the memory.

Pulling out her phone, she texted Will.

What is Greg's title again at work? I would ask Julie but you know how she is. I am trying to brag to my friend Sue, but I can't seem to remember it!

Will responded instantly. He was a very diligent man, and a swarm of love filled in her chest.

Hi mom! He is the communications director for the New Hampshire Senate.

That was it! Nancy scanned the sea of doors, her eyes settling on one at the very end of the hall. A memory of Julie walking through that door flashed at her, and then it was gone. She hurried forward, breathless as she stood in front of the door.

Greg Brooks. Communications Director.

Some communicator he was.

She closed her eyes, raised her hand into a tentative fist, and knocked.

JULIE

Julie drummed her fingers on the kitchen table, staring out the window, willing Greg to pull back into the driveway. So far, it wasn't working. She collapsed in a heap into one of the delicate upholstered dining room chairs she had forced Greg to redo last year. She glanced around the room at the perfect decor. She'd spent so much time fussing and frittering about the way it looked.

And for what?

They never had guests over.

All they did was work and drive to fertility appointments. Greg had been so excited to have big dinners and game nights, but the longer it took for Julie to get pregnant, the more she had let everything else go. She pressed the palm of her hand into her forehead.

How had she gotten here?

Suddenly, her phone buzzed and shimmied across the table. She snatched it up. Will.

"Finally," she muttered, hitting answer.

"Hey, Jules, what's up? Did you call me earlier?"

She fidgeted with the edge of the placemats she had to have last year from an upscale home decor store downtown. It was always awkward with Will. Despite being brother and sister, they were not that close. They only touched base around holidays, birthdays, and family events. It wasn't often that they texted or got together, even though they lived ten minutes from each other. Will had two kids, a beautiful wife, and frankly, an awesome life. It didn't seem that much bothered him. He just showed up for the next life event and boom, there it was, just as he had expected it to be.

Julie wondered how it must feel to be so cavalier.

So sure of everything.

So laid back and happy.

"Jules? Are you there?"

"Yeah, sorry. Have you talked to Mom recently?"

Will laughed. "Yeah. She just texted me actually and asked me what Greg's job title was."

Julie froze. Why was she asking Will that? She gripped the phone harder in her hand. "She is out of control."

"Yeah, I should probably bring the kids over to see her soon."

Julie swallowed and cleared her throat. "I just had lunch with her the other day and she got a call from a memory clinic." Julie paused briefly and then barreled on before she lost the courage. "I obviously pressed her about it and then she denied it, but then I got a call from Ally's husband Cade."

"What the heck?" Will laughed nervously on the other end, and she heard the kids screaming in the background.

"So anyway, Mom was at Ally's house and hit Cade's car."

"Wait. What?" Will's concerned tone spilled through the phone.

"I know. So, I went over to her house to check on her, and her car was running in the driveway with the door still open. I confronted her, obviously, and she broke down and told me she had been diagnosed with Cognitive Memory Disorder."

Julie closed her eyes and took a deep breath. Maybe this would have been better to tell Will in person, but she didn't trust herself to not cry, because all she could think about was the journal with her mom's sloppy, huge capital letters telling her that Ally was pregnant.

"Whoa. For real? What the. Are you sure? Where is she now?"

"I don't know, it was a lot to take in, but I think we have to meet with her doctors and come up with a plan. I don't think she should be alone anymore..." Julie trailed off, unsure of what to say next.

Will was silent on the other end. She felt bad for dropping this on him, but what else was she supposed to do?

"Will? What do you think?" She was spiraling now. Maybe she shouldn't have left her mother alone at all.

"All right, well, I'll put a call in to the doctor and go over and see her. We will figure this out. Don't stress about it. Talk soon, okay?"

"Okay," she said quietly, "Let me know what you think after you talk to her."

"On it."

Julie set the phone down on the table. Will had always been the shining star of the family. The one who swooped in and saved the day. Cleaned up the mess. Made the plans. Gave the best gifts. Coached all the kids' sports teams and still had time to go over and mow the lawn for their mother. It had always just been *easier* for him. Right down to having the picture-perfect family.

She pushed the thoughts of her mind. She had always let him assume that role, and she wasn't about to try to change things now. It felt good to know Will was going to take over because she had other shit to deal with.

There were two things left she had to do before she could up and leave. First, she needed to track down Greg, apparently before her mother did. She looked at her phone. Greg would probably still be at work. It was time that they had a conversation. A conversation about their marriage. About their future. About the baby they clearly were not having.

As she backed her car out of the driveway, she tried calling Ally one more time, but there was no answer.

It seemed that everyone in her life was more than happy to let her go.

ALLY

Cade had not returned to my room, and I was beginning to think I had spooked him. Perhaps he was pretending he wanted the baby when, in fact, the thought terrified him more than it terrified me. The doctor had paid me a visit, explaining that I had vasovagal syncope, which only occurred in a small percentage of pregnancies.

"No need to worry, Ally. Everything looks great from the scan. The fainting you have been experiencing is simply from your blood pressure dropping. Try to lie down and take deep breaths when you begin to feel dizzy. I would also recommend not eating or drinking when you feel a spell coming on. You should be good to go home within the hour."

I had wanted to inform him that telling a pregnant woman not to eat or drink was a cruel joke and that I still did not know where my husband was. I would have assumed that replenishing my fluids and my protein levels would increase my level of awareness. I decided to let the conversation go and avoid alerting him that Cade was missing in action, as they say in the movies.

I was not particularly religious, but I did pay a proper thank-you to the heavens above for giving me space from Cade, even though it was slightly suspicious he had not returned. Frankly, I was relieved Cade seemed to have disappeared. There was so much I had to say to him, but I needed time to process everything. I could use the quiet car ride home to think. He did not deserve this mess I had put us in, that was for certain. I was still set on not having the baby, yet when I heard that the baby was fine, my whole body relaxed.

How could I be relieved that the baby was healthy yet still not want to become a mother?

I had done a lot of thinking while waiting for the MRI results. What if I allowed Cade to believe that I would be having the baby? It would buy me some time to develop a better plan of action. I had basically already alluded to that in our conversation. He could carry on thinking he was to be a father, and I could prolong breaking his heart. I knew that, morally, this was not the right thing to do, but the thought of telling Cade that I could not have the baby sounded so exhausting.

I was so tired. This was precisely why I didn't want to have children! I saw how tired the new mothers looked. I had never been so tired in my whole life, and the baby wasn't even here yet.

There was a slight issue at hand now that I had been released from the hospital. I did not have a car as it was still parked over at the doctor's office. In all of the chaos, I had forgotten to discuss this matter with Cade. Julie was not returning my calls, which was also probably for the best. However, I did need transportation home, and I was becoming quite ravenous. I had ordered a vegetarian burger from the hospital menu to appease Wanda but as soon as her shift ended, about eight hours too late in my opinion, I had shoved the cover back on the tray and pushed it to the edge of the room.

Now I was sitting on a bench in the waiting room contemplating on whether or not I should order a car service. I had never used one of those lift apps before. The thought was appalling to me. Climbing into a stranger's personal car and trusting them to drive me home? This was how murders took place. People these days were so willing to hop into any situation and hope for the best.

Julie always made fun of me for my views on the subject.

"But what about taxis? I have seen you take those before when we visited the city!"

I had reminded Julie that a taxi was a bright-yellow vehicle with a large beacon on top that alerted everyone it was a business. A transactional ride that citizens had an unwritten agreement amongst each other to watch out for. If you saw signs of a struggle or a fast-zooming taxi, you knew the person inside was at risk. What do you do when you see a suspicious or speeding car without any labeling? Nothing. You look the other way. All while a poor woman could be in distress right before your eyes.

My phone battery was slowly dissipating, and I decided to give Julie one more ring. Holding the phone up to my ear, I waited absentmindedly as it rang, watching a mother and a toddler wrestle with a plant on the waiting room table. The toddler wanted very much to "dig" out the plant, and the mother, for obvious reasons, was trying to lure the tiny terror away from it.

"DIG. DIG. DIG," the toddler yelled continuously, his voice becoming more desperate and a bit closer to a screech with each pronunciation. The mother looked around nervously and tried her best to scoop the toddler up in her arms. The little boy did not take to this tactic well and immediately began protesting in a fit of shrieks and swift leg kicks. I shuddered at the thought of being stuck in that situation.

"Ally?" I jumped and focused my attention back to the call. Julie had answered!

"Julie." I straightened out my spine and eyed the toddler. "I have called you several times. Where have you been?"

"It sounds like you're at Chuckie Cheese, what is going on, Ally?"

I waved my hand; even though Julie couldn't see my gestures, I felt like it was necessary. "Listen, Jules. I am in a bit of a predicament. Could you pick me up at the hospital?" I asked, closing my eyes briefly to let a wave of nausea pass by.

The other end of the line was silent for a moment.

"Please, Julie. It is not an emergency, but I am without transportation and I cannot seem to get ahold of Cade."

"Okay, yeah, I will come pick you up. I just have to run a quick errand and then I'll be there."

I closed my eyes again. Thank goodness. "Thank you, Jules, I will explain when you arrive."

"No need to explain, Ally, I already know everything."

I froze, the other end of the line dead. Did Julie know about the pregnancy? But how? I hadn't told anyone. Except for Cade. Oh, this was very unfortunate. In all the chaos of the day, I had forgotten to tell Cade that Julie didn't know about my pregnancy.

Yet, I still didn't understand why Cade and Julie would have been chatting today. That definitely didn't make any sense. Something wasn't adding up, and I was going to get to the bottom of it.

NANCY

At first, nothing happened. She stood there staring at the door, waiting to hear footsteps shuffling up to it. Raising her fist, she hovered it there. Should she knock again? Leaning forward, she pressed her ear against the mahogany. It felt cold against her skin. She listened closely. There was a rustling of papers and a closing of drawers.

He was in there! She pulled her hand back and knocked again. Enough with being polite. She needed to speak to him right now before her brain dipped out for the day.

"Greg! I know you are in there. Open the door, please, it's Nancy. I need to speak with you." She knocked again, this time with more authority, and just as she was about to try the doorknob, the door flew open.

Greg's eyes widened as he stared at her. Nancy imagined it would take him a minute to sort out why his mother-in-law was knocking on his office door in the middle of a Monday. She peered around him and narrowed her eyes. There were a very expensive roller suitcase and a sleeping bag tucked into the corner.

Greg seemed to regain his composure and followed Nancy's gaze to the collection of overnight items. "Nancy, ahhh... Hi, how are you? Are you all right? You look a little bit..."

Nancy waved her hand, pushing past him and then turning around, placing her hands on her hips. "Well? What do you have to say for yourself?"

Greg laughed nervously. "Nancy, I am not sure what is happening here. Julie and I had a little fight, that's all. I am guessing you spoke with her?"

Nancy swallowed down her nerves and reminded herself that she had to get this out while she still could. "Just a little fight, or just a little bit of an affair?"

Nancy had snooped through Julie's phone when she had gone to the bathroom at lunch. She had just wanted to be a part of her daughter's life! She had seen the way Greg had been responding to Julie. Short and dismissive. Like a man who had checked out. There was another memory that Nancy couldn't quite grasp, from a few weeks before. She couldn't see it now, but she had written it down in her notebook.

A hint of fear flashed through Greg's eyes, and Nancy knew in that moment her assumptions were correct.

"I may be the weird mother-in-law that everyone makes jokes about, but I don't miss a beat. I know you have been cheating on Julie, and if you don't tell her, then I will."

Greg scoffed and ran his hands up his face. "Nancy, you don't know what you are talking about." He looked nervously at the door and then took a step back. "I have a busy day today. I can't have this conversation right now." He turned and went back around behind his desk with its gold-plated name tag and exquisite pens.

Nancy stepped forward and lowered her voice. "You have fooled everyone with your good looks, fancy job, and well-to-do lifestyle, but you haven't fooled me. I never liked you from the moment I met you, but Julie was happy, and that was all that mattered to me. I can see now that I was wrong. How dare you put Julie through all of this and let her continue trying to have a baby?!" She was shouting now, and it felt good to shout!

It was liberating. Finally, she was the one with the power!

Greg glanced around, his eyes darting to the door and back.

Like a rat in a cage. He opened his mouth, and she jabbed her finger at him.

"Nope. No, you don't. Julie is beside herself about this baby she can't have, and if you so much as give her one more sense of false hope, I will put everything on blast. All of it."

"This is ridiculous, Nancy. I love Julie. You don't have all the facts."

"I have enough facts to know that you have been unsupportive. That you have been tinkering around with other women!" She pointed in the direction of his bags. "And that you left her!" She took a step toward him, straightening herself out, trying to become taller. "Well, at least you had the right idea there. It's time to let her go. She needs to be set free from you so she can come to terms with the fact that not only will she not be getting pregnant, but she will also be losing her husband."

Just then the door opened, and Nancy spun around. She gasped, taking a step forward.

There was her daughter.

Standing there with tears streaming down her beautiful face.

Julie didn't have to say anything for Nancy to know that she had heard everything.

JULIE

Julie stood frozen in the doorway to Greg's office. She was trying to digest everything she had heard. Trying to digest that her mother had beaten her to it. That her mother was standing there shouting at her husband with her hair matted down on one side and her jacket buttoned up haphazardly.

Julie shook her head. Her mother had officially lost it, but she had also put Greg in his place. She didn't know whether she should scream at both of them or hug her mother.

"Mom? Greg, are you serious? I mean—"

Greg cleared his throat and walked out from behind the desk, eying Nancy wearily. "Jules, I am so glad you are here. I was just trying to explain to your mom that we had a little fight, and well..."

Julie held up her hand, cutting Greg off. "That's enough out of you, Greg," she spat. "We don't need your pathetic excuses right now. You are a poor excuse for a man. Bowing out of this relationship because it got stressful and then cheating on me! While I was at the doctor's office these last few months trying to figure out how to have your baby."

Greg took a step forward. "Are you fucking kidding me? Now you're accusing me of cheating?"

"Don't. I have to get this out."

She glanced over at her mother, who was nodding in encouragement.

"I thought I was being overly emotional, like you always tell me." She could feel the tears coming, but she pressed on. "I thought I was making things up in my head. You staying late at work and spending more time out on the weekends. I thought..." She trailed off, feeling like her heart was splitting in two for the third time this week. "I thought you needed space because of everything, but really you don't even care about me."

Greg scoffed and ran his hands down his face. "You've got to be kidding me right now."

Julie wiped her eyes and felt herself deflate.

As hard as it was to face, she somehow felt lighter.

Free in a way.

As if she finally had permission to give up.

"I can't believe I am actually saying this right now, but I think maybe it was a blessing we couldn't have a baby." She looked at Greg, waiting for a sign that maybe he still cared, but there was nothing. He just stared at her, a blank expression plastered across his face.

She exhaled, trying to calm herself down. "Now that you've shown me who you truly are, or I don't know? Who you turned into?" She threw her hands up, realizing that it really was over.

Maybe it was better this way.

Maybe this was happening by design.

Because she sure as fuck did not want to have a baby with a man like this.

Narrowing her eyes, she looked directly at Greg and whispered, "I don't want my child having a father like you."

Her mom walked over to her and laid her hand on her arm. "Julie, let's go."

"Mom, it's okay. I've got this." She turned her attention to

Greg, who was trying his best to look like the victim, slouched over by his desk. "It's over, Greg. The rest of your stuff will be in a pile on my front lawn. I suggest coming to pick it up before it rains."

She turned and gently patted her mother's hand. "Come on, I'll follow you home."

Without looking back, she left him standing behind his desk, speechless. Her therapist would have a lot to say about this later. Up until this moment, she had still been clinging on to the hope that she could salvage their relationship. That Greg would come around. That she had been imagining everything.

The reality of what she'd said started to sink in. She really wasn't going to have a baby with him now.

It was over.

Her mother was clinging to her arm and throwing her worried glances, and Julie was fully aware she was shaking.

That tears were streaming down her cheeks.

That while she wanted to blame everything she had just heard on her mother's newfound memory issue, she knew deep down that it wasn't a mix up. She knew deep down that Greg had cheated.

She was finally seeing him for who he was. She had married an unsupportive asshole who only cared about himself. Somewhere along the line, he had changed for the worse.

And maybe, in a different way, so had she.

Once she got her mother settled in her own car, she checked her reflection in the rearview mirror. All she saw an emptiness in her eyes that matched the ache in her womb. She tried to rub off the smudged mascara and straightened herself out. She looked back toward her mother, who was sitting in her own car, staring absentmindedly out the window.

She would deal with the unraveling of her marriage later,

but first she needed to get her mother home and tell her thank you.

Then she planned to pick up her best friend, who was carrying the one thing Julie wanted more than anything else in the world.

ALLY

Julie was taking much longer than I anticipated. I longed for a hot shower in my clean bathroom and a few hot buttered rolls. Perhaps when I got ahold of Cade, I could summon him to retrieve me a basket of them from Killian's. That was one of the perks of being pregnant; people wanted to help you.

The waiting room was quieting down, and based on all the signs, I realized that this was the emergency room. I had been so focused on finding a ride that I hadn't noticed. A pang of sympathy shot through my chest for the mother with the screaming child. Hopefully everything was all right.

I stood up and switched chairs so I had a better view of the emergency dispatchers at their stations behind the glass partition. One of them was filing her nails, looking rather bored. The other one was scrolling furiously on the computer, perhaps online shopping or investigating an ex. The phone rang, and the one filing her nails jumped as if she had no idea there was a phone next to her.

She answered the phone at what I would consider an unnecessary volume. "Emergency Department, how can I assist you?" I watched as her face turned into a frown, and she glanced at her coworker, motioning her over with her hand. The coworker slid over, clearly enjoying the fact that her chair was on wheels. The one with the nail file, which she was now using as a pointer, jabbed at something on the screen, and they both nodded solemnly.

"All right, we are clearing a bed now. I will alert the ICU. Yes. So sad. Okay."

The one who had been scrolling began talking too loudly. Surely, they had been trained to keep their voices down and not inflict trauma out into the ethers of the waiting room. Something about a man in his early thirties. Terrible car accident. Might not make it.

I shuddered. This was too much doom and gloom for me.

As if on cue, the emergency doors slid open and Julie strode through, looking rather upset. My stomach dropped. Surely, she couldn't be this upset at me. It wasn't as if I had made it my life's mission to go out and get pregnant and rub it in her face. I must agree, it was rather unfortunate how everything was unfolding. I worried about Julie. With each passing day she appeared more and more fragile, like crystal glass stemware packed in a moving box without proper wrapping paper. Bound to break once it was set into motion.

I stood up and tried my best to act not pregnant as I made my way over to Julie. I didn't think I looked any different physically, so that was helpful. I saw her glance immediately at my stomach, as if she were daring it to reveal a baby.

I had half a mind to ask her if we could stop on the way home at one of those drive-through restaurants. I had seen a commercial in the waiting room for a frozen drink that I needed to have immediately. The company had also advertised its French fries. Under normal circumstances, I would have been appalled at someone who would eat such a greasy mess of a meal, yet I was at this time rather intrigued by them. The way they had glistened with a light layer of salt on top had left my mouth watering.

Julie turned on her heel without a word and headed back out into the cold evening air. I thought about telling her she was lucky to not be pregnant, as I was realizing that all the health awareness I had proudly carried around was now being tossed out the window along with the rest of my plans for the future. I decided it was probably best to keep this to myself for now. I could remind her of this later, when she looked more confident.

Like the normal Julie I was used to.

The one who didn't let a single soul step in the way of what she wanted.

I settled into the passenger seat and grimaced at the lowness of Julie's car. I preferred to ride up high; it was a much safer option. Sitting in these low fancy cars was basically a walking advertisement to slide up underneath a sixteen-wheeler and kiss the rest of your life goodbye. A tin can was what my father used to refer to these cars as. Then he would grab an empty beer can from the trash and crush it between his fingers. *"See, Ally? You don't want to end up as a crushed tin can."* I shuddered at the thought.

Julie looked over at me and rolled her eyes. It was clear that she was agitated, but I was too tired to let it bother me.

She cleared her throat, and I could tell it was taking a lot for her to speak. "Are you okay? I mean, is the, well, is the baby okay?"

I nodded and covered my ears as an ambulance and a fire truck blew past us and into the emergency room bay. Certainly, they could have turned off the sirens as they pulled into the hospital. Everyone understood that they had arrived. Something about loud noises made it feel like someone had reached inside my body and given my insides a little twist.

It was one of the reasons I had refused to move from our small home. Recently, Cade had found a larger house with a finished basement, closer to downtown and with a newly remodeled kitchen. When we had viewed the home, I insisted that he drop me off at the end of the block so I could do a practice walk and make sure everything was quiet on the loop that I had mapped out.

It had in fact not been quiet. There had been a four-way intersection that I would have to cross in order to get to the quieter side streets. Two separate trucks had revved their engines in a false sense of power as I had crossed through. Once I was on the "quieter" streets, as the real estate agent had generously labeled them, I was met with lawnmowers, a run-down house that someone was clearly fixing up with loud power tools, and a home that was apparently running a landscaping business out of their barn. There had been much too much traffic and not one but two cut throughs, inviting a sea of sports cars and dump trucks to zoom and clatter their way by my delicate ears.

"Jules, I know this is a bit of a shock to you. I, I am not sure what the correct protocol is, but I do want you to know I never intended to hurt you."

Julie sighed so deeply it seemed as though all the air had leaked out of her body, leaving her slightly smaller in front of the steering wheel.

"I know, Als. It's just that— I guess I don't even know what to say."

I looked over at my friend, trying to find the right words to say myself. We never quarreled. We were always on the same team, mad at the same person. Or lifting each other up when the other was having a bad day or week or month. That was the magic of having a best friend. One of you was always thriving, while the other might have been down and out. It was a beautiful balance of unspoken words and connections that needed no explaining. No matter what was happening in my life, I knew that one conversation with Julie would raise my energy and set me back on straight. This walking on eggshells feeling was very out of sorts for us, and I was unsure of how to navigate it properly.

Julie barreled on, cutting through my thoughts. "Greg cheated on me. It's over, Als. And my mom, she, she has some sort of memory disorder. I found out all of this in like the last twenty-four hours. I kept calling you and texting you, and I didn't know where you were." She sniffed, wiping her eyes. "I needed you."

"I thought there was something peculiar about your mother when I ran into her at the grocery store the other day."

Julie turned and looked at me, eyes flashing. "Hello. I just told you my husband has cheated on me and that is what you are focused on?!"

"I would argue that your mother losing her memory competes quite strongly with Greg cheating."

Julie scoffed. "Are you serious right now?"

I reached out gingerly and turned the steering wheel, so we were no longer drifting off into a looming gully. "Tin can," I whispered to myself.

Julie rolled her eyes and refocused herself back on the road.

I did silently agree that she had a point. How does one determine what affects someone else the most? It really wasn't up for me to decide. I imagined that finding out your husband had cheated on you would be devastating. If I was being frank, I would say that Greg cheating didn't surprise me.

The problem was, I also understood why someone might betray their partner, because hadn't I done the exact same thing by misleading Cade?

NANCY

Nancy had promised Julie that she would stay
put until tomorrow when Julie had composed herself and
would come back over with Will to sort everything out. This
would have been perfectly fine with Nancy if she had remembered that she had promised this to Julie, but by the time she
had made herself a sandwich and a cup of tea, she had
forgotten all about her pledge to stay home.

If she were being honest, she had forgotten a lot of things.
Some big chunks of her life had slipped away as if they had
never been there in the first place. That was the ironic part
about losing your memory. Once it was gone, you were bliss-
fully unaware that it was ever there to begin with. So you kept
plugging along, thriving on what memories were left over, like
a squirrel working through the last bits of his winter stash.

Yet it was those moments when everything seemed to come
back. When all the memories reappeared like a bright flash in
front of your eyes, and you realized the devastating reality of
what was happening. Those were the days where you clung so
hard to the details that it hurt. You could feel the pain sawing
away at the burrows in your heart. The deep corners where you
kept your children and all the people who would hurt much
more than you would hurt, once you could no longer
remember.

Nancy had been on point this morning during her outing,
but this afternoon it was all slipping away. She knew there had

been an outburst with Julie, but when was there not? Oh, how she had wished that the notebook had been with her!

She moved to the room where she kept her notebook. The one that everyone gathered in to have meals. What was that room called? It was right on the tip of her tongue, but she couldn't quite grasp it. She pulled at the wooden handle in the thing that held sections that rolled in and out, feeling rather aggravated with herself.

She let out a small gasp. There it was. Her notebook!

She opened it, flipping hastily through the pages until she got to the last one. It helped to restore some of her memory. Ally was pregnant. Greg had cheated. She had hit Cade's car. This line made her chuckle. How mad Julie must have been!

She searched the latest entry for a mention of Dean, but there wasn't anything. Where was he? She hadn't seen him in what felt like decades. She glanced at the clock on the wall. It was almost dinnertime. He should be home in about an hour. Just enough time for her to run an errand.

An errand that was very important.

One that couldn't wait another day.

JULIE

JULIE HAD PLANNED TO BE BIG MAD AT ALLY WHEN she picked her up from the hospital, but as soon as she saw her, she'd felt herself soften. By the time they were in the car, Julie had basically lost all her steam, and only a few remnants of anger remained in the air as they tossed words back and forth like a clumsy tennis match. But when Ally had argued that finding out about her mother was just as bad as Greg cheating, Julie had felt her chest refill with anger, like one of those high strikers at the summer fair. All it needed was one hit for it to fill back up.

There was only one other time in their friendship when Ally had kept something from her. It was at the beginning of senior year, and they had both finally heard from all the colleges they had applied to. The plan was to stick together. Attend the same college, be roommates but see to their different degrees. By that point, Ally had basically been living with Julie and her family. Her mother had even found an old twin bed at a yard sale and set it up in the office for Ally so she could have her own room.

Nancy took the girls prom dress shopping, and Ally had insisted on wearing those fancy gloves that went all the way up to her elbows. At first, Julie had thought she was kidding, but then when Ally explained it was a great way to look proper and avoid the nasty germs from their drunken classmates, Julie had burst out laughing. Her mother had nudged Julie in the side and whispered, "Everyone is entitled to their own style. Let the girl wear what she wants."

Ally started using their address to receive all her mail, and she used Nancy as her emergency contact on her school forms. That was how Julie discovered Ally's secret. A large envelope had landed on their kitchen counter. Nancy had called up to the girls, letting them know another college acceptance letter had arrived. Julie could still remember looking over at Ally, who was already moving quickly out of the room and toward the stairs.

Her mother had been cleaning up the kitchen and frowned, watching Ally scatter from the room. "You girls are applying to more colleges than I can keep track of. Which one is this, Ally?"

Julie's chest had tightened. They'd heard back from every school they had applied to. The envelope in Ally's hand only meant one thing. She'd applied somewhere else, behind Julie's back. She narrowed her eyes and crossed her arms. "Yes, Ally, which one is this?"

Ally clutched the envelope harder and stared at them both. "I'd rather open this one in private, if you don't mind."

Nancy smiled and patted Ally's arm. "Of course, dear! Jules. Let her look at it on her own. You two are tied at the hip; it would do you good to take an hour apart. Why don't you come with me to the store?"

Julie had stared at Ally in disbelief. Had she really applied to a school without Julie's knowledge? Later, after Ally had fallen asleep, Julie had snuck into her room and opened her top dresser drawer, where she knew Ally kept all her important items. The envelope was sitting right on top. Pulling it out quietly, Julie had tucked it under her arm and tiptoed out of the room. It had felt like betrayal; to know that Ally had made a huge life decision without Julie. They were supposed to do everything together. What if Ally chose to go somewhere without her? They had agreed to attend Brown University, far enough from their small town in New Hampshire to feel exciting, but still close enough to head home for the weekend when they needed a reprieve.

After she had opened the envelope, which held Ally's acceptance letter to Oxford, Julie hadn't said a word and Ally never mentioned it. Now, looking back, a pang of guilt lodged itself in Julie's chest.

Julie looked over at Ally now, who had fallen asleep with her head on the window. Had her silence, her resentment, her fear of being without Ally, hindered Ally's future?

She couldn't let that happen again.

She needed to talk to Ally.

To tell her it was okay with her that she was having a baby. Just like she should have told her it was okay to go to Oxford without her. She couldn't let Ally make a decision again because she was worried about leaving Julie behind.

They had managed to do everything together up until this point, but becoming mothers was something neither of them could control. Julie had just never imagined it happening this way.

All their dreams seemed so out of reach now.

Even their friendship.

Just like the baby she couldn't have.

ALLY

As Julie's car pulled into the driveway, I was jostled awake by it sliding into park. I sat up expectantly. My stomach reminded me by making a rather loud gurgling sound that it was time to enjoy a large meal. I planned on ordering a large pizza with a salad to start. I had been dreaming about dipping the pizza into the house dressing. When I had driven by the restaurant the day before, the sign had said, *homemade house dressing*, and I couldn't stop thinking about it. The baby had complete control over my appetite. I wondered if it would come out asking for pizza.

I peered out the window, looking for Cade's truck. Had he pulled it into the garage? I frowned, seeing now that the garage door was open and his pickup was not there.

Julie tapped her fingers on the steering wheel. I looked over at her, opening my mouth and then closing it again. I wanted to say more about the baby, but I didn't know how to say anything without her misunderstanding my words. How could I explain to her that the last thing I wanted was the baby that was growing inside me? That I didn't even want to stay married to Cade anymore. Not because I didn't love him, quite the opposite actually. I loved him so much that I knew I had to let him go. Unfortunately, my plan to travel was a solo mission, and in order to complete it, I would have to leave everyone behind. This was, of course, something I should have done right after high school.

"Julie, I-I am unsure of what to say." I fumbled over my words and stared ahead at the empty garage.

Julie wiped a single tear from her face. It was dark, but I knew she was crying. I could tell by her trembling lip. "Als, I get it. I, I just have a lot going on. I think I need a break. From everything."

I nodded in understanding. I had been waiting for her to admit this for a long while. The fertility treatments weren't working for her, and well, it appeared she had lost an important part of the equation: Greg.

"Yes. This makes sense. You might feel better taking some of the pressure off for a few months, you know. Let yourself off the hook for once. I mean, that is, if you are planning to take Greg back?"

Personally, I wouldn't have given the man a second chance, but I also wasn't three years deep into a fertility nightmare. That was what I referred to it in my head sometimes. Julie's fertility nightmare. I made a mental note to never tell her that. That would probably be socially unacceptable and hurtful.

Julie snapped her head in my direction. "What? No. No, I'm not. That's not what I mean. I'm not giving him another chance, but that's bedside the point." She sighed and ran her hands down her face. "I mean I need a break from all of this." She made a sweeping motion with her hand in my direction.

Something in me snapped, and I felt my frustration rise. "Well, Julie. I am sorry that you feel resentful of my ability to create a baby. It was certainly never my intention to rub it in your face, which is why I had been keeping it a secret. I never planned for any of this to happen."

I paused, pressing my own hands to my head. I was beginning to feel my body temperature rise. My skin felt agitated. Like my insides wanted to jump up and run away. Usually, I was very levelheaded, but it appeared that with pregnancy your emotions took you for a rollercoaster ride.

I started tapping my hand on my knee to trying to regulate my anger, but it persisted. "Julie," I said carefully. "I am feeling rather annoyed."

Julie's face quieted, and she tried to cut me off, but before she could get a word in, I barreled on.

"No, Julie. Let me get this out. In case you don't remember, I don't like children. I don't want to have a baby. And I know it is practically impossible for you to understand how someone could feel that way, but I do. And, if you could imagine how upsetting it is for *me*, to be carrying a baby, well, you might understand a bit more. So, good for you, for opting out of my situation."

With that, I opened the car door and stood up, much too fast, I might add. My body wavered in the evening air, like a weak tree during a winter storm. This was probably from the lack of nutrients.

I tried to think about what I had in my fridge, but all I could recall was deli meats, which I had just learned were off-limits to pregnant women. I was appalled when my app suggested I heat the meat up in the microwave to kill off listeria. I would never be eating a floppy piece of deli meat again, pregnant or not. And I certainly wouldn't be exposing my food to the radioactive poison of a microwave. Shouldn't the app be warning pregnant women about that?

I held on to the top of the car to steady myself because of course I was towering over it. I felt a strong urge to kick the car once or twice with my shoe, but I refrained.

"Tin can," I muttered and slammed the door behind me.

"Ally! Wait. I, I—"

I spun around on my heel and looked at her expectantly. "What? What is it, Julie?"

"I just. Well, are you okay? Where is Cade? I don't want to leave you alone if you know, you need someone."

I could feel that burning behind my eyes again. Pregnancy really was something else. I studied my best friend's face in the evening light. Something told me that after today, we would never be the same. Something had broken between us. We had kept things from each other. Things we shouldn't have. I couldn't ask Julie to be my caretaker now. It was cruel.

I straightened up and nodded. "I am quite all right, Jules." I held up my phone as if it was proof that I did not need her. "Cade has just texted. He is on his way home."

Julie smiled sadly. "Okay, well. I'll talk to you soon then."

I couldn't bear to stand there a second longer, and I certainly couldn't admit to her that I had lied.

Cade hadn't texted me, and I had no idea where he was.

NANCY

N ANCY PULLED UP TO THE BANK AND REACHED across the seat for her notebook. She would bring it with her wherever she went now. She wasn't going to make that mistake again. So far, she still had enough of her wits about her and knew exactly what she was doing. In fear that tomorrow she might not remember, she had to make the transfer today.

She would divide it up in three ways.

One third to Julie.

One third to Will.

One third to Ally.

Will didn't really need the money; he was already quite successful, but fair was fair. Nancy hoped he would be smart with it. Put it into a high-yield savings account or even invest it!

Dean would be so happy. He had wanted to tell the kids about it when they were still in high school, but Nancy would not allow it. She could still hear him peppering her.

Think about it, Nancy! They could buy a house on campus and rent it out to all their friends. Make their money back! Ally could travel!

But Nancy was insistent that they wait. She had heard too many stories about kids inheriting fortunes too young and blowing it on sports cars and luxury vacations and shopping sprees. She wanted them to go to college first. To find careers they loved. Learn how to navigate life. She was so proud of each of them. They were all now in a spot in their lives where they could inherit a large amount of money and make smart choices with it.

It had been the right choice, and she couldn't wait to tell Dean tonight at dinner. What a wonderful surprise it would be for him! Perhaps she would stop by the store on her way home and pick up a bottle of their favorite chianti.

Marching up to the doors of the bank, she caught a glimpse of her reflection. Her hair was strewn about and in need of styling. Her outfit was a mix match of casual and professional. She realized now that the blazer she had on didn't really go with the sweatpants. She'd been so excited to get to the bank she hadn't thought much about her outfit.

She frowned, realizing she hardly recognized herself. A pang of pain lurched through her chest. What if by the time Julie had children, she wouldn't know who they were? What if Julie decided it was not safe to let her hold them?

Or worse than all of that, what if she never found out whether Julie got to become a mother?

She wasn't ready yet. It was too soon. It was too much. But she had to keep moving forward for her children. She had to square this away and go back home to wait for the ending of her story to begin.

As she made her way up to the teller, she realized she probably should have made an appointment. The young woman behind the counter smiled warmly at her, giving her a boost of confidence. There was no time for small talk, so Nancy dove right into it.

"Hi there, I need to transfer some funds to each of my children please."

The young woman raised her eyebrows but smiled politely. "All right, let me see if there is a banker available for that."

Nancy nodded and looked around. Was she supposed to wait

here or have a seat? She shifted on her feet and checked her pocketbook. All the documents she needed were right there along with the notebook if she forgot anything. She had written herself a detailed note in case she got lost during the conversation.

"Nancy?" A middle-aged woman in a power suit came around the corner and looked expectantly at her. If she had an opinion about Nancy's outfit, she didn't show it.

"Yes, that's me. Thank you." Nancy hurried over to her, hoping this would be a quick process.

The banker sat down behind a desk and smiled again. "All right, what can I do for you today?"

"I need to transfer each of my children a substantially large amount of money."

The banker paused mid-typing and looked up then quickly resumed typing and nodded. "Are you the only name listed on the account?"

Nancy paused. Was she? "Well, yes. Actually, no. My husband Dean will be listed there as well."

The banker raised her eyebrows. "All right, well, we will need his signature in order to make the transfer."

Nancy rubbed her fingers between her eyes. This was fine. She would just drive home and ask him to sign it. "Okay, I understand. I can do that."

The banker agreed to get everything in order and passed a folder of papers across the desk to her, explaining where she needed signatures and what needed to be filled out. "Bring them back any time before 5 p.m. today, or we are here tomorrow morning at 8 a.m."

Nancy smiled and shuffled out of the bank. She would need to drive straight home to retrieve Dean's signature.

By the time she pulled into her driveway, she had to check her notebook to remind herself what her plan was. But once she was inside the house and calling Dean's name, she could feel her alertness slipping away.

Where was Dean?

Why wasn't he answering her.?

She didn't see his worn-out workbooks or his jacket hanging on the hook. She couldn't even remember what kind of car he drove. Not that it mattered, because there wasn't a car in the driveway to look for. Maybe he had gone to get something for dinner and had forgotten to let her know.

She opened the machine that held cold items and stared blankly at the contents. None of the items that Dean loved were there. She should probably give him a call and remind him that he was out of everything. When was the last time she had done a proper grocery shopping? She knew he liked chive cream cheese with his morning bagels and plain cream with his coffee. Grapefruits and cottage cheese. Pickles. Whole ones, not sliced. The precut cookie dough, straight out of the bag, no need to cook it; as a late-night snack.

She knew all these things, but something told her she was missing something big.

Something that she should have known but just couldn't quite remember.

ALLY

The doctors said I would most likely feel exceptionally tired for a few days considering the falls and all the commotion. They had recommended rest, and I had promised them that I had someone at home to care for me. At the time that was not untrue.

I thought that I would have Cade.

I thought I was going to summon him for hot buttered rolls.

It was apparent now that I was very wrong about that. He still was not answering his phone. Surely, he wasn't angry with me? I assumed he was out on a drive, thinking about everything that had unfolded. About the fact that he was going to become a father. I wished that he would answer my calls soon because as of right now, he still thought I was in the hospital.

Plus, I wanted to tell him about Julie. I knew he would have something smart to say. Something that would make me feel better. Despite everything I had put him through, he would still be there for me. No matter what. Somehow, that made me feel even worse. It also made me question all of my original plans. I had been so willing to leave Cade high and dry before this pregnancy occurred. To set off into the sunset, quite literally, on an airplane. To be on my own and see the world for myself.

Now that I was on my own in a sense, considering I didn't know where Cade was, and that I had navigated the beginning of this pregnancy by myself, I wasn't so sure I wanted to be alone anymore. Cade really knew how to help me regulate my nervous system and keep me on track.

He knew all the things I liked and all the things that upset me.

Abrupt noises and slow drivers.

Brightly lit rooms and loud talkers.

Glade PlugIns.

I had told him that if he ever brought me to a home or an Airbnb that had Glade PlugIns that first, I would call poison control, and second, divorce him. In addition to all those horrors there was the threat of unexpected gifts and anything that resembled the feeling of silk. He knew not to surprise me with clothing or a new throw blanket.

He was my other half, and yet I still felt as though something was missing. I still felt as though I was moving through life in someone else's shoes. That I had just been taking the steps toward what I thought I wanted, when in reality, what I wanted deep down was something else entirely.

I decided to draw a bath and pull out my journal. The one with the map of all the places I wanted to visit. Perhaps I could become one of those influencers who just traveled around the world with their infant. I shook my head. It sounded like a terrible idea and one I could not get behind. I had made a conscious choice to not have a baby for this very reason. Yet here I was, pregnant and stuck in the exact scenario I had desperately tried to avoid. It was not that I didn't think traveling with a baby and accomplishing your dreams was possible.

It was that I did not want that for myself.

As much as everyone in my life poked fun at my odd behaviors and unique tendencies, I had dreams of seeing the ancient pyramids of Egypt and touching Uluru in Australia. I wanted to wander through the Colosseum and walk the length of the Great Wall of China. I could not imagine doing any of that with a baby, and at the same time, I also could not imagine terminating this pregnancy and destroying both my husband and my best friend in the process.

I placed my journal neatly on a dry towel outside of the bath and thought about what I would have for my next meal. I regretted not bringing a snack into the tub with me. If Cade were home, I would have asked him to run out to get me an ice cream, like all the pregnant women do in the movies. I always thought it was peculiar. Why didn't they just buy ice cream at the store during regular hours? But now I understood. Pregnancy had a mind of its own. You could very well have been at the store earlier that day and been thinking healthy thoughts. Then later, when the sun had set and you were alone with your thoughts again, all you could think about was gallons of ice cream.

Perhaps I would need to purchase one of those bath trays that I saw people using online. I could watch my guilty pleasure, *The Bachelor*, while I relaxed in the bath eating crunchy snacks or enjoying a banana split. Cade always poked fun at my love for the show, but I stood by my argument. It was a wonderful way to virtually travel and experience different parts of the world while witnessing the possibility of love, all the comfort of your living room.

Suddenly, my phone began buzzing, startling me. The caller ID was a number I did not recognize. I scowled. Telemarketers these days had no boundaries. You would think they would at least stick to normal business hours.

I placed my phone down on the side of the tub and leaned back to close my eyes. Perhaps if I tried meditating, I would be met with an answer about the baby. Just as I started to focus on relaxing my mind, my phone buzzed furiously for a second time. I reached for it, seeing that there was a voicemail.

Now they were leaving messages? They had a lot of nerve.

Just as I was about to delete the message without listening to it, the text preview populated underneath. *Hello, this is The Miranda Hillsman Memorial Medical Center, we are looking for the wife of Cade Webster. Please return our call as soon as possible.*

I frowned. Why would they be calling back and asking for me in that manner?

After I got out of the tub, I changed into my softest pajamas, all while carefully avoiding Cade's brand-new pair of athletic socks that lay in a heap on the floor. Looking at the fabric of his socks made me feel nauseous. I shuddered and moved out of the room. Picking up my phone, I dialed the number from the hospital. It was answered almost immediately, and I pulled the phone away from my ear a bit as the man's voice came booming out.

"Miranda Hillsman Memorial Medical Center ICU."

"Oh, I am sorry. I received a call back from this number. I was discharged a few hours ago."

"From the ICU?" the man barked back at me.

I wanted to point out to him that if I had just been discharged from the ICU, I most likely wouldn't be making a chipper phone call, but I kept that to myself.

"No, not from the ICU. I am pregnant and had an MRI earlier today. I received a message to call this number back as soon as possible."

"What's your name?" the man said shortly. Clearly, he was having a bad night.

"Ally Webster."

"Oh." The man fell silent.

I waited, starting to feel rather annoyed.

He cleared his throat and spoke again. "Ally, yes. I am sorry to inform you, but your husband has been in an accident. Can you come to the ICU right away?"

I pulled the phone away from my body as if it was infected with poison. With trembling hands, I reached for my sweatshirt and fumbled around for a pair of cozy socks.

"Ally? Are you able to come?"

"Yes. Yes. I am on my way," I whispered back, completely unsure if I could actually move.

JULIE

Things she needed to file away in her brain until a later date: divorce and Ally's pregnancy. If only it was that easy. She knew what her therapist would say: *It is best not to bypass everything that is happening. Practice self-compassion. You have a lot going on. What could you do that counts as self-care right now?*

She felt like she could practically be her own therapist at this point. She had all the tools in her back pocket, but the problem was she didn't feel like using them.

She was done having hard conversations.

She was done trying to explain to people how alone she felt.

She would rather just pretend all of it wasn't happening.

They would have to be put on hold until she sorted out this issue with her mother. Julie had woken up this morning to her phone full of notifications and missed calls from ol' Nancy herself. By the time she had gotten her mother back on the phone, she was in full panic mode. Making zero sense.

Julie knew she should be more compassionate. She should probably be more upset, but at this point she was out of tears. Instead, she just felt frustrated.

Frustrated because she didn't know how to handle this.

Frustrated because so much of it was out of her control.

Frustrated because Greg had turned out to be a lowlife.

Couldn't her mother just wait until next year to lose her mind? Julie knew she was being a monster, but that didn't stop her from feeling the anger and resentment. Everyone was having a big crisis, and it felt as though they all expected her to pick up the pieces.

Deep down, all she really wanted was for someone to pick them up for her.

For someone to tell her everything was going to be okay.

She knew she wasn't going to get that, but she had texted Will and told him they needed to have an emergency meeting. At least they could navigate their mother together.

Pulling into her mother's driveway, she looked around the yard for any signs of weirdness. So far, everything checked out.

Inside the house, it was quiet.

"Mom?"

Nothing.

"Mom? It's Jules. Where are you?"

Still nothing.

"What the fuck?" Julie muttered.

She made her way into the kitchen and heard a clattering sound coming from upstairs.

"Hello? Mom?"

Her heart skipped a beat. Was that sobbing she heard?

Running up the stairs, she followed the sound of her mother's cries, opening and closing various doors before she found her sitting on the floor in her walk-in closet surrounded by Dad's old belts, shoes, and ties.

"Mom?" Julie asked softly, "What are you doing?"

"Oh, hi." Her mother looked up at her blankly. "I was trying to find your father's favorite shirt. I wanted to take him out to dinner tonight to tell him some good news, and well, I can't seem to find him or the shirt."

Julie stared down next to her mother and inhaled slowly. What was the correct thing to do in this situation? She remembered watching *This Is Us*, one of the last episodes, when Kevin, had wanted to keep correcting Rebecca. One of the other kids played along and let her believe that Jack, her husband, was still alive.

That felt right in this moment. To let her mother believe he was still here.

She knelt on the ground next to her mom and slowly started putting the pile of ties and belts back into the bin that had tumbled off the shelf.

"Dad is on a work trip, remember?" she said cautiously, placing an old hat of his back on the hook. It still smelled like him, and she felt her throat tighten up. "He won't be back until next week. I bet he took his favorite shirt with him."

Her mother sniffled and wiped her nose, making a mess of her face. Julie cringed, trying to remain calm.

Her mother stared at her for a few seconds, almost as if for a fleeting moment, she knew. But then her eyes shifted back to that blank look, and she nodded. "Right. Silly me. I was so excited to see him, I just, I just forgot."

Julie exhaled. This was probably best. "It's okay, Mom. Let's go downstairs. Come on."

Once they were settled in the kitchen, Julie noticed the notebook was sitting on the table. Underneath it was some sort of folder. She fought the urge to rifle through it. She had a feeling it would send her mother into a spiral if she saw her leafing through the papers.

She glanced over her shoulder. Her mother had muttered something about going to the laundry room, and she doubted she'd have enough time to peek right now.

"Julie?" Her mother's voice traveled down the hall.

Julie could hear her lumbering toward the kitchen.

Deep breaths.

"Can you drive me to the bank? I need to make a deposit, and it has to be done today, before they close."

Julie spun around and looked at her mother, who was suddenly in a new outfit with an agitated look in her eyes.

She did not feel like driving her to the bank right now, but she certainly couldn't leave her alone again because she would definitely drive herself. "Sure. Okay. Let's go."

Her mother brushed past her and scooped up the notebook and folder underneath. "Great, thank you, dear."

Damn it. She should have looked at the papers when she had the chance.

Julie pulled her phone out and sent Will another text.

SOS. Mom has officially lost it. She thinks Dad is still alive. We need to call that assisted living place ASAP.

ALLY

One would argue that despite the tragedy unfolding, this could be the ideal situation for me. My husband, whom I continued to put through the ringer, was quite possibly dying. If he was dying, I wouldn't have to worry about telling him that I had changed my mind. That I couldn't spend the rest of my thriving years with a small sticky human with his or her own opinions and agenda following me around day in and day out.

That I wasn't set up for this kind of life.

That I had made a big mistake.

Of course, I had thought about all those things on my drive over to the hospital, not because I was a horrible person, but because I was a practical one.

I also thought about how much I wanted Cade to live.

I thought about that cheesy saying, "You don't know what you've got until it's gone."

I understood now more than ever that Cade was my comfort. Even though he did many things to annoy me on a daily basis, he was also my home base.

He was the person who looked past all my unique attributes and loved me for who I was.

He was the one who could always calm me down, no matter what the situation was.

The one who knew I loved hot buttered rolls and tables by the exit.

Who knew what I was thinking before I even opened my mouth.

Who trusted me with every fiber of his being, even if lately I had continued to give him every reason not to trust me.

I reminded myself not to panic. I did not have all the facts. That I was acting from a place of emotion, which was never a good idea. There was a high probability that he would make a full recovery. I did not even know the extent of his injuries. There was no need to jump to conclusions. I needed to stay calm, positive, and focused on making it to his bedside.

By the time I parked the car and made my way back into the emergency department for a second time, I was feeling rather weak. Luckily, I had half a mind before I left the house to shove an array of crunchy snacks into my bag. I was determined to get better at this pregnancy thing.

As one of the nurses smiled sympathetically at me and led me to Cade's room, I tried to give myself a pep talk. I had just seen Cade hours earlier. I was aware that being in the ICU meant he was hurt badly, but it was nothing we couldn't overcome. In a few years from now, we would laugh at this moment. We would talk about how I had left the hospital alone in search of Cade only to have to return to find him.

As soon as I entered the room, my stomach dropped, and I felt heat building behind my eyes. I was not prepared to see him lying in a hospital bed, wires and tubes strewn about. My stomach tightened, and I had to sit down in the hard plastic chair to steady myself.

"Cade," I whispered.

He did not respond.

Cade already looked dead. I would have believed he was if I didn't see the slightest rise and fall of his chest or hear the steady beep and gurgle of the machine carrying the responsibility of his life in its square little box.

I walked gingerly up to the bed and leaned over his body. Clearing my throat, I spoke softly to him. "Cade, can you hear me?"

My voice sounded like an imposter. Tears welled up in my eyes and threatened to spill over. I wiped them hastily with my sleeve.

I had to stay strong for Cade.

"If you wake up, I promise to have this baby." I squeezed his hand, half expecting him to wake up at the pressure I was causing.

He didn't move a muscle.

I looked at him, determined to make something happen. "I will take out all the best parenting books from the library and let our child eat cotton candy at the fair, and then wipe their sticky fingers all over my car's interior." I almost smiled, thinking about how much Cade would enjoy that. "I will let you turn the basement into a playroom, and I'll tear up my five-year plan and throw it in the fire. I will do whatever you want. Just please wake up."

I waited for him to move, but still nothing happened. Perhaps I should have screamed all of that to him. Maybe his hearing had gone in the accident. I pictured myself teaching our child sign language to communicate with their father. Certainly, that would help them become more well-rounded.

"Ally?" A voice cut through my thoughts, and I jumped, my free hand flying up to my chest. This was proving to be too much for my nervous system.

The doctor looked at me sympathetically and stepped forward, checking Cade's eyes with a small light. He turned and looked back to me.

"Ally, I know how hard this must be to see your husband like this. I'm going to jump right to the chase. Right now, there is no brain activity. Unfortunately, during the impact, his head received the brunt of the crash. In addition, he has some internal bleeding to his spleen that we are monitoring. It looks like we might be able to hold off on surgery for now."

I swallowed, forcing down a bit of bile, and wondered if this would be an inappropriate moment to fish a cracker out of my purse.

My husband was no longer the husband I knew and loved. I looked back at his body.

He was there, but not in the way he should be.

Cade was no longer Cade.

I brought my hand to my mouth, closed my fist and inhaled, trying to control my emotions.

"Ally? Are you all right?"

I covered my ears with my hands and said nothing. I could not take in any more information at this time, and I could not form a proper sentence. I did not have any words that were able to become a sound. If I did, I would tell the doctor that of course I was not all right. Surely, he had more intuition than that. What an ignorant question to ask. *Are you all right?* As if he was asking a sweet old lady who was trying to make her way through the self-checkout at a busy CVS. That would be the correct time to ask someone if they were all right.

Read the room, I thought to myself.

The doctor put his hand on my arm. I bristled and pulled away, fully aware that this was rather rude of me. I did not care about manners right now. The doctor could manage his own emotions. I was sure he was trained to handle grieving next of kin, and he seemed to have forgotten his training.

He withdrew his hand quickly and brought his attention back to the paperwork in his hands. "You are welcome to stay here as long as you need. For now, we are going to monitor Cade and see if there is any improvement. If after a few days there is not, we will need to think about next steps. About what you would like to do. About what Cade would have wanted in this situation."

I looked up at the doctor, appalled. How could he dismiss Cade's chances so quickly?

"What are the odds that he could wake up?" The words tumbled out of my mouth in short bursts. Each one harder to get out than the last. I felt like I couldn't take a full breath, as if all of the air was being robbed from me. My stomach felt as though it had done a complete flip, or maybe that was the baby.

The baby.

The doctor cleared his throat and looked at me uncomfortably. "Right now, there is no brain activity. It is of course up to you, if after a few days there is no improvement." The doctor shifted on his feet, looking very worn out. "You can move him to a long-term care facility, but the chances of him waking up or becoming the person that you knew are basically non-existent." His eyes softened, and he looked at Cade, then back to me. "I know this is incredibly difficult, but again. I would suggest taking some time to think about what he would have wanted."

This couldn't be real.

I stared at him, my mind struggling to come up with a response. The doctor was already talking about him as if he had already died. I felt like screaming at him, but I just stared straight past him, at the small window.

Of course, I knew what Cade would have wanted. We had the conversation countless times. I almost smiled thinking about it now. When you have a conversation like that, you never imagine that it would actually happen. It is much easier to make a joke about it. To toss scenarios back and forth with your best friend or your spouse. To have a plan in place for the thing that would never become a reality.

Not to us.

To other people we heard about on the news or were acquainted with through a friend of a friend on Facebook's newsfeed.

It wouldn't ever happen to us.

"But it had," I whispered to Cade, my body folding over as sobs rifled through me.

NANCY

Nancy patted her pocketbook like an old friend. It deflated a bit against the weight of her hand, much like her brain did when someone asked her an important question. Inside it held her copy of the signed papers. Since Dean was away, she had simply forged his signature before walking back up to the woman at the bank. She would have saved herself a lot of trouble if she had just remembered to do that the first time around.

She looked over at Julie, who was biting her bottom lip and deepening that line in the middle of her forehead with an omnipresent frown plastered across her face. She had always been so serious. Even as a little girl, she walked around with a permanent scowl as if she was waiting for someone to wrong her. She could still hear Dean: *Jules, if you keep scrunching your cute little face up like that you are going to be mighty unhappy when you are forty and you're stuck with a big line down your forehead.*

Nancy had always scolded him when he said that. *Stop giving her a complex! She's a thinker. Let her think.*

Nancy smiled now, grateful for the memory. She didn't know how much longer she would be able to remember things like that. The doctor warned her that some things would go slowly and others all at once.

Her daughter glanced over at her and raised her eyebrows. "What are you smiling about?"

Nancy sighed. She had learned to not take Julie's accusatorial tones so personally, but sometimes she wanted to say to her: *It wouldn't hurt to lighten up a bit.* Or, *I am trying to imprint memories of you as a little girl into my brain for eternity. I am so afraid I am going to lose them! I am so afraid one day I will look at you and not know who you are!*

You know what, she thought to herself. Maybe that was what she should say! She didn't have time to walk on eggshells around her daughter anymore.

"I am thinking about you as a little girl. Always so precocious and ready for a fight. I guess that hasn't changed, has it?"

Now it was Julie's turn to sigh. Nancy saw her soften, just a tiny bit. That was always how it was with her. She required just the right amount of teasing and peppering, but not too much. Nancy wondered if she should have explained that more to Greg. He probably was a bit scared to spend the rest of his life with Julie.

Nancy knew she shouldn't press, but that was what mothers did. Plus, she didn't know if she would get another chance to ask, so she barreled on.

"Are you going to continue with your fertility treatments?"

Julie snapped her head over in the direction of Nancy and then spun it back on the road ahead. "I don't want to talk about that right now."

Nancy nodded. She understood, but she also wanted Julie to understand that they might not have that much time left to talk about it. Not while Nancy could offer helpful advice or be a support system, anyway.

How did you have all the hard conversations with your children before it was too late?

The ones you knew would upset them.

The ones that you so desperately needed the answers to but were also terrified to uncover.

The ones you couldn't bear not knowing, but at the same time, were worried that the truth might unravel you.

Nancy looked out the window. The street they were on looked unfamiliar. She couldn't place where they were. Frowning, she gave her pocketbook another pat. The contents protested inside, and she heard the important papers crinkling.

"Why are you patting your bag like it's a cat?" Julie grumbled

Nancy shifted in her seat and tried to find something else to say. "Where are we going? I thought you were bringing me home?"

Julie didn't answer. Nancy squeezed her pocketbook tighter as her daughter kept staring straight ahead; her silence threatening to spill over like a hot cup of coffee with not a whisper of room for anything else.

JULIE

WILL HAD AGREED TO HAVE THEM AT HIS HOUSE FOR an intervention. Julie hadn't even told him about Greg yet. She didn't have it in her. Not today. Not tomorrow. Not in a month.

Maybe next year.

Same with the Ally situation.

Next year sounded good. When the baby was a year old and Julie was living in a tiki hut in Bali. The one upside to her mother slowly forgetting things was that she seemed to have forgotten about going to Greg's office and all about Ally.

She didn't want Will and his wife, Heather, to think she was being dramatic either. Julie knew that her looming divorce was going to upset the apple cart as it was. It wasn't a thing in their world. They had a jam-packed schedule and a perfectly manicured lawn. There were kids' sports games to attend and date nights to be had. There were photos to be taken and weekends at the ski house and summer cottages on the beach.

There wasn't space for Julie and her messy life.

There wasn't space for Julie to be crying about her best friend having a baby.

Plus, having a mother with memory loss didn't fit into Will's agenda, but he would take it on with some indirect avoidance. He would act as the hero at first, taking charge and making calls. But Julie knew as time went on, he would let things fall through the cracks. She was afraid he would visit Nancy less once she was in a home. Which would mean that

Julie would have to be the one to do it. Which would mean realistically she couldn't pack up her life and move to an island unless she wanted her mother to sit alone in a nursing home by herself. She couldn't do that to her.

Her mother deserved more.

So much more.

More than Julie had ever been able to give her as a daughter.

At least now, she could make up for it.

She could be there for her now. For all the times she had been downright awful to her as a teenager; heck, as an adult. She knew that the way she acted with her mother was borderline abusive, but she had been hurting so badly inside that she didn't know how else to act. All she had been able to do was focus on was the pain.

The shame.

The unwavering guilt.

The resentment.

All the worst emotions, according to her therapist.

She would try her best to be there for her mother, but she was terrified she would fuck that up too. She was terrified she wasn't strong enough. Could she really watch her mother's memory slip away day after day, knowing that she could have been a better daughter?

They pulled into Will's plush circular driveway with its trimmed hedges and beautiful garden. Julie drove all the way around the loop so that her car was ready for a quick exit. She glanced over at her mom, who was rummaging around frantically in her purse.

"Mom? What are you looking for?" She could hear the clatter of loose makeup. Coins and keys and paper receipts shuffling and clanging. The sound always drove her up a wall, ever since she was a teenager. She had vowed never to carry one of those pocket mirrors or a lipstick so she wouldn't replicate the sound.

So far, she had held true to it.

Her mother looked up from the bag, her eyes heavy with confusion. "My disposable camera. I can't find it." Her voice was rising with panic. "I must have left it at home."

Julie inhaled her reaction and exhaled it out as a long breath instead of words. Her camera? What year was this? 1998?

She should probably just roll with it.

"I am sure you can use Will's and he can print you out some copies."

Her mother sighed and started shoving her jacket into her purse, the way a toddler would try to put clothes in a washer.

"Come on, Mom, let's go inside."

Will was already out in the driveway looking at them expectantly. His older daughter, Willa, appeared at his side. Julie still couldn't believe they named her after him. "Hey, guys!" Will called out, still unsure of what he was supposed to be doing, like this was the first time he was meeting his biological parent.

Julie rolled her eyes and marched over to Willa. She scooped her up in a big hug and snuck a new bracelet and a piece of candy into her hand. Leaning over, Julie whispered, "Shhhhh, don't tell your dad." She winked and stood back up, Willa grinned and shoved the goods into her pocket.

Her mom started chattering to Will and she decided to leave him to deal with it, giving him no warning that she was currently stuck in the late nineties.

She went inside to find Heather, Will's wife, in the kitchen, putting out a spread of cheese and crackers. Julie inhaled deeply. There was something baking in the oven, and an overwhelming sense of comfort hit her. As much as her brother and his wife annoyed her at times, she loved coming over here.

It was always so grounding.

It was what she wanted for herself.

A cozy home with kids and cooking and memories. How did it all come to her brother so easily while she had to fight tooth and nail every step of the way? And then just when she thought she had built something, it all went up in flames before she even really got to enjoy it.

"Perfect timing." Heather smiled and held up a glass rimmed with salt. "I'll make you one too."

Julie laughed and sat down at the large island.

"So," Heather continued. "How are you holding up? I have been telling Will that he needs to like, do something?" Heather threw a hand up, clearly annoyed. "You know how he is; he avoids the situation until he literally can't anymore."

Julie sighed. She did know. "It's fine. I knew he would come through."

Heather's face deepened. "Do you think it's really that bad?"

"Honestly, I do. She has been keeping a notebook of all the important information, so she doesn't forget."

Heather's eyes widened. "A notebook. Holy shit. What am I going to tell the kids?"

Just then, her mother and Will walked through the door.

Heather looked at Julie with a flash of panic and slid the margarita across the counter, moving back into hostess mode. "Nancy, hi! You look great. Do you want some cheese and crackers?"

Julie watched her mom smile at Heather, her eyes scanning the room as if she was trying to commit it to memory.

Will looked at Julie and smiled nervously. "Mom, why don't you sit with us in the living room. We have something we want to talk to you about."

Once everyone was settled, Julie looked at Will, hoping he

would kick off the conversation, but before he could open his mouth, her mother cleared her throat.

"I have an announcement. I wanted to wait until your Dad was back from his trip, but I can't get ahold of him in time, so I am just going to tell you all now."

Heather looked over at Julie and mouthed the words, "What the fuck?"

Will leaned forward, putting his hand on their mother's shoulder.

Julie shook her head vigorously. She should have warned Will about going along with whatever her mother believed. "Will, I think–"

But Will was already going for it, cutting her off. It was like watching a toddler one second before they took a crayon to the wall, impossible to stop.

"Mom, Dad is dead. He, he died a few years ago."

ALLY

I was still holding Cade's hand an hour later, reviewing the conversations we'd had over the years around this very topic.

"Well, it is very simple for me," I had explained. "I certainly do not want to be left rotting in a bed for years on end."

Cade's eyebrows had widened, and I could see he was holding back a smile. "Well, that is one way to put it."

I'd frowned at his teasing. "My father used to talk about his friend Billy, who was in a terrible car accident when they were in college. He had left no instructions for his family on what to do in this type of situation. He had one of those mothers, you know, the hovering ones? That never let their children grow up and still do their laundry and pack lunches for them at age thirty-five?"

Cade had laughed, that full-hearted, deep laugh that I loved.

"She refused to pull the plug. She kept poor Billy in that bed for twenty years. As my dad always said, I never want to end up a vegetable like Billy."

Cade had remained silent for a few minutes, staring at me. When he spoke, his voice was lower. "Sometimes when you tell me stories from your childhood, I don't know how you turned out the way you did. But I am so glad you did, because I love all of you. The weird parts. The way you are unafraid to discuss the scary sides of life." He'd leaned forward and given me a kiss. "I will make sure you will never become a vegetable. Promise that you will do the same for me?"

I had promised, of course. At the time, I had felt secure and relieved to know that Cade would never let me suffer. But I had never really considered how it would feel to be the one making the decision.

But now I was in the scenario we never thought would happen. I was the one who was being forced to keep the promise. I knew what I had to do but, I didn't know if I could actually do it. I pressed my fingers to my forehead and tried to think about if the roles were reversed. Cade would certainly uphold his end of the promise. He knew how serious I was about this sort of thing. How could I betray him now?

I was the only person who could make this choice for him.

I looked around the room. How long should I allot for myself to sit here?

Nothing was changing.

Cade had not moved.

The doctors had not come back.

I was beginning to feel upset about the constant buzzing and beeping from the machines. I could only handle background noises for so long before they started to upset my nervous system.

I would need to alert Julie. I was unable to make any sound decisions at this time without her. My stomach flipped and flopped, threatening me with repercussions if I did not eat something soon. Instinctively, I placed my hand over it, hoping that would signal to the baby that it would have to wait a bit longer. There was nothing I could do at this time to nourish it. I had fed it crackers and supplied it with a bit of water. That would have to be enough.

I thought about Cade's aunt and uncle. They were the closest thing he had to parents. I would have to call them soon.

Some of his friends from basketball; he was in a league that met every Thursday night. His best friend, Frankie. All of that could wait until later. I would have to come up with something to say. I didn't have any strength to hold space for other people's reactions to this. I barely had enough left for myself.

I pulled out my phone and stared at it. All of the little icons made me feel a bit nauseous. Cade always poked fun at me because I had the brightness setting on my phone set very low. The blue light from screens these days was atrocious. It accosted my eyes and sent my brain into a distressed state. I imagined that since I was pregnant, this sensitivity would only be heightened.

While I was staring at my phone trying to decide what to do, the door opened and a nurse appeared, her gums flapping loudly with gum. I grimaced and then set my face to a stoic expression.

She slowed down her chewing and smiled at me sympathetically. "Ally, I am one of the ICU nurses. I just wanted to check on you and see how you were doing."

I sat up straighter and frowned. "Shouldn't you be checking on Cade? He is the patient."

The nurse stopped chewing. She had a lot of hair, all piled up in one big bun on top of her head. It bounced a bit when she chewed, threatening to spill over. I wondered if she felt each flop and fumble of the bun as she moved about. Surely that would drive a person mad.

"I will check on Cade, of course, but unfortunately there is not much we can do for him at this time. If anything was to happen, the machines would alert us."

She returned to chewing and placed her hand on my arm. I fought the urge to ask her to remove it. Her hospital attire smelled very strongly of toxic laundry detergent. I considered letting her know that the chemicals from that detergent were slowly seeping into her skin as she went about her business, chomping away. But I refrained. It was not my responsibility to make others understand the everyday poisons in the world. They had the same access to information that I did.

She took her hand off my arm and put her hands on her hips. This seemed like odd behavior, but I watched and waited because what else was I supposed to do in this moment?

"Ally. I know you must be in shock and unsure of what to do next." She paused and looked at Cade, and then back at me. "Excuse me if I am overstepping, but I know that you are pregnant and were just discharged yourself a bit ago. You must be exhausted, and frankly, you look it. Cade will be here in the morning. I am working the overnight shift tonight, and I will take good care of him. I think it would be best to call someone to come pick you up. You need rest. And food. Do you want me to call someone for you?"

I stared at her.

She wasn't even out of breath after all of that, just chewing along, waiting for a response from me. Even though I did not approve of her gum habit or her rancid clothing, I knew that she did have a point. I was not doing myself any good sitting here and pondering about what to do next. I looked at Cade and then back at the nurse. She still had her hands on her hips, a signal that she was not going to move until I gave her the answer she wanted.

"All right. I will put in a call to my friend to come pick me up. Do you promise to keep a watchful eye on Cade?"

I didn't trust myself to drive right now.

I needed Julie to do that for me, even though her little car was arguably a less safe option.

I needed her to be with me.

She stopped chewing again and dropped her hands from her hips. Leaning forward, she put both hands on my shoulders. I thought about plugging my nose, but I was too tired to make the statement. "I will watch him like a hawk."

I nodded and felt hot pricks at the back of my eyes. She nodded back and looked at the phone in my hand, waiting for me to make the call.

I unlocked the screen and hit Julie's name.

Sighing as it began to ring, knowing very well this might unravel me.

NANCY

NANCY LOOKED AT HER SON BLANKLY AND THEN back to the pretty woman sitting next to him. She tried to find her name in the back of her brain, but it was too far away, like the gas tank when you park just out of reach from the pump. Nice girl, a little over the top, but nice. Nancy was happy for them. They looked like one of those couples you would find in a picture frame from TJ Maxx. She shook her head and stared straight at the blank TV screen. A black hole, similar to her mind.

Dean couldn't be dead. She had just seen him a few days ago, before his work trip. No, no. It must have been a mistake. He had been at the store! Just the other night, stocking up on all of his favorites because she had forgotten to get them during her last grocery trip.

She felt herself leaning forward, panic climbing up her chest. Her throat was tight, as if she couldn't swallow all the way.

What was that girl's name? Maybe she knew that Dean wasn't dead too. If only Nancy could remember her name, she would ask her to clarify.

Nancy held up one trembling hand and pointed it at the girl.

"You," she said with a shaking finger. "You live with Will and you know."

She couldn't remember what it was called when two people

stayed together forever. "Explain to them that Dean isn't dead."

Everyone fell silent. They all stared at her with nervous expressions. It was making her nervous to see their reactions. She wanted to tell them that the words had come out all wrong, but she couldn't find the words!

The girl was frozen on the spot, like a dog who had just been caught snatching a sandwich off the table.

Nancy frowned and waited for someone to speak.

Panic rose in her chest. "Where is Dean? Someone get Dean on the phone!" She was aware she was yelling, but it was as if she had lost control of her body. Her head pulsed with fear. She started rocking back and forth lightly, trying to shake the memories loose, but they just wouldn't come.

"Mom. Why don't we go outside and get some fresh air?" Her son was standing now, desperate to put a stop to her outburst. He had always avoided confrontation. Ever since he was a little boy. Once in elementary school, he had a few of his friends over for a playdate. One of them was very fresh. Nancy could tell right away that he was going to be a problem. Bossing everyone around, no manners, sloppy and rude. When it was time to go, the boy came down the stairs carrying Will's favorite Lego plane.

Nancy had stopped him and said, "Oh whoops! The plane stays here."

The little boy had shouted, "No! It's mine now."

She remembered Will's face, like a deer in headlights. He had mumbled, "It's okay, Mom, he can have it."

Nancy sighed.

Hot tears pricked the back of her eyes.

Her sweet, sweet son. She should have made the boy leave the airplane, but she could see in that moment that would have been worse for Will, so she had let the boy take it. And in that moment, she had taught her son not to speak up. To just let someone else walk all over him. It had bothered her for years. Not to mention Legos weren't cheap and he loved those sets so much!

She wouldn't make that mistake again. She straightened up and looked at Will. "I shouldn't have let him take the airplane."

The pretty girl very matter-of-factly said, "What the fuck?"

"Heather! Come on," Will muttered, shooting the girl a look.

Nancy silently cheered. Heather! That was her name.

"Mom? Are you okay? Do you want me to get you some water?

"I shouldn't have let him take the airplane." Nancy cried. The panic was pulsing through her body, and she didn't understand why everyone was looking at her like she was a delicate flower.

Nancy watched Will look at Julie, who was walking out of the room, phone pressed to her ear. It didn't seem like a good time to be taking a phone call, in Nancy's opinion. Will turned his gaze back to Nancy and gave her that same look he had when he was a little boy.

Deer in headlights.

She knew the things coming out of her mouth didn't make sense to them.

She wanted to explain.

She wanted to tell them about the airplane.

That she was so sorry! So sorry for everything, but what was the point in trying to explain why you made a choice in the past when everyone else was so focused on the present? How was it that you spent your whole life homed in on getting to the next thing and the next thing only to all of a sudden forget what it was that you even wanted?

There was one thing she still knew. She wanted to help her

children. They weren't ready to be without her! They needed her. Julie needed a baby. Nancy needed to comfort them. She glanced nervously at Will. He would be eaten up by that girl. She was ruthless.

Maybe it wasn't too late to stop them from being together.

Nancy looked at the girl again and sat up straighter. "I don't like you."

"Ummmmm. Okay." The girl stood up. "I am going to go make another drink. This is out of control."

Nancy sighed. She wouldn't get very far with this conversation. She would have to wait until the girl had gone home. What was her name? She had already forgotten. It was all becoming too much. She had so much to say, but she just couldn't access it. It was right there. So close!

Her poor son looked at her and then to the doorway, as if he would rather be anywhere but here. Nancy stood up and walked over to Will and wrapped her arms around him, sobbing into his chest.

She was crying for everything she remembered right now that she knew she would lose very soon.

For all the memories she wouldn't be able to make with her children.

For all the ones she had already lost.

For all the unfairness of it all.

For what this would put them through.

For Dean because she just didn't understand where he was and why he wasn't helping her.

Suddenly, Julie reappeared in the doorway.

Nancy sniffled and turned toward her.

Her daughter's voice traveled through the room, quiet and concerned, landing around them like a sudden storm.

"I have to go. Ally is at the hospital. Cade was— He is— There was an accident."

JULIE

Ally had called and texted her repeatedly during the whole scene in the living room at Will's. Finally, Julie had gotten up to call her back because watching her mother talk as if they were living twenty years ago was too much for her to handle. It was slowly breaking down what was left of her heart, moment by moment, memory by memory. Will looked like he had seen a ghost, and Heather, well, Julie didn't have time to think about that.

If there had been time, Julie might have had a breakdown right there in the driveway of Will's house. But there wasn't. Cade had been in a bad accident. Ally needed her. All she had said was, "Julie. It's Cade. He has been severely injured. Can you please come right now?"

As she raced over to the hospital, she ran through possible scenarios in her head. Cade would be fine. He had to be. Her mother was definitely going to need to be put into assisted living.

She picked up her phone and looked at it, half hoping Greg had sent her a text. Nothing. He had completely fallen off the grid, and honestly at this point, it didn't even fucking matter anymore.

Even though she had basically ended things at his office, she was going back to the doctor's next week to discuss next steps. Even though he had cheated on her. Even though she had acted like she didn't care about having a baby. But she'd been lying to herself. Infertility wasn't something you could just turn off.

The desire to have a baby wasn't something you could just swipe left on.

She slammed her fist against the steering wheel and screamed at the top of her lungs. Her therapist had told her to do that when she was feeling overwhelmed. *"Your emotions have nowhere to go if you don't learn how to express them. If you let the overwhelm stay, then your brain and body will find an alternate place for them, usually in here."* Her therapist had pointed to her chest. *"So, it turns into anger and resentment and then slides right back into overwhelm. Then, you are stuck in a loop, and that's where the constant anxiety settles in. That's when you are stuck in a perpetual fight or flight."*

Julie had nodded when her therapist explained all of this.

Her therapist had stopped and looked at her. *"I am getting the sense that you are agreeing with me but it's not really sticking. Do you want me to go slower?"*

In that moment, Julie had felt like flipping the table that sat in between them.

"Julie, I know how hard it is to want to have a baby and not be able to."

Julie had wanted to challenge her and shoot back. *No, you actually don't.* She had seen framed photos of little kids on her therapist's desk, just another reminder of what she couldn't have.

"Disallowing yourself to experience joy because it feels too scary is only going to deepen the pattern that you are used to, which are your old favorites. Guilt, shame, fear, anxiety. I know this is hard for you to see, but you have conditioned your body to feel safer with those emotions, and we want to get you to a place where you can feel safe with happiness. With joy. With love."

Julie narrowed her eyes and looked at her therapist. What she really wanted to say was, *Great. Figure out how to heal my womb, and I'll easily step into joy.*

It was the last appointment she had gone to. She just couldn't bring herself to keep sitting in all the pain anymore. She understood therapy was supposed to help, but all it did was make her feel tired and sad.

She said a silent prayer that Cade would be okay.

She couldn't deal with Ally being pregnant and a widow.

Someone had to help Ally become a mother, and if Julie had to do it, well, it would basically kill her.

As she pulled into the parking lot, she checked her face in the rearview mirror. Despite all the stress and insanity, she still looked somewhat presentable. She hurried through the cars and into the hospital. By the time she was walking through the ICU doors, Will had texted and called her twice. She silenced them. He could handle this one on his own.

Ally was sitting in a chair, staring at the wall. One hand sat on top of Cade's and the other rested on her belly. Julie stopped in the doorway. She didn't know if she could do this. She didn't know how much more sadness she could handle.

She leaned against the doorframe and took a breath.

He didn't look like Cade. He looked bad. Really bad.

Julie took a step forward just as Ally looked up. Straightening her shoulders, she pulled her hand off Cade's and made eye contact with Julie.

Something inside Julie broke in that moment.

Her best friend looked so fragile and small.

Ally had always been a very private person. She never wanted to bombard people with her issues or feel like a burden. It had taken Julie and her mother almost two years to convince Ally to take over the office as her bedroom. To leave clothes in the drawers and feel comfortable enough to waltz into the kitchen and help herself to a snack without Julie present. Julie knew it had taken a lot for her to call and ask for help.

"Ally, I don't even know what to say," Julie whispered as

she tentatively searched Ally's face, trying to figure out how to navigate this. She opened her mouth and then closed it again. Everything was thick and murky and too slow, like they were both moving through molasses.

Ally looked at Julie, her eyes rimmed red with sadness. "I have to make a decision," she said softly, her voice breaking.

Julie stepped forward, and Ally stood, looking at her. She looked as though all the energy had drained from her body.

That all that was left was a shell, the person inside it almost completely gone.

Ally's hands were shaking, and her lip trembled.

"Oh, Ally. I am so sorry." She took another step forward, knowing that her friend needed her to be her support system in this moment and for so many moments to follow. "Ally, I am here. You are not alone."

Ally sniffed and wiped her eyes. "I will not allow Cade to lie here and rot. It's not what he wanted. I have to... I have to say goodbye."

Julie took another step forward and wrapped her arms around Ally, letting her best friend fall apart. And as Ally fell apart, so did Julie.

The two of them together, holding each other up.

The two of them and their broken emotions and missing parts.

This was how they made it through life. One supporting the other.

When one was unstable, the other was the rock. Right now, Julie had to be the rock. Divorce, infertility, and a mother with a detonating memory were no match for the loss of your husband.

Or maybe it was.

It didn't matter.

All that mattered to Julie was being there for her best friend.

Even if her best friend had the very thing she wanted more than anything in the world.

Even if it would slowly eat away at her inside every day.

She would always be there for Ally.

And Ally would always be there for her.

ALLY

Five Months Later

One hundred and fifty-three days had passed since I lost Cade. Not that I was counting.

At home, I was still catching myself looking for the ring stains his glass cups would leave on our end tables at night. Whenever I heard the jingle of Archimede's collar, I half expected to hear Cade's voice following it. Poor Archimedes. I had committed to long daily walks with him so he had something to look forward to. Losing Cade had been hard on him, plus it was good for my physique.

I did not hide my pregnancy snacks anymore. Partially because my cravings had changed and also because there was no need to. I was no longer nauseas, just rather large. I was trying to control my diet, but it seemed to be an uphill battle. I still thought about what it would have been like to have Cade do that midnight ice cream run for me. Sometimes at night, I thought about venturing out and doing it myself, but I didn't. It wouldn't feel right to go without him, so I didn't go at all.

Cade's office was full of baby paraphernalia, and I ignored it on purpose. There had been a few times where I considered returning all of it and donating the funds to a local shelter, but that would probably be the end of my friendship with Julie.

Julie really out did herself with the baby shower. She had been coming over to sort through everything. Harassing me about hanging up the tiny baby clothes and putting up sun-blocking shades in the windows. I kept arguing with her that it seemed backward to try to trick a baby about the sunlight. Surely, they were wired the same way as us. Once the sun sets, it was time to sleep. Why does a baby require so many gadgets and gizmos? From what I understood, there would not be much activity for the first six months or so.

My feelings about motherhood had not changed. I was not ready to be a mother. My baby deserved someone who was.

Someone who longed to hold a newborn in her arms at 2 a.m. and sing it out-of-pitch songs.

Someone who would fuss over what the proper nutrients will be as it begins to eat real food.

Someone who would be understanding about a mess and welcoming to tears and tantrums.

I knew I could not provide all of that to a tiny human.

So, I had a new plan. A gateway plan that would eventually lead me back to my original five-year plan. I was sitting at a coffee shop waiting for her to arrive. I chose to meet her here because she would have to be somewhat contained. I would be able to speak through what I needed to say without a big event. Perhaps this was going to be a mistake, but nothing about this had a rulebook.

I stood slowly and waddled over to the counter. The barista smiled at my belly. This was how it was now. Not one adult in public had the common decency to look me in the eye. Instead, their beady little eyeballs made a mad dash for my huge stomach. Last week at the post office, a rather pushy woman had actually reached her hand out to touch it. I promptly slapped her hand away and scolded her. The look on her face was astounding, as if I had done something unthinkable. The woman had touched my stomach! Without my permission. And then she had the audacity to be miffed that I slapped her hand away?

This world was becoming too much for me to handle.

Precisely why I couldn't raise a child of my own.

I thought about telling the barista that it was rude to stare. Instead, I held back. I had bigger fish to fry today. Later, I was going to take myself out to dinner to enjoy a basket of hot buttered rolls.

Cade would have wanted to do that for me.

He would have wanted me to be waited on and taken care of.

He would have been so excited to see my giant belly.

My eyes began to feel hot. I pushed the heat away with my palms, forcing it instead, to travel down my torso. The barista was asking me what I want to order, but I was too busy ripping off my jacket.

"Are you okay?" She leaned forward over the counter as if that was going to save us. I fantasied about answering that question truthfully and watching her face melt with panic.

"I am perfectly fine," I snapped. "I will have a large iced mocha with extra ice." I paused, leaning forward to mimic her body language. "So much ice you wouldn't even believe it."

"Ummmm, okay." The barista tapped and typed into the screen. "Lots of ice, got it."

Satisfied, I turned to walk slowly back to the table. Suddenly, I was doubled over in pain. Reaching for the nearest chair, I squeezed the back of it so hard my knuckles turned white.

No. I refused to go into labor at this dusty coffee shop. It was much too early. I waited until the pain subsided, and then I looked around. No one had seemed to notice my minor mishap. Everyone was too engrossed in their laptops and lattes.

I pulled out my phone and caught myself going to text Cade. That had been happening more often than I anticipated. Sometimes in the morning, I would absentmindedly put out his favorite coffee mug or leave a few pancakes still warm under a towel, thinking he would come down the stairs any minute, ready for his morning run.

But he was gone.

I was alone, about to have his baby.

Without him.

Wasn't this what I had wanted?

To do things on my own?

I was still quite sure I didn't want to have this baby, but it felt more convoluted now that he was gone. Now that this baby was really the only part of him I had left.

This baby that was the size of some ground vegetable.

Mostly as a distraction while I tried to figure out what to do next, I scrolled through my phone until I found that ridiculous pregnancy app. As it turned out, it had become quite useful, however I still did not approve of their comparisons to food. I knew from the update that last week my baby was the size of a bunch of leeks. I had considered writing in to the company and asking them who had decided that a bunch of leeks was the best they could come up with? They were flimsy, varying in size and weight, and were not a food that many people purchased!

The app dinged at me, cheerful and excited to discuss more baby updates. *Your baby is the size of a Napa cabbage!* I sighed. I would be giving birth to a Californian vegetable.

Gathering my handbag, I walked back over to the counter and waited for my mocha to be delivered. If I was going to have a baby today, I would certainly need a bit of caffeine to get the job done.

"Ally Arlington!"

The barista yelled my name like it was the final inning of a baseball game and I was in the stands across the field. I looked around to see if anyone else thought this was a bit over the top, but no one had even flinched. I noticed that the pain was gone now. Perhaps it had been a false alarm. I had read up on those in the app. Braxton Hicks. They sounded like a country singer that had never really quite made it to the top of the charts. Maybe that was why the name had stuck, because they were contractions that never amounted to anything.

I was happy to have my old name back. It suited me. Julie had been appalled that I did not want to keep Cade's last name after he was gone. I did not understand it. Why would I want to carry around the name of a man who was no longer here? My life would go on without him, and I had to be my own person. Plus, I wanted to get my new luggage set monogramed with my initials. Ally Webster would have shortened to AW, and I certainly didn't want to be recognized as a mediocre root beer for the rest of my life if I didn't have to be.

I grasped my mocha and took a giant sip. Hurrying as fast as my large body would carry me, I pretended to be doctoring up my drink at the little station where the sugars and creamers were, just so I had a moment to think.

Everything felt fine.

It was definitely a false alarm.

Just as I picked up my drink to have another glorious sip, the pain shot through my abdomen again. My knees buckled, and I gripped the edge of the counter with one hand and grimaced as the next contraction moved through me.

This really was unfortunate.

I did not want to cause a scene here in the coffee shop. People would be fussing and panicking if I told them I was in labor. I knew from my research that premature labor was not ideal. Usually, the baby needed a bit more time before it made its debut. I was not entirely upset about the situation; however,

I did worry that it might make it harder for the baby being so small.

Everything would be fine, I told myself. The doctors would sort it out. I would have to redirect her to the hospital instead.

By the time I reached the car, I realized that driving was going to be somewhat of a challenge. I had faced larger ones than this, though. Such as becoming pregnant when I never wanted to be and then losing my husband to a terrible car accident.

I would get through just fine.

I pulled out my phone and sent a quick text.

Change of plans. Meet me at the hospital. It's time for the baby to come.

After a very uncomfortable drive where I had to pull over two times to sit through very real contractions, I finally arrived in the parking lot. It took another ten minutes for me to make it to the front entrance. I tried to act as if everything was fine, but I did think a few patient visitors were worried about me as I passed them heading inside.

I walked calmly into the hospital's main entrance and looked around. The woman at the front desk was smacking her gums loudly. Too loud for my liking. What was it with hospital employees and gum? Without looking up from her computer, she blew a huge bubble. I watched it as it grew bigger and bigger until most of the woman's face disappeared behind it. Finally, it popped. It was a louder noise than I expected. Disgusted, I watched as the woman peeled the stray pieces off her lips and shoveled it all back into her mouth.

I would not be asking her for assistance.

I glanced toward the elevators.

No.

Not today.

I would not allow myself to take the risk of riding on the elevator while in labor. At least that was what I suspected anyway. Perhaps there was still a chance these were the fake contractions. Although I believed there would be more of a warning from the app if they were actually this painful. I considered calling Julie, but I knew that if I got her on the phone, she'd be distracted from getting here, and I didn't need a lecture about the baby that was not even in the world yet. What I needed now more than anything was for my best friend to be here by my side.

"Ma'am? Are you all right?"

I spun around, appalled at the voice who had the audacity to call me a "ma'am." Was nothing sacred anymore? Surely I hadn't aged that much. Add that to the list of reasons why I didn't want to have a baby. Suddenly you were labeled as a ma'am and tossed away into the mom category, never to be redeemed again.

There was a doctor standing near me, a concerned look on his face. In his hands he was holding a lunch box. One of those grown-up ones that I had seen people who work in office buildings carry like a little satchel. Back and forth from their home to work. I would love to see what he packed for lunch. For principle, really. I heard a statistic once that doctors and nurses had some of the unhealthiest eating habits, due to their demanding schedules.

This doctor looked very fit, though, and I imagined inside his lunch box he had neatly organized carrot sticks with hummus and a bran muffin. Perhaps a fancy can of soda water. One of those new age brands that promised you would receive all the herbs and flavors you could ever need in a single carbonated tin can. I never understood the phenomenon. Why not just purchase the real thing and leave the artificial flavoring to the candy companies?

"Ma'am?"

The doctor had moved closer. I took a step back, and that was when I realized. The floor seemed to be wet. You would think there would have been a sign. One of those janitor ones. *Caution: wet floor.* I looked around and then down at the floor again. My pants were damp. I tentatively patted the pockets of my jacket and then my purse. Perhaps my bottle of water leaked on me while I was driving. Surely, I would have felt it. Just as I began to connect the dots, the doctor took a step toward me and spoke again.

"Ma'am. I think your water broke. Let me get you a wheelchair."

I clasped my hand over my mouth and then quickly removed it. What a rookie move. It was probably covered in germs from the door handle. Quickly, I tried to rummage around in my bag for my portable hand sanitizer, but then the pain hit again and I leaned forward, clutching my stomach and wishing I had more privacy.

"I am fine. Where is the stairwell, please?"

The doctor frowned and looked to the receptionist. "Kim? Can you call for a wheelchair and notify labor and delivery we are coming up."

I held out my hand and opened my mouth to protest, but then another contraction hits and I almost doubled over at the pain. This seemed exceptionally cruel. I hardly had time to respond to the last one. The doctor was at my side in seconds, and I grasped his arm so tightly I could feel his muscles twitching underneath his scrubs.

"It's too early," I muttered through gritted teeth.

The doctor showed no emotion, only action. Somehow, he had produced a wheelchair and was guiding me into it.

"How far along?" he asked as he began pushing me past the receptionist, who was back to typing on her computer, snapping her gum and completely unfazed by the scene in front of her.

"Thirty-two weeks." I gasped, leaning forward over my purse as if it was going to save me from all of this. I waited for the doctor to say something about how this was not good, but he didn't. He just nodded and picked up the pace.

That was when I realized we were heading straight for the elevator.

"Oh. No. No, thank you."

He was already hitting the button on the side, over and over again. Like an impatient toddler. I wanted to let him know that I didn't think that would get the elevator there any quicker, but I didn't have time for that. Instead, I tried to push myself up and out of the wheelchair, which as it turned out, was harder than expected given my circumstances.

"I don't do elevators," I muttered as the doctor scrambled to help me.

"Please. Sit. You don't want to distress the baby anymore. Your water has broken, so the baby is coming whether we like it or not. The elevator is very safe. Trust me."

I glanced at his badge for the first time. Nathan was his name. I committed this to memory so I could send a proper thank-you card to the hospital after this is all said and done. "Nathan, I appreciate your help, but I will be taking the stairs."

As soon as I got the words out, another contraction slammed into me. Simultaneously, the elevator doors sprung open, and I was forced back into my chair, completely helpless as the pain washed over me. I closed my eyes and put my hands over my ears. The sounds of the lobby, of the elevator.

Of all of it. It was too much.

When I opened them again, we were in the elevator. Going up. I was in so much pain that I did not even say anything. I just stared at Nathan's sneakers, which were rather scuffed up and dirty for a high-end doctor like himself. I noticed one of the laces had a little trinket tied to it. A small heart. I glanced up at him. I now saw that his badge said cardiology.

His lunch box was missing.

It was the last thing I noticed before everything went black.

JULIE

Julie looked out over the well-manicured lawn
and watched as her mother threw bread into the pond a few
hundred yards away. There were an insane number of ducks
surrounding her, all quacking and flapping in excitement. It
had been her mother's most consistent request whenever Julie
called to ask her if she needed anything.

Just more bread for the ducks, she would say matter-of-
factly. As if this had been her career for the last forty years.
Feeding ducks in a man-made pond inside an assisted living
facility.

Her mother turned back to her and smiled. It was one of
those big, dumb smiles that used to annoy the fuck out of Julie,
but now it felt comforting. She would never be able to understand why someone who had lost so much could still be so
happy, but it was a reminder to her that is was possible.

Julie smiled back. It was easier now to not feel so upset
with her mother's aloofness. She'd been working hard on
lowering her stress levels, and she'd found solace with a new
somatic therapist. Slowly, she was becoming softer. Julie understood her mother more now, which felt odd because her
mother was slipping away from her in so many ways, but at the
same time, they were growing closer.

She watched her mother throw another piece of bread to
the ducks. There was still so much to get through with the
divorce from Greg. Everyone at work told her how lucky she
was that they didn't have kids yet.

"It's so much harder once kids are involved. You are just dividing up your assets. That will be a breeze."

"My friend Lindsey's divorce lasted three years! Her husband wouldn't agree on anything. They are still fighting over a dining room table!"

Julie knew all of this was true, but she would still have given anything to have a child to fight over. She wondered, more than she would like to admit, if getting pregnant had been easy, would they have stayed together? Or would they have ended up split regardless?

It was something that she would never get the answer to.

Just like she would never get the answers as to why Ally was left as a widow, pregnant with a baby she never even wanted.

Or why her mother lost the love of her life and then her memory, all within the span of a few years.

Maybe it was for the best. Maybe sometimes the pain of losing someone or something you love was too great. So great that the universe made other plans for you. So you wouldn't have to keep suffering in silence.

Her phone buzzed in the pocket of her jacket. She pulled it out, reading the text quickly.

Change of plans. Meet me at the hospital. It's time for the baby to come.

The phone slipped from her fingers and tumbled into the wet grass. At that same moment, her mother looked over at her again. She didn't smile. She just nodded. As if she knew.

Julie waved to her; it was a wave that told her everything, without saying anything at all.

Her mother smiled again, this time a softer smile. A smile that said, *You can do this.* It was Julie's turn to nod in response. Before the tears came, she spun on her heels, heading back into the foyer of the building.

After explaining to a staff member that she had to leave

unexpectedly, she gave them specific instructions to double-check on her mother, and then she hurried out to her car. On the way to the hospital, she called Will and told him what was happening.

It's too early.

Will assured her that everything would be fine. Heather's best friend's baby was born at thirty weeks, and now he was the star of the little league team and had recently taken a pair of scissors to the side of his father's truck, claiming he was practicing real life art in the driveway.

Julie laughed and hung up. By the time she was in the parking lot, she had called Ally three times and sent her about seventeen text messages. She ran into the main entrance of the hospital and breathlessly asked a receptionist, who was chewing gum very loudly, where labor and delivery was.

When she got to the maternity ward, the doors were locked. There were instructions explaining that only immediate family was allowed in. Julie frowned and jammed her finger into the buzzer. The woman on the other side of the glass eyed her suspiciously and buzzed her in.

"Hi, my best friend is in labor." Julie leaned on the counter, trying to catch her breath and calm herself down. "Sh-she drove herself here, and she isn't due for two more months. Can you tell me what room she is in?"

The woman slid a sheet across the counter and tapped at the top of the page where it read: *no visitors allowed after 4 p.m.*

Julie slid the sheet back to the woman and leaned forward, her eyes flashing. Anger rose in her chest, threatening to spill over.

Not today, lady. Not today.

"Listen. She has no one else. Her husband died in a car accident two months ago. Her father is three sheets to the wind somewhere in upstate New York, her mother is working overtime, and she has no siblings." Julie slammed her hand down on the counter, causing the receptionist to jump.

"Sorry. I didn't mean to yell. It's just that." She closed her eyes for a second, trying to ground herself down. "Let me start over, okay? I am her person. She needs someone with her. Please. I am begging you. Tell me where she is. I refuse to let her deliver this baby alone."

The woman said nothing but picked up the phone and pressed a few buttons. Someone on the other end picked up. "Hi, Jackie. Can you tell me what room number Ally..." the woman paused and looked at Julie.

"Arlington," Julie said quickly, relief flooding through her body.

"Ally Arlington is in." Slowly, the woman's face fell. Her scowl transformed into a tight line. Her eyebrows went from angry to concerned. Julie's chest tightened. The woman nodded, writing something down, and then hung up the phone.

"What," Julie pressed. "What happened?"

The woman handed Julie a piece of paper. "Ally is in the operating room. Emergency C Section. She lost consciousness in the elevator. They are not sure what is wrong yet."

Julie was already running down the hall.

The woman yelled after her. "Third door on the left, but they are not going to let you in there! You are not immediate family!"

Julie didn't give a flying fuck what they considered immediate family.

Ally was her family.

And she would get into that operating room.

ALLY

THE FIRST THING I FELT WAS PAIN. IT WASN'T AS
sharp as I expected, but dull. A quiet pulsing in my abdomen.
The nausea was back. It was different this time. Not the ever-
pressing sickness that I felt in the beginning, but more of a
threatening nausea. The kind where by the time you register
that it had complete control over you, it was already too late. I
vomited into one of those horrendous kidney-shaped buckets
that hospitals insisted on using. Did they do that as a reminder
that it could be worse? At least you still have all your organs,
they seemed to taunt. Or did they want you to remember the
worst kind of swimming pool design so that you would be
distracted from what is really happening?

There was a nurse at my side. She had placed a cold towel
on my forehead, and although I considered asking her to
remove it for sanitary reasons, its relief was so immense that I
allowed it to stay. That was when I really opened my eyes and
realized what had happened. I jolted upward, but the searing
pain lowered me back down. My eyes filled with tears, and they
spilled out of the corners, dripping slowly into my ears. If Cade
were here, he would know that I did not like tears in my ears.
He would have been there with a towel. But of course, he was
not, because he was gone. I tried to wipe them on my own, but
my hands were weighed down by IV's and exhaustion.

The nurse took another towel and dabbed my ears. I appreciated her attention to detail. If I'd had more strength, I would
have thanked her and also let her know that she missed one

spot. It was all I could think about; the remaining wet spot on my right earlobe. The same sort of feeling when you go to the hairdressers and they slather a huge glob of conditioner behind your ear and never wipe it off, too busy with the gossip and hustle and bustle of the salon.

That was why I always washed my hair before I headed to the salon. I had it down to a science. If I left my house immediately after I get out of the shower and kept my hair wrapped in a towel, it would stay wet enough for the hairdresser to cut it. That way I also avoided the toxic hair products they tried to push on you like drug dealers.

There was another thought that overpowered everything else. It was the moment I realized what had happened. My heart clenched. The baby. Where was the baby?

"My... the... the baby," I managed to say as a heavy lump formed in my throat, making it hard to articulate the thousand pressing questions that were trying to push their way past the nausea and into my vocal cords.

The nurse grabbed my hand and squeezed it. "Don't worry. She is fine. She is just fine. A little peanut. They have taken her to the NICU. She needed a little help breathing, and it will be a rocky few weeks, but she is strong. You can see her in just a little bit."

I swallowed and forced myself to say the words even though I was not sure I was ready to. I didn't know if I would ever be ready to say them out loud.

But they had to be said.

For my sake.

For the baby's sake.

For everyone.

"I don't want to see her."

The nurse froze and then collected herself in the blink of an eye. She patted my hand, which felt superficial and clunky since there was an array of needles sticking out of it. "Don't worry, dear. That can be normal. You just went through a great ordeal. Once the nausea wears off, you will be back to feeling more like yourself."

I swallowed hard and straightened out my head, forcing my chin up as if I was standing and wanted to appear in charge. "I won't change my mind."

I knew what she is thinking. But she didn't understand. Not many people ever would. Except for Julie. And that was all that matters.

As if on cue, Julie was at my side. I looked at her and the tears came again. White-hot pricks of pain. Behind my eyes and in my abdomen. I grimaced, wiping my eyes and my mouth. I tried to say words, but nothing came out.

Julie smiled, and I looked at her.

She nodded.

I nodded.

She knew what I needed right now without me having to say it.

"I'll go be with her. Don't worry, Als. She won't be alone ever again."

Oh, Julie. I knew how hard this was for her. I knew it must have been taking every single ounce of strength she had in her body to go and be with my baby. The baby I didn't want.

I wished I could explain everything to her, but my brain was foggy and I was so very tired.

I wanted to tell her everything right then, but I didn't. I gave myself permission to rest first. I closed my eyes and relief washed over me.

I knew how much weight Julie's statement carried.

She won't be alone ever again.

I knew Julie would make sure that baby was never alone. She would make sure that she had a completely different childhood than I had. One with a stable home. One with consistency and happiness.

That she would be loved and cared for and held.

That she would be sung to at three in the morning.

That she would be the first to be picked up at preschool and have the loudest clapping mother in the crowd at her kindergarten graduation.

That she would have a parent home for dinner every single night.

That she would be encouraged to try new things but never be forced to do something she didn't love.

That she would always have a mother that would put her first every single time.

That she would be loved.

Loved so much by a mother who wanted nothing more than to love a child of her own.

JULIE

Julie was sitting next to the tiny incubator with her hand resting inside, one little tiny finger clasped over hers. Sobs bubbled up and out of her chest against her will. She was openly sobbing in the NICU for a baby that wasn't even hers.

Sobbing uncontrollably for how unfair all of this was.

How unfair it was that this little baby would never get to meet her father.

How unfair it was that Julie wished and prayed and did everything in her power to have a moment like this.

How unfair it was that her own mother would most likely never be able to see Julie become a mother, at least not in a coherent way.

How unfair it was that Ally had no interest in being a mother, yet here she was with this tiny human who was relying on her for everything.

The nurse in the NICU looked over at Julie with a concerned expression on her face. Julie wiped her eyes with her other arm and straightened up. She needed to stay composed. For the baby's sake. She would never forgive herself if she was kicked out of here. Ally asked her to stay with the baby, and that was what she would do, even if every second that passed felt like a dagger digging deeper into her heart.

She wasn't sure how much time had passed, all she knew was that she didn't let go of that baby's little hand.

She watched as her tiny chest rose and fell.

She sang to her as the nurses came by and took her vitals.

She hummed and whispered and loved that baby in every way that she knew how.

One nurse had left and another had replaced her. All she cared about was making sure Ally's baby was loved. That she had someone there for her. Advocating for her. Supporting her. Loving her.

The new nurse made her way over to Julie and put her hand on her arm. "The baby's mother is coming down. She wants you to stay. Normally we wouldn't allow this, but given the circumstances..." The nurse smiled softly. "I won't say anything."

Julie nodded, unable to speak. She kept her gaze on the baby. She wondered what Ally was planning to name her. They hadn't talked about a name. About the possibility that Ally could become a mother two months earlier than they anticipated.

Instead, Julie had gone into hyper planning mode. Throwing Ally a huge baby shower even though she protested every step of the way. She created the registry and researched the best strollers on the market. She went to the baby store and filled the cart with all of the newborn necessities while Ally moaned and groaned behind her, making hilarious comments about all the stuff. She silently inhaled the newborn baby clothes and wrote out the thank-you notes to each of Ally's guests.

If she was being honest with herself, she pretended it was all for her. That she was the one having the baby. Ally had waved her hand when Julie had asked her about the theme for a nursery.

"A theme? As in a literary theme? I suppose we could do Alice In Wonderland *or Jane Austen, but both of those feel rather sophisticated for an infant."*

Julie had rolled her eyes and set out to plan that part solo.

Julie had gone back to her old therapist once more, who had a lot to say about Julie being so involved. She had pointed out that this was probably going to be very painful once the baby was born. She used terms like disassociating and avoiding.

That was when Julie fired her therapist for good and switched to the somatic healer.

All that mattered was that planning for that baby had gotten her through the last several weeks. As she went through the logistics of divorcing her husband and moving her mother into the assisted living center, it was the one thing that had brought her joy in a time full of despair and disappointment.

The door to the NICU opened slowly, and there was Ally.

Julie looked up at her friend.

Fragile and stoic at the same time.

Julie knew that Ally hated receiving help, so the fact that she was letting a nurse push her in a wheelchair was a huge moment of surrender. She smiled weakly. Ally shrugged and rolled her eyes at the nurse behind her.

Julie sniffled and fought back the tears that just kept trying to come.

Ally was next to her now.

Silent.

Staring at her daughter.

Suddenly, Julie realized that her hand was still inside the incubator. Quickly, she went to pull it out, but the little fingers gripped back, as if the baby was saying, *Don't leave me.*

Julie's heart shattered into a million pieces, and a small gasp slipped out of her mouth.

Tears hit the back of her eyelids.

Tiny hot pricks of deep, deep pain.

This was not her baby.

Before she could remove her hand all the way, Ally's shaky hand was on her arm.

"No. Keep it there. She needs you."

Julie shook her head. "No, Ally, she needs her mother now." She was trying so hard to hold it together. She couldn't let Ally see her pain. It wasn't fair.

Ally was allowed to become a mother, even if Julie wasn't.

Julie slowly tried to wiggle her hand out of the incubator once more, sitting up straighter, swallowing down all the sadness in the world in one breath.

Ally squeezed her arm. "Exactly. She needs her mother. You are her mother, Jules."

Julie froze. It felt like her heart had stopped. It felt like the world was spinning around her and she was somehow floating. Again, the baby squeezed Julie's finger.

Ally smiled. "You were always her mother. You always will be. She is your daughter. Not mine."

"I-I, I am not sure what you are saying? Are you..."

"Julie. I am giving the baby to you. Consider it a formal adoption. You are her mother."

"Ally, you can't be serious? I mean— How would? But—" A cry escaped her, and with it all of the emotions shuttered out of her, slowly at first, then all at once. Hastily, she wiped the tears that were streaming down her face with her free hand. The baby's little fingers squeezed back, as if she knew.

As if she knew that she was holding her mother's hand.

As if she knew all along that she would be hers.

Julie looked up at Ally. How could she feel such happiness and sadness at the same time? Her heart broke for what felt like the millionth time, but as it broke, it also healed.

For herself. For Ally. For Cade. For everything they had been through.

Ally straightened out her shoulders as if she was attending a business meeting. "I am not sure what is appropriate for this sort of thing, you know, who should be the one to pick the name. I do have one suggestion; in case you are open to it. I think you would like it."

Julie nodded, unable to get any words out. She was in shock. Happy shock. Her throat swelled and her heart felt as though it was going to beat up and out of her chest.

Ally shifted in her seat and smiled. "I thought Minna would be a nice name. It is unique, but not too over top like the names celebrities use these days."

Julie laughed, the tears now fully falling down her face. "I, I love it. Minna." She tried the name out, whispering it over and over again. Minna, Minna, Minna.

Her daughter, Minna.

"I also wanted to share with you the meaning. You know, that is an important part of choosing a name, or at least that is what the baby apps have been telling me. After much consideration, I chose it because it means *mind* or *loving memory*. Well, actually, Minerva was *to remember*, but I didn't like that one as much, and I think a name can mean whatever you want it to." Ally looked over at Minna then, her eyes full of wonder and peace. "I wanted to, you know, choose a name that honored everyone we have had to let go. In order to get here. Your dad. Cade. Your mother. Myself even."

Julie opened her mouth, but still there were not words, only emotions flooding through her a mile a minute.

Minna.

For all the people they had to let go.

And now she was here.

She was here, and she had made Julie a mother.

The two women sat there in silence, crying over everything.

Saying nothing but understanding everything.

Every single inch of her body shook. Expect for the hand

inside the incubator, where her daughter clutched her finger. That hand was as steady as a rock because she was a mother now and that was what mothers were.

They were steady when their children need them.

They were omnipresent.

They did not falter.

They did not waver.

They were there.

Always.

Every day.

Protecting their children, the best way they knew how.

With a love that knew no bounds.

With a love that didn't know the difference between a biological or adoptive mother.

Between good memories, bad memories, or no memories at all.

Epilogue

Ally

THE SOUND OF JET ENGINES AND TAXIS FILLED MY ears; all this noise was going to take some getting used to. If I wanted to travel, I had to become accustomed to various sounds and experiences. My flight didn't leave for a few hours, so I was still standing on the curb watching them drive away. I kept my gaze locked on the very safe SUV until it rounded the bend and disappeared out of sight.

A whisper of fear traveled through my body, but I knew that this was the right choice.

It had been all along; I just didn't see it until the very end.

I had pondered this a lot over the last year. If Cade had lived, would I have made the same choice? I'd maybe never know, but I liked to think Cade's accident had a purpose. That he died so his child could live. Maybe a part of him knew that if he had pushed me, I would have done the opposite, just so I didn't feel trapped. Just so I could be free.

Thinking about that now gave me what they called goosebumps. After seeing our baby out in the world, as a real tiny human, I could not imagine the alternative; an ending where Minna never came to fruition. That surprised me every day.

I was aware that Minna was not mine. She was not ours. She was Julie's, but I still liked to think about her as ours sometimes. In honor of Cade. I thought he would have liked that. Even though he was gone, there would always be a piece of him here in Minna, and that was something beautiful. Julie reminded me of this every day, and I thought she was right.

Julie had also agreed with me when I proposed she would

need a proper vessel to transport Minna in. She was not allowed to drive Minna, or any baby for that matter, in that tiny tin can of a car. Julie had laughed out loud when I'd asked to meet with her about the topic and then went to the dealership that very day to trade it in.

After many lengthy discussions, Julie and I decided that my house was the proper place for a baby to grow up, plus, it was much easier to transfer the home to Julie than it would have been to redo that elaborate nursery she had decorated. Plus, Greg had kept their luxury condo in the divorce. And since I wouldn't be needing a home anymore, it only made sense.

It wasn't every day that you signed over your newborn and your home to your best friend, but I figured one day perhaps I could write a story about it. I had seen that some of those memoirs did quite well. I already had a little outline in my brain. My five-year plan could be a big part of the story. My travels, my upbringing. Julie, Nancy, Cade.

All of it.

All of them.

Everything I was still yet to learn.

I turned and looked at the busy entrance to the airport. There was a moment of hesitation as I thought about all the germs lurking inside. About all the elevators I would ultimately have to ride on during my trip across Europe. About all the fears I would have to overcome.

Sometimes though, when you wanted to accomplish your dreams, you had to do things that were really scary. That were way outside of your comfort zone. You had to weed out all the riffraff, all of the opinions of the people in your life, and instead get clear on what you wanted for yourself. I had already done one scary thing, and handled a lot of opinions on the matter, and it had led me here; so I was beginning to believe this was definitely true.

Giving up the baby to Julie had been the most terrifying and emotional moment in my life, and that was saying a lot, as I had just buried my husband.

But having a baby wasn't my dream.

It was hers.

My dream was to travel and see the world.

To find the best hot buttered rolls in France and to see all the ancient history of the world.

To live the life my mother was never able to live or to give me.

I was healing generational trauma, as my therapist liked to say. Therapy had been Julie's idea. I was reluctant at first, but it had proved to be quite helpful. I could still hear Julie's words in my head. *"Ally. Your husband died, and then you gave your baby to me. I think maybe a little bit of therapy would be beneficial."*

She did have a point.

When I had said goodbye to Cade in that awful hospital room, I had known in that moment that I couldn't terminate the pregnancy. In some ways, it was a relief to have made a decision. In other ways it was suffocating, because it wasn't the decision I ever intended to make.

Life was funny like that sometimes.

I knew from experience that you could be really set on doing something and then a chain of events could send you in a completely different direction. Later, when you were on the other side, you couldn't imagine doing what you had originally planned.

Some people would call that fate.

In those moments after Cade died, I had known the baby would be born, but what I hadn't known was what I would do. Looking back, I went into what my therapist referred to as denial. I was unwilling to address the elephant in the room. I pretended that it wasn't happening. That I wasn't going to be a mother.

Instead, I carried on with finalizing my five-year plan, even though I didn't really have the funds or the resources to travel. Cade hadn't set up a will, and we didn't have much in savings. That was all on our to-do list for the future. I kicked myself daily for not being more pressing with Cade about it at the time. Now I told anyone I met about the importance of planning for death.

That was how I had come up with the idea to give the baby to Julie. I didn't know why I hadn't thought of it sooner. I had been on a walk with Archimedes, thinking about how if I became president, I would require high schools to mandate a course on taxes and life planning. This led me to think about the logistics if I had kept the baby.

I needed an updated will and a plan. I couldn't ask my mom to take the baby in the event of my death, as she was getting older and still working overnight shifts. She wasn't fit to be a mother to a small child the first time around; it certainly didn't make sense to have her give it a second go at it thirty years later.

Obviously, in the event of my death, Julie would take the baby.

I had stopped dead in my tracks, no pun intended.

Julie would take the baby.

I had gotten to work on all the back-end paperwork directly after I returned from the walk. Cade's funeral had cost more than I imagined.

I was lost and alone.

I couldn't even ask my best friend for advice, because what would I have said? *Hi, Julie! I am planning to give you the baby and rob a bank so I can travel!*

She wouldn't have let me.

She couldn't know until all the plans were set.

Once I had a plan for the baby, I needed a plan for myself. The five-year plan, of course. But what about Archimedes? How could I leave the baby, my best friend, my dog, my whole life behind? How would I execute it without any money?

Sure, there was the option to travel light and stay in hostels, but I wasn't really cut out for that sort of trip. My exposure therapy had been going well, but not that well. I imagined it would take me several more years before I was ready to stay in a dingy hotel room or sleep at a bus station; if that sort of thing was even permitted. I wanted to have enough money to feel safe. To take care of myself. To eat delicious food and splurge on every historic tour that was offered.

It was several days after Cade's funeral when everything changed, again.

I was at home, mopping the downstairs. Archimedes had created a huge disaster in the kitchen. A mix of muddy paw prints and a tub of hummus stolen off the counter. He had been acting up since Cade passed. I didn't blame him. I wasn't sure how I was supposed to explain death to a dog, so I just loved him as much as I could. I took him on long walks; as long an old bulldog could really walk. I provided him with gourmet treats and special visits to the pet store. We spent time at the beach, watching the seagulls and picking up litter. So much litter; it was very disappointing. I wore gloves, of course. I hoped that overseas there would be more respect for the environment.

Then there was a knock at the door. Perplexed, I had peeled back the living room blinds to get a peek at who was invading my privacy. The last person I had expected to see was Nancy, and quite frankly, I was unsure if she was allowed to be out on her own.

"Nancy? What are you doing here? Are you all right?"

Nancy glanced nervously over her shoulder and shuffled inside. "Don't tell Julie. Or Will. They think I have gone and lost my mind."

I thought about pointing out that they did indeed have a valid point, but I figured that was a bit insensitive given the circumstances.

Nancy smiled softly at my belly. "I know how torn you must be about this pregnancy. Julie will be okay, dear. Don't worry about her. She is as strong as an ox. She will get through it. Her time will come."

I shifted uncomfortably on my feet. Partially, because they were beginning to swell and partially because I did not like sentimental conversations. Also, because I really wanted to reassure Nancy that Julie's time would definitely come. Very soon.

"Can I offer you a tea or something to eat?"

Nancy looked at me then, as if she had no idea why she was there. Looking back, I thought she forgot for a moment. That would have made sense for someone with a declining memory.

She pulled out a piece of paper, studied it for what seemed like quite a long time, and then retrieved an envelope from her purse. An old gum wrapper fluttered to the floor, followed by a few crumbs. I fought the urge to pick them up. I made a mental note to re-Swiffer that area after she left. Nancy didn't even seem to notice. Instead, she thrusted the envelope at me.

"Here. This is for you. It's your third of the money. You have always been like a daughter to me. My third child, if you will. It's only fair you also receive this, and frankly, you need it more than the other two probably do."

I opened the envelope and nearly fell over. Reaching out, I grabbed the edge of the counter to steady my breath. "Nancy. What is this?"

"It's your third of everything, like I said. I have sold the house and combined the profit from that with the money that Dean and I had been investing in since Will and Julie were tiny. Plus, Dean left me a large lump sum when he passed. I don't have any need for it, you know, with my condition. It should be plenty for you to live comfortably. To travel and do all of the things you have always wanted to do."

She looked down at my stomach. In that moment, I was almost positive that she knew. She knew what I planned to do. Nancy reached out and put her hand on top of mine.

"What you are doing for Julie. It's something I could never repay you for. But this will help." She patted my hand and smiled sadly. "I might not be able to remember this moment for very long, but I want you to remember it forever, Ally. You are a magnificent young woman. You are strong and smart, and you never waver from who you truly are. That is something that a lot of people can't say for themselves. You don't let anyone else's opinion change your mind. You have always been you. I know your life hasn't been sunshine and rainbows, but you have a heart of gold underneath all of that quirkiness. I know that your baby will too. You are the best kind of friend any mother could wish for their daughter to have. I hope you will visit me sometimes. You and Julie and the baby."

She paused and squeezed my hand.

I wiped a tear from the corner of my eye and waited, knowing she had one more thing to say.

She smiled sadly. "Make sure you remind Julie that is it okay to let me go. And, Ally? Please don't forget me, even if I forget you."

Epilogue

____

NANCY

HER DAUGHTER WAS HERE. SHE KNEW BECAUSE SHE recognized her voice. She heard the nurses talk sometimes, about how she had lost her memory. On the days when she knew who she was, she listened to them, taking it all in. It was sort of like watching one of those things on the black box. She couldn't remember what they are called, but that was okay.

She wanted to tell them that she used to be all consumed with her life, too, but that it wasn't really worth all the fuss, because one day you just might forget everything.

She didn't though, because she didn't want to sound depressing.

Nancy didn't view what had happened to her as sad, mostly because she couldn't quite connect the dots of everything that she'd lost. But when she heard her daughter's voice, she was reminded.

Suddenly.

All at once.

The memories came in flashes, like lightning.

If she closed her eyes and listened, she could see it all unfold. It was almost like waking up from a dream. For a few moments, you still had a grasp on it. But as the reality of waking up set in, the scenes you saw so clearly just moments before faded.

Unless of course, you were one to keep a notebook by your bedside. Then you had a great chance of holding on to the memories, even if sometimes when you read them, they didn't all make sense.

Her nurses didn't know about her notebooks. She kept them hidden under her mattress and tucked away in various spots in her room. When her daughter, she couldn't remember her name anymore, moved her into this place, she had requested one thing.

Funny enough, she could still recall bits of the conversation.

"I would like ten spiral notebooks, please. Nothing fancy, just the ones from the drugstore."

Her daughter had stiffened and given her that furrowed brow look that she had worn around for the last thirty years. "Is that allowed?"

"Of course, it's allowed. This isn't jail. I think even jail lets you have notebooks, anyway."

Her daughter had laughed and promised she would bring them.

And she had. A huge pile of them. And every so often, she brought more. Just a few at a time. One slipped in her giant thing that she wore on her shoulder that held all the contents you needed. Sometimes one was tucked under her arm, and today, well, today was the best delivery yet.

The little girl wobbled up to Nancy, a huge gummy grin on her face. She held out the notebook and said, "Gramma! Book!"

Nancy kneeled down to her level and smiled. "Thank you so much, this is just what I needed!"

The little girl leaned forward and hugged Nancy. It reminded her of when her daughter was little. She could still feel the push and pull of being the one thing that your child needed.

How at times, it was the most overbearing thing in the

moment. But later, you would realize how fleeting those moments actually were.

How quickly your children grew up on you.

How hard it was to let them go.

How you longed to hug them just once more, without feeling like there was a time limit on the length of the hug, like a traffic light turning from yellow to red.

You only had a few seconds before your chance was over.

The little girl pointed to the pond and said, "Ducks."

Nancy nodded. "It is time to feed the ducks. I am glad you reminded me."

She looked at her daughter, who was smiling. One of the biggest smiles she had ever seen. The furrowed brow had faded, and there was a light in her eyes Nancy hadn't seen in years.

There was joy.

There was love.

There was happiness.

There was a mother. The thing her daughter had always wanted to become.

Two mothers, in fact.

Two mothers who loved their daughters so much that it hurt.

One kind of love that Nancy could never forget.

ACKNOWLEDGMENTS

I've been dreaming of writing acknowledgements for six years and I am finally here! This means I have six years to get through, so buckle up.

Firstly, I'd like to give a shout out to my kids for coming into this world and tipping me over sideways. You two have taught me about a new kind of love. A love that hurts and stretches and pushes you into a whole new identity. I find myself writing about parenting, about mothering, about family in every single book I've written.

To my dad, Bob Bean for sharing his love of reading with me and for handing me The Hobbit in third grade. Thank you for always having a book in your hand and showing me that reading is an excellent escape. Your humor and wisdom and classic one liners have found their way into my books and I hope I have made you proud.

To my mom, Peggy Bean. Thank you for your unwavering belief in me. For always finding a way to make my dreams happen. For always reminding me that those big dreams are possible. You've been holding the vision alongside for me through this wild life and I'll be forever grateful.

To Erin Holt who has (at times against her will) learned everything about the publishing industry (and the divorce process) and listened to hours and days and year's worth of voxes about my path to publication (and the rest of my insane life). Thank you for always being down for my delusion and believing in me. For being the absolute best friend anyone could ask for. For coming into my life and gently nudging me in the right direction- let's just say, the gravy train is ovvvaaa.

See you at all the places and spaces that you know I am planning to go.

To everyone in the Bean family for giving me the most colorful and insane childhood (with a special shout out to Phil, Scott, Iain, and Al)- thank you for giving me centuries worth of material and memories. I wouldn't have it any other way and I love you all so much.

To my brother Robbie for always being the grounded, kind, funny best pal growing up and teaching me about sibling relationships. I love to write about them, and you are a big part of that.

To Samantha Bean-Lyford for being my very best friend since day one. I love you. I know we will never be able to put into words what we've been through together but just know that I'm sprinkling it all throughout my books in my own special way.

To Kellan Maloney for being another shining example of a best friend- as well as a confidant, design witch, reader, and so much more. Thank you for always making me a new website when I need one (which is way too many times at this point). I love you forever.

To Sarah Ridzon for being one of my first readers and always shouting from the rooftops about my books long before they were published. It has always meant the world to me and I love you.

To Liz Libby who read a very early copy of this book and sent me the most encouraging message.

To Ali Ofstedal for your wisdom, weekly guidance, channelings, and constant encouragement. Thank you for listening to me talk about my books and agents and autopays incessantly. You are a global treasure, and I wish that everyone got to have an Ali in their life.

To Kristin Dwyer for all your advice, wisdom, humor, and

insanely talented story brain. You have this special, magical gift of being able to read someone's story and know exactly what they are trying to do, and I am so lucky that you were willing to read some of mine. Thank you for believing in Ally and Nancy and Julie from day one. I am so grateful for you and everything you do for me and so many other writers.

To Marissa Young for being my absolute best book friend. For reading this story (and many more). For helping me with branding and social media ideas. For listening to me talk about rejections and characters and publishing. For always, always reminding me that I am meant to be doing this. I am truly so grateful for our friendship and I appreciate you.

To my aunt Cici for being another early reader and cheering me on. I value your insight and appreciate all your encouragement and support.

To Emily Varga for giving me endless advice, support, and encouragement- and being so welcoming to me from day one on that bus in Scotland. You are a vibe and a shining example of what a bad ass bitch really is.

Shout out to Jamye Smith for literally walking me through the self-publishing process and spending hours with me on zoom and answering all my insane questions. You are generous and kind and the best.

And to Chelsea Walker for reading this story (with a newborn no less) and giving me invaluable insight and notes. Thank you.

To Aurora Whittet Best for designing me the most beautiful cover and for being patient with me as I learned how to self-publish and format a book. For Andrea Halland for proof reading this and reminding me that commas exist- any grammar mistakes are my own.

To my OG critique group- Sue Hincenbergs, Amanda Vano, Jessie Squires, Genevieve Lyons. Thank you for all the opening chapter reads, conversations, support, jokes, cheering, and for being expanders for me. We are all just getting started. To Jamie Kenny Clark for reading an early version of this book and being my first real CP. Whenever I think of you, I laugh. You are brilliant. Thank you for believing in my characters from day one. To my critique group from Scotland. You all read the opening pages in 2021 and gave me invaluable feedback and encouragement. I will always appreciate each one of you.

To every agent that told me no but gave me personalized feedback and told me to keep going. Thank you for being kind and sharing your time and expertise with an aspiring writer. It means more than you know.

To Steam House, my hot yoga and pilates studio. Thank you for being a steady rock for the last eleven years. For allowing me the space and time to write books while I ran a business and learned how to be a mom at the same time. The community, the teachers, the energy- it has all been a collective part of this journey and I am so grateful.

Thank you to all the little shops, boutiques, bookstores, and people who have already offered and will continue to offer to sell my book. Your support and willingness to share my work is everything.

And finally, to anyone who has cheered me on over the last several years -whether it was on social media or in person or some other way. And to anyone who reads this book and recommends it to a friend. Thank you. Each share helps get this book into the hands of more readers.

To whoever made it this far- I hope you loved this story and I am so grateful that you decided to pick up. Thank you for giving it a chance.

About the Author

Emily lives on the seacoast of New Hampshire with her two boys, senior pug, and one child proof cat. She owns a hot yoga & pilates studio and holds a BA in English from the University of New Hampshire. When she's not writing, she can be found drinking too many matcha lattes, walking outside, and adding to her TBR pile. (photo by Marissa Young)

www.ingramcontent.com/pod-product-compliance
Lightning Source LLC
Chambersburg PA
CBHW052155160726
47990CB00015B/1797